EVERYTHING BUT—

The Sarge, Devlin Tracy's dad, was happy. Trace had agreed to join his detective agency, and father and son were going to make a helluva team.

Trace was happy. His girlfriend, Chico, no longer threatened to leave him. She would join him and Sarge to give their agency her inimitable feminine touch.

Chico, maybe, was the happiest of all. She had a firm promise that she was getting a gun and, even better, would be allowed to use it.

All three had everything they wanted. Except for one thing. One very big, troubling, and increasingly dangerous thing:

A killer who slew at will, and came up smelling like a poisoned rose. . . .

TRACE
TOO OLD A CAT

WARREN MURPHY

A SIGNET BOOK

NEW AMERICAN LIBRARY

PUBLISHER'S NOTE

This novel is a work of fiction. Names, characters, places, and incidents either are the product of the author's imagination or are used fictitiously, and any resemblance to actual persons, living or dead, events, or locales is entirely coincidental.

NAL BOOKS ARE AVAILABLE AT QUANTITY DISCOUNTS WHEN USED TO PROMOTE PRODUCTS OR SERVICES. FOR INFORMATION PLEASE WRITE TO PREMIUM MARKETING DIVISION. NEW AMERICAN LIBRARY. 1633 BROADWAY. NEW YORK. NEW YORK 10019.

SIGNET TRADEMARK REG. U.S. PAT. OFF. AND FOREIGN COUNTRIES
REGISTERED TRADEMARK—MARCA REGISTRADA
HECHO EN CHICAGO. U.S.A.

SIGNET, SIGNET CLASSIC, MENTOR, ONYX, PLUME, MERIDIAN and NAL BOOKS are published by New American Library, 1633 Broadway, New York, New York 10019

First Printing, August, 1986

1 2 3 4 5 6 7 8 9

PRINTED IN THE UNITED STATES OF AMERICA

For Estelle Blair, Tony Spiesman,
Susan Lauman, and Michael Madonna,
always with thanks

1

It was a habit acquired during thirty years on the New York City police department. What Retired Sergeant Patrick Tracy called it was "making a rough cut." Essentially, it involved noting as many facts as he could about someone, on the first meeting, making a snap judgment about the person, and fitting him into a pigeonhole where other people had fit comfortably at other times in Tracy's experience.

It was hard to explain, and when he tried, some would say that it was just jumping to conclusions or looking for an excuse to hate at first sight. Tracy didn't understand this thinking and was eager to point out that judgments he made were based on experience, not whim.

"Look," he might say. "You're walking through a dark alley at midnight, right? Then, suddenly, you hear a sound and you look up and some guy jumps out of a garbage pail, and he's swinging a tire chain in his hand. He's nine feet tall and he's got a scar that runs from his left temple to his right ear. Right? You with me so far?"

Perhaps a nod. Then, "Now it's true," Tracy might say, "that this gentleman may have gotten that scar during sabre training at old Heidelberg. And it's true that he might be a visiting professor of psychology from the University of Kenya, here to study the impact of unexpected stress on the American urban dweller. All that's true," Tracy might say, nodding. "That's what he might be. He might just be a visiting professor. But I would suggest that you might be better off assuming that this guy is up to no

7

good and you'd better lay him out with a two-by-four before he gets you. Wouldn't you?''

Sometimes a nod and Tracy might continue, "See, that's a rough cut. You make a judgment based on available information. Sometimes you're right and sometimes you're wrong, but at least you can live with most of your judgments because you don't have to wait and wait and wait for the last shred of evidence to come in. Later you might get new evidence and use it to make a new rough cut. And that's the way it works.''

"You're a racist," he was once told.

"See. You just did it," Tracy said. "You made a rough cut. That's a very good start.''

"It's racism and you're a racist.''

"It's efficient living and you're an asshole," Tracy had said. "Now I did it too, 'cause that's also a rough cut. The truth might be that you are a thinking, caring person, but my life is made much more livable by assuming that you're an asshole.'' Then he walked away. The fact that the man he had been talking to—a dentist—was later arrested for diddling his women patients while they were under anesthesia, only served to convince him even more that he was right. Rough cuts stuck with him.

So when a man's outline appeared through the frosted glass of his office door, and the form ignored the PLEASE KNOCK sign and pushed the door open, these were the factors that went into Tracy's rough cut:

—The man was wearing a dark shirt and, God help him, a white tie, under a chocolate-brown pin-striped suit that cost a lot of money, with shoes that might have cost even more, oxblood things they were, with little leather tassels.

—Thick black hair so neatly razor-trimmed it looked as carved as the feathers on a wooden duck decoy. A pencil-line mustache that Tracy thought had looked good on Errol Flynn and David Niven and made everyone else who tried it look like a department-store floorwalker.

—Thick lips, thick eyelashes, skin as smooth as the surface of a maraschino cherry, a fleck of white behind the right jaw where the barber had powdered him after the shave, a fresh manicure with high-gloss polish so no one would miss noticing that he was the kind of man who got manicures.

—Little scowl lines alongside the mouth. What did they mean? Petulance? Cruelty? He met Tracy's eyes directly He was used to being the boss.

Those were the things Tracy saw immediately, and his mind ran them past images of thousands of people he had seen in his life, and he made an immediate rough cut:

A young man who might or might not be in the mob but wanted everybody to think he was. A young man who had been pampered since childhood by women of all sorts and was spoiled by that. A young man who didn't care about rules because he wanted to do what he wanted to do, and if the rules didn't permit it, then that was the fault of the rules.

The man pushed the door shut behind him with a bang but didn't even blink at the sound. He was used to slamming doors, Tracy thought.

"You Tracy?" the young man said.

"Yes. What can I do for you?"

"I got your name downstairs in the restaurant," the man said. "I need a private detective. You any good? This isn't much of an office."

"I only keep this place because the denizens of the underworld feel comfortable meeting me here," Tracy said. "Most of my business I handle in my penthouse at the World Trace Center."

The young man wasn't listening to him. He had walked past Tracy's desk to the windows that looked out over West Twenty-sixth Street and waved, presumably a signal to someone waiting on the street below. Then he turned and stepped toward the far wall where two *Playboy* centerfolds were taped up. Patrick Tracy had thought they gave his office a certain seedy panache, only partially realized by the scuzzy secondhand furniture.

The man looked at the pictures for a long time as if trying to memorize them. "Christ," he said, shaking his head. "There's some women in the world, ain't there?"

Tracy knew a no-answer-required statement when he heard one, so he looked back down at the desk where he had been working on the firm's profit-and-loss statement for the first six months of the year. Every time he looked at the dismal accounting, he thought of something he had read years ago, a French writer's last will and testament, which went: "I have nothing; I owe much; the rest I leave to the poor."

Even by those standards, Tracy didn't have anything to leave to the poor. He decided he was being rude to his guest. Maybe God had sent this piece of provolone to rescue him.

The man was touching one of the centerfolds with his right index finger.

"My wife looks like that," he said. "Except my wife's got bigger jugs. And her nipples are bigger too."

Next, it would be her orgasms, Tracy thought. He said, "Why don't you sit down and tell me why you're here? Besides your wife's sex life." He gestured toward the sofa.

The young man eyed it with suspicion and said, "I'd rather stand up. Sitting ruins the creases." He brushed at imaginary dust on his trousers.

"Suit yourself," Tracy said.

"I do," the man said. He guffawed. "A little joke. We were talking about suits."

"I personally think levity in the workplace is over-rated," Tracy said. "So what can I do for you?"

"It's my wife. I want you to follow her."

"Why?"

" 'Cause she left me. She run off to join some hippie-shit rice-eaters or something."

"No law against that," Tracy replied. "So why should I follow her?"

The young man dismissed the entire history of western law with a wave of his hand. "I don't care about no law," he said. "Look, she's gonna sue me for divorce."

"She tell you that?"

"No, but I know it. And I don't want her holding me up, so I want . . . you know, I want to have a bargaining chip when that time comes." He looked over his shoulder again, out into the street.

"Tell me about your wife leaving you," Tracy said. "Why? When?"

"I told you why. She went and joined some pack of towel-heads. She's like a goddamn Hare Krishna with hair."

"And jugs," Tracy said. "Don't forget the jugs."

"Right," the man said.

"So this is like a religious cult she joined?" Tracy said.

"That's right. That's the word. Cult. She joined a cult. She's a goddamn cult-ist."

"Did she have to leave you to join a cult? Couldn't she stay married to you and go join that religion too?"

The young man shook his head. Not a strand of his hair moved independently of the lacquered mass. "Not in this world," he said. "No way I was gonna let her go sitting around or begging on the street. Make a fool of me. Suppose somebody saw her who knows me? What kind of dumbo do I look like?"

"Very good questions," Tracy said, suppressing all the answers that jumped into his head. He looked down at his profit-and-loss statement. The things he would do for money. "Maybe we should start at the beginning. What's your name?"

"Angelo Alcetta. My friends call me Sonny."

Tracy had looked up quickly at the name "Alcetta," and the young man grinned. "You've heard of me, huh?"

"I've heard the name before," Tracy said.

"Well, don't believe everything you hear," the young man said. "We're in the food-importing business. That's all." He seemed disappointed when Tracy did not force him to defend the proposition that his family was not part of the Mafia, but when Tracy was silent, he went on with his background. He was thirty-three years old and lived in Brooklyn, where the family's business was located. His wife's name was Gloria and they had been married for four years with no children. "No fault of mine," he said. "I think she's steroid or something 'cause I pronged her enough to knock up a girl's school, but it just didn't take." About six months earlier, she had become interested in the teachings of "some swami or something."

From then on, Alcetta said, "I wasn't good enough for her. Nothing was good enough for her no more. A nice Catholic girl, what gets into somebody like that, to go jerking off for some guy with a dish rag around his head?"

Three months earlier, after a particularly bad argument, Gloria had waited for Angelo to leave the house and had then packed her things and moved out. She had called him with her address, an apartment building on West Eighty-sixth Street, but she refused to see him. He had spoken to her on the telephone but had not been able to convince her to return home. Then he had gone to "like the swami's headquarters or something, some dump downtown," and spoken to her there, but she had refused to return home.

"Did you speak to the swami?" Tracy asked, not because it mattered but because he just had to hear that conversation recounted.

"He wouldn't talk to me. Like high and mighty, he wouldn't talk to nobody like me, so I told him what I thought of him, curry-breath bastard, and told him that I'd like to bash both their heads in, and that's when Gloria told me that she was probably going to file for a divorce. Of course, she said she wouldn't want nothing, but you know how it is," Alcetta said, glancing over his shoulder toward the street below.

"No. How is it?" Tracy said.

"Women always say they don't want nothing and then they get some lawyer who says, 'Hey, baby, your husband's got a thousand million dollars and I'll get it all for you, just drop your drawers.' " He nodded once, sharply, to emphasize a point well made.

"Do you have a thousand million dollars?" Tracy asked blandly. "Think carefully about answering because it'll help determine my fee."

"I got enough to get along," Alcetta said.

"So what do you want me to do?"

"I want you on her case. Find out what she's doing and who she's doing it with. She's screwing around with somebody, maybe even that swami."

"If you're sure of that, why do you need me?"

"I'm sure she's screwing around with somebody, 'cause

I know her, but I can't prove it or nothing. I want you to find out what she's up to. Maybe she's doing drugs or something. Maybe that swami's got something going with drugs, that Indian shit, coyote or something. I hear these people are always smuggling in aliens. Maybe Gloria's doing that. You find out how she's breaking the law and you get me pictures or evidence or something and I'll pay you good." He stood up straight and Tracy noticed that he was shorter than he had seemed to be. "I've got money," Alcetta said.

"Seems like a lot of trouble to go to," Tracy said.

"Hey. It ain't your money she's going to be coming after."

"Suppose I just find out that she's gainfully employed and can support herself and doesn't need alimony from you. Wouldn't that help in a divorce?"

"Not as much as something that'd send her to jail," Alcetta said. He opened his hands at his sides, palms up, in a gesture of confusion. "You want this case or not? What kind of business you run here, Tracy?"

Tracy glanced down at the profit-and-loss statement, then back at Angelo Alcetta, whose friends called him Sonny.

"Angelo," he said, "it will be a great pleasure to represent you. Welcome to the happy family of Patrick Tracy clients."

"Save the welcome. What's the fee?"

"I'll give you the rock-bottom number."

"How much?" Alcetta said.

"Seven hundred dollars a week. Of course, that's not around the clock, but it's selective surveillance."

"That's pretty steep," Alcetta said.

"You get what you pay for in the world," Tracy said. "You want the best, you've got to pay. A lot of people charge a lot more than that too. How'd you come to me anyway?"

"I heard there was some private eyes hung out downstairs in the restaurant. I went there to see but the guy there said there wasn't nobody there but you were up here. Seven hundred a week, maybe I should have waited for one of them down in the restaurant."

"One's a broken-down pug and the other one's a one-armed communist," Tracy said. "Neither one of them could find a bass drum in a phone booth. You want good work, Angelo, you came to the right place."

Alcetta seemed to ponder for a moment, then said, "Okay. Seven hundred a week sounds all right. But you do just a couple of days first and then let me know how you're doing and I'll see should you do some more."

"When do you want me to start?" Tracy asked.

"Right away, naturally."

Tracy was about to tell him that weekends were the worst time to start a surveillance, because people were put out of their usual Monday–Friday routine and were therefore harder to keep an eye on. He decided not to confuse the young man with too much information.

"Fine," he said. "The first three days are payable in advance anyway."

"That's . . ."

"Correct. Three hundred dollars," Tracy said.

Alcetta took a billfold from an inside jacket pocket, opened it, and gave Tracy three fresh new one-hundred-dollar bills.

"And sales tax," Tracy said.

"Hah?"

"Four percent sales tax," Tracy said, shaking his head sadly. "Us and hairdressers and interior decorators. We've got to charge four percent."

"They got all the fags," Alcetta said with a smirk.

"Just pay the twelve dollars," Tracy said.

"I don't like paying no sales tax," Alcetta said.

"Pay the twelve dollars."

Alcetta rooted around inside his billfold and finally brought out a ten-dollar bill. "I got no singles," he said.

Tracy took the ten. "You owe me the two," he said.

"Oh, here." Alcetta handed the detective a small glossy photograph. "That's my wife. One of the ones I took of her with her clothes on." He guffawed again.

Tracy looked at the photograph of a lovely redhaired woman with a strong intelligent face and a smile too natural to be adopted only for a photo session.

"Very pretty," he said.

"And some knockers too," Alcetta said.

"I'll start right away," Tracy said.

"Okay." Alcetta looked at his wristwatch. "Christ, I got to get out of here. I got business. You call me like on Monday?"

Tracy nodded and Alcetta walked toward the door. Tracy rose and stopped him. He towered over the younger man by at least four inches, and while Sonny Alcetta had the shaped look that came from working hard at body-building, Tracy had the look of bulk that came from being, by nature, a big man. He reached into his top left drawer and removed a business card from a box of a thousand. This was the way, he thought. In business a year, and he'd already given out a half-dozen cards. At that rate, he had a 141-year supply left. If he didn't move and change his address.

"Here's one of my cards," he said. "Call me anytime."

Alcetta took the card and read it before putting it into his jacket pocket.

"Here. Take some more," Tracy said. "I'll bet you've got many friends who could use a good private detective."

"Okay, okay. Enough with the junk cards," Alcetta said, but he stuck those cards in his pocket too, then left the office.

Tracy went to the window and looked down. A brown Lincoln was parked at a fire hydrant across the street. He saw Alcetta walk across the street, climb into the back seat, and the car drove off. As it sped down the street, Tracy noticed a bumper strip on the rear of the car. It read:

ITALIANS MAKE THE BEST LOVERS.

"God save us everyone," Tracy mumbled.

2

Two miles uptown, in one of those transitional Manhattan blocks where multimillion-dollar brownstone mansions mixed with pricy boutiques and chi-chi little restaurants, two men sat alone in the dimly lit kitchen of one of the restaurants.

The black man stirred his coffee at the small stainless-steel work table, put his spoon in his saucer, and drank slowly from his cup before he said, "Let's just try to make this work for a change."

"There you go again," his companion, a white man, said. "Of course it's going to work. Don't my ideas always work?"

The black man rolled his eyes. They were alone in the kitchen and their voices echoed metallically from around the high-ceilinged room.

"Well, don't they?" the white man demanded.

Detective William (Tough) Jackson refused to answer. He looked at the white coffee mug that was almost hidden inside his huge black hand.

"Don't be stubborn," the white man persisted. He was leaning back against one of the sinks in the kitchen, waving at Jackson with the coffeecup in his right hand. "If Ed Razoni tells you it's going to work, it's going to work. That's that. Would I lie to you?"

"Not about anything unimportant," Jackson said. He looked across the room at the white man and smiled. "You forget, you've been my partner a long time."

"Too long," Razoni grumbled. "You want, we'll do it your way. You get a job as a dishwasher here. A couple of

years from now, when they show up, you can put down
your sponge and go out and shoot them."

"That wasn't my idea," Jackson said. "My idea was
that we wire Tippi for sound, and when they come in to
shake him down, we nail them."

"Too complicated," Razoni said. "First of all, we're
not supposed to arrest these guys. Just discourage them.
So we get Tippi involved and then we've got to book them
and then we're jerking around in court for the rest of our
lives, and then they get off anyway because Tippi wasn't
wearing a sign that says, 'Attention, you thieving bastards,
I am wired for sound.' My way's better." Razoni slammed
his coffeecup onto the drain board of the sink. "Shit,
Tough, why do we always get crap jobs? What the hell is
so important about the mob shaking down some restaurant
owner? What the Christ did he expect? If you open a
restaurant, the mob's gonna want to be fed. Everybody
knows that. So what's the big deal?"

"Yeah. But, you know, he gets the mayor's ear and the
mayor gets the commissioner's ear and the commissioner
gets Captain Mannion's ear and Captain Mannion gets our
ear . . ."

"Yeah, and he'll get our asses if this doesn't work,"
said Razoni disconsolately.

"Don't worry about it," Jackson said. "It'll work.
Your plans always work. I have it on the highest authority."

"I don't like this kind of work anyway," said Razoni.
He looked around for his coffeecup, then poured more
from the electric pot in the corner of the kitchen. "Tippi
threatens to go to the *Times* with the story. Let him go to
the *Times*. Who the hell cares? Only fags read the *Times*
anyway."

"The captain cares," Jackson said patiently. "Think of
all those people out there in this great teeming metropolis
who would be outraged if they thought us cops let thugs
run around loose, shaking down poor little restaurant
owners."

Razoni sighed and sank his tall lean frame into the chair
across from Jackson. "It's all *Miami Vice*'s fault," he
said.

"What's *Miami Vice*'s fault?" Jackson asked.

"Everything is. People watch that show, those two fags running around, and they expect cops to do that shit. Cops don't do that shit. Cops give tickets. Arrest people who already confess. Aaaah, screw it. When they come in, don't screw it up, right? Please. I'm the manager and you listen, and when they threaten me or ask for money or something, then you come out and we show them the evidence and then tell them to stay out of here."

"I've got the drill," Jackson said wearily. "I just wish you had gotten a wire from our radio people at headquarters."

"Oh, bullshit," Razoni said. "You try to get anything out of them, you spend six weeks filling out forms. That is my own personal tape recorder and it works like a charm. All you got to do is point it and press the record button. Even you ought to be able to figure that out."

"I'll try to remember," Jackson said blandly. "Ed, do me a favor."

"Now, you're going to ask me not to shoot anybody," Razoni complained. "I'm getting tired of you always asking me not to shoot anybody. Shhh. I hear somebody. Now, listen, you stay out here and keep your eyes open. And remember, point that thing and press the record button, and don't screw up because you be the witness."

"I be the witness, I be the witness. Yassuh, yassuh."

"Oh, shut up," Razoni said. He stood and smoothed the back of his dark-blue mohair suit and walked through the kitchen door out into the main dining room of the small restaurant.

Jackson quietly removed the two cups from the table, in case anyone looked into the kitchen, then moved behind the partially open door.

"Sorry, gentlemen, we don't open till four," he heard Razoni say. Not bad, he thought. With Razoni, one never knew what to expect. If his temper got the better of him, he might just as easily have gone out, punched one man in the face in place of "hello," and threatened to shoot the other man if he blinked.

"We know you're closed," Jackson heard a gruff voice answer. "Where's Tippi?" Jackson pressed the record button on the tape recorder, which he held in his hand. Nothing happened. There was no whir, no movement. Jackson pressed the button again. Nothing. He looked at the recorder. It had no tape in it. The idiot had forgotten to put tape in it.

"Mr. Tippi's not here today," Razoni said blandly, his voice artificially loud to carry into the kitchen.

"And who are you?" the gruff voice asked.

"I'm Mister Randisi. His new partner," Razoni said.

Behind the kitchen door, Jackson shook his head and stuck the small tape recorder in his pocket. From the corner of his eye, he saw something flashing, on and off, on and off. It was the phone on the wall behind him. Someone was calling and that might be Captain Mannion, their boss, who knew they were here.

Quietly, Jackson lifted the receiver and turned his back to the door. "Hello," he whispered.

"Who's that?" It was Captain Mannion's voice.

"Jackson."

"What's the matter with you? You got a cold?"

"No. Can't talk now."

"Oh, for Christ's sake," Mannion said. "Well, listen to me then."

Outside, in the dim dining room, shadowed by the heavy drapes drawn tight over its windows, Razoni sized up the two men who had entered the restaurant. The one in the brown pin-striped suit was the leader because he liked to smirk and pose a lot. The one in the cheap suit was the muscle. He liked to scowl. Razoni wanted to know where the leader had bought that brown suit.

"Do you know why we're here?" asked the one in the pin stripes. Razoni wouldn't have worn that dark shirt and white tie with that suit. That shirt and tie looked ridiculous. But the suit was nice.

"No," said Razoni.

"Tippi's supposed to have some money for us."

"Well, I don't know anything about that," Razoni said. "What company are you with?"

"Listen, asshole," the other one snapped. "We ain't with no company. We ain't with nobody but ourselves. And we told Tippi and we ain't telling you again: if you think you're running some restaurant around here, you need our services."

"What kind of services?" Razoni asked.

"The kind of services that make sure that this don't happen to you," the man said. He stepped forward to one of the tables, picked up a chair that sat upside down atop it, and slammed the chair down on the table, breaking off one of the chair's legs. "That kind of service," the man repeated. The man in the brown pin-striped suit guffawed. "Charlie Ribs gives good service."

"Oh, I see," Razoni said.

"It just don't happen to no chairs neither," Charlie Ribs said. "Sometimes it happens to the people who own the chairs."

"I got it," Razoni said. "And you can prevent it?"

"Mr. Alcetta can," the man said, nodding over his shoulder at the man in the brown pin stripes. "He can."

"You can?" Razoni said.

Angelo (Sonny) Alcetta nodded.

"For how much?"

"Now you're catching on," the muscle man said.

Alcetta said, "Five percent of receipts, and there was supposed to be five big ones here today."

Razoni said, "Big ones? You mean thousands? Of dollars? That kind of big ones?"

"We sure don't mean rubber dicks, them kinds of big ones," the muscle man said. "Yeah, thousands of dollars big ones."

Razoni nodded. That should be enough to play out this game. A threat, a demand for five thousand dollars, a witness behind the door, a tape recording. Enough to work with.

"You're both under arrest," Razoni said, his hand reaching behind his back and drawing the snub-nosed .38 revolver from its holster on the back of his belt.

"Hey, what's going on?" Sonny Alcetta said.

"I'm a police officer and you've just threatened me and tried to extort money from me. You're under arrest."

"Extort? Extort?" Alcetta said. "I don't know nothing about no extort. Do you, Charlie? All I remember is you trying to get us to give you a bribe." He smiled at Charlie, who said, "That's right. That's right. You was looking for a bribe."

Alcetta smirked. "Your word against ours," he said jauntily.

"Tough," Razoni called over his shoulder. "You can come out now. It's safe."

Jackson ambled out of the kitchen slowly, moving to Razoni's side. Even though Razoni was tall and broad-shouldered, he seemed like a stunted sapling next to Jackson's tree-trunk six-foot-six and 245 pounds.

"Here's my witness," Razoni said. "He got it all on tape too."

"Ed, I want to talk to you," Jackson said.

Razoni waved at the men with his revolver. "You two sit down and don't get cute."

He waited until the two men had seated themselves, then walked behind Jackson toward the kitchen door.

"Well, what do you want?"

"I just don't want you to threaten to play the tape for them," Jackson said.

"Why not?"

" 'Cause I didn't get anything."

"You what?" said Razoni, turning toward Jackson, a look of agony on his handsome angular face.

"You forgot to put tape in the machine," Jackson said.

"You must have dropped it, you big clumsy oaf," Razoni said. "There was tape in that machine."

"There wasn't any."

"Well, the hell with it," Razoni said. "We're not going to book them anyway. And besides, you heard everything."

"I didn't hear anything," Jackson said.

"I can't believe you. Why not?"

"I was talking on the phone," Jackson said.

"Oh, I see. That's good. At least you weren't wasting your time. You were talking on the phone. Good. And how's everything home. Wife all right? The kid, the nasty one, he all right too?"

"I was talking to the captain," Jackson said. "He said just finish up with these guys and go down and see him. He wanted to talk to us."

"Well, for Christ's sake, why didn't you say so?" Razoni said. "You can't ever get to the point."

He walked away from Jackson toward the table where the two men sat, watching the detectives intently, trying to overhear what they had been saying.

Razoni holstered his pistol.

"I've decided to let you two men go," Razoni said.

Sonny Alcetta smirked. "I thought you might. How much?"

"What did you say?" asked Razoni pleasantly.

"I said how much?"

"That's what I thought you said." The smile still on his face, Razoni raised his knee and kicked the man from the chair. He hit the floor with a thud.

"I don't know what you do with other cops, but don't try to bribe me," Razoni said. He turned toward the other man. "And you called me an asshole," he said.

Charlie Ribs raised his hands toward his face. "I didn't mean anything by it," he said.

"Good," Razoni said. "I don't mean anything by this."

His hands darted forward, brushing aside the other man's hands. He grabbed the collar of the man's jacket and slammed his head forward onto the table.

The head hit with a thunk that echoed through the room.

"What do you think, Tough?" Razoni called out.

"Not loud enough," Jackson said. His voice was a deep bass and resounded through the dark restaurant.

"That's what I thought too," Razoni said. He pushed the man's head back, then slammed it down onto the table again.

"That's better," Jackson said.

Razoni nodded and released the man's collar. He brushed imaginary lint from the sleeves of his suit jacket.

"Now, you two, listen," he said. "You go back to whoever sent you and you tell them that Mr. Tippi is a very good friend of the police department and if they try to lean into him again, they will find themselves in very deep trouble." He spoke slowly, his voice rising and falling for emphasis, as if lecturing young children "Which is not to mention the trouble you two shits will be in because I will personally wipe up the streets with you. Is that very clear?"

There were two answering grunts.

"I don't hear you," Razoni chided. "Louder, please."

"Yes."

"Yes."

"Good," Razoni said.

Sonny Alcetta flinched as Razoni extended a hand toward him, but the detective simply picked up the billfold and looked through it. He examined the driver's license. "Angelo Alcetta?" he said, disbelievingly. "You should be ashamed of yourself, doing this kind of work." He took a hundred-dollar bill from the wallet's cash compartment. "This is for the chair." A business card slipped from the wallet with the bill and fell onto the table. Razoni looked at it.

"Patrick Tracy, Private Investigator." he read aloud. "Angelo, what do you need a private detective for?"

"It's personal," Alcetta said.

"I'd hate my last memory of you to be that you were uncooperative," Razoni said.

"My wife. He's checking on my wife."

"You think she's cheating on you?" Razoni asked.

Glumly, Alcetta nodded. "She left me," he said.

"Can't blame her," Razoni said. He stuck the business card in his jacket pocket and tossed the billfold onto Alcetta, who was still on the floor. I think you two ought to leave now." Alcetta got to his feet quickly, brushed off his suit, and walked toward the door. The other man, nose dripping blood on his suit, followed.

"Don't figure on coming back," Razoni said.

Just before the two men started down the restaurant's stairs, Razoni called out, "Alcetta?"

"What?" the man said, turning warily.

"Where'd you get that suit?"

Alcetta brushed dust from his lapels. "I had it made in London."

"Nice suit," Razoni said. The two men started down the steps and Razoni called out, after them, "But get rid of that shirt and tie. You look like an idiot."

After the two men left, Jackson said, "What's-his-name, Alcetta, you know him?"

"He's a jerk," Razoni said.

"You sounded like you knew him," Jackson said.

"That's what I mean. He's a jerk," Razoni said. "The Alcettas are a big mob family in Brooklyn. Now what kind of family member would be doing this cheap muscle-man shit unless he was a loser? Mafia fathers don't let their kids do restaurant shakedowns. They send them to law school or something so they can learn to steal legally. He's got to be a real prince, this one."

"All of you Italians are," Jackson said. "Real princes."

"Oh, shut up. What does the captain want?"

"He didn't say."

"One thing you can count on," Razoni said. "If it's work, it's a shit job. That's all we get are shit jobs."

They locked the restaurant door and walked down the short flight of wooden steps leading to the street. The stairs creaked under their weight, even though both men moved lightly, like athletes.

Halfway down, Razoni said, "I hope if he has work for us, it's real police work, not like this crap." Three-quarters of the way down, he said, "I didn't like this assignment from the start. I don't like tape recorders and all that shit." At the bottom of the steps, Razoni said, "And besides, your idea for handling it was stupid. Would anybody take me for a restaurant owner?"

"No," said Jackson. "Everybody looks at your clothes and they take you for a pimp."

"Who asked you anyway?" Razoni demanded.

In the brown Lincoln limousine driving away from the East Side restaurant, Sonny Alcetta rubbed his sore wrist and looked at the thick neck of Charlie Ribs, his driver.

"Assholes," he said.

"That's right, Sonny. They're assholes, all them cops."

"Big high and mighty. How much can they make any-way? Twenty, twenty-five a year?"

"That's about it," Charlie Ribs said.

"Turning down some dough like they're big crusaders. You can buy 'em all for a dime."

"That's what I think too, Sonny," said Charlie Ribs.

"They think they're hot just 'cause they got some piece of tin in their pockets. Well, fuck 'em. They don't get a single dime from us."

"That's right, Sonny. Not a fucking dime."

"Aaah, fuck it. Let's go out to Aqueduct and make some real money. One of the guys told me there's this horse going in the fifth and the fix is in and he's supposed to go off at sixty to . . ."

3

Trace's Log: Tape recording damnedest the last from Kansas City in the matter of the late and unlamented Robert Napier, Devlin Tracy reporting, early Friday morning.

Pardon me while I burst into song:

> Nothing's going down in Kansas City
> And I'm about as low as I can go.
> La, la, la, la, la.

I forget how it goes. Anyway, the last crime in this town was the Cardinals choking in the World Series. What do you expect from a team who had a player named Walking Underwear?

Anyway, no crime here. That's right, folks. Old Robert Napier did indeed die in a boating accident and good old Garrison Fidelity Insurance Company is going to have to pay off on the policy.

Talk about one dull week. I have pooched around this city for a full week and found nothing more interesting than a woman with a low forehead and morals to match who knew the family and who took me by the hand and less public parts and showed me that the accident was indeed an accident. Stupid old Cap'n Bob couldn't swim, and if you're gonna go fishing from a boat, you should be able to swim or wear a life jacket.

He didn't, and now he is dead and his wife didn't have anything to do with it, except perhaps to wish hard for such a happy ending.

Damn. I really needed a murder.

This has not been one of my real best weeks ever. A week in Kansas City to start with. And is that a stupid name for a city in Missouri? If you're going to be in Missouri—and who the hell would want to be?—at least have the sense to call yourself Missouri City. Not Kansas City. I think there ought to be a federal commission to go around America renaming names. Like in New Jersey, North Bergen is south of Bergen County. Does that make any sense to anybody? Aaah, the hell with it. Nobody listens to me anyway. So I got a week here in Missouri City to start with and no crime to continue with and so no cut of what the insurance company would have saved to finish with. Now, if I had found out that the old lady had wrapped stupid Napier in ten-pound test nylon line and chucked him overboard, I would have saved the company two hundred thousand dollars and got a piece for myself. Now, all I get is my retainer and whatever I can steal on expenses. And how much could I steal here? What is there in Missouri City that you could pretend you spent money on?

And where the hell is Chico? I've called the condo three times in the last week and she is never there. All I hear is my own voice on that stupid tape machine, and if I wanted to hear my own stupid voice on some stupid machine, I wouldn't have to go to stupid Missouri City to do it.

So Chico's not around and that's not helping my week either. I wonder if my father ever has weeks like this. Knowing my mother, I guess so. Sarge, I guess, has decades like this.

I'm so depressed I con't even feel like drinking. I feel like a damn businessman in a damn strange town and I'm not a businessman and I don't want to be a businessman. I don't like businessmen. The only one I think I'd like is whoever named that luggage Amelia Earhart luggage. Now, come on, is that the greatest name for luggage you've ever heard? Amelia Earhart luggage. Fifty years' experience of being lost in transit. Now, there's a guy I'd love. Him and the first person ever to call his eatery the Terminal Restaurant. And maybe that guy who runs a string of pizzerias named John's and he advertises, "Women, if you're tired of being stuck in the house, go cruising till you find John's." Great commercial. All the rest of the businessmen in the world you can have.

So what was I talking about? Right, drinking. I can't remember things anymore and I think I'm getting What's-his-name's disease. Drinking. Right. I used to think I was going to drink until I had tasted every kind of drink in the world.

Well, did you ever see blue liqueur? I've been seeing that bottle of blue goo since I first started hanging out in saloons when I was a kid and I never saw anybody drink any of it. Actually, I think there's only one bottle and they ship it around the country like a rotating trophy and every bar gets a chance to have it on the shelf for a while. Like a Christmas fruit cake. There's only one of them in the entire country, but nobody ever eats it and they just keep mailing it around from family to family.

Anyway, last night, the big breakthrough. I drank some of that blue liqueur. It tasted like blue liqueur, which is to say it tasted like dragon barf. It's a big moment, though. Now, there's nothing left in the world that I haven't drunk, and if they don't start inventing some new liquor pretty soon—maybe something nice in a black—I may just decide to reconsider my position on drinking.

You can tell I miss Chico. Where the hell is she? I'm running off at the mouth this way because I drank all night, I haven't been to bed yet, I'm bored, and I'm afraid to go to bed because my plane's in just a few hours and I don't want to miss it.

Yes, midwestern-type folks, I'm leaving and it is a far, far better thing I do than I have done for the last seven days. I'm going to buy Chico a present, maybe something nice in a T-shirt. Actually, she's something nice in a T-shirt. I bet nobody ever gave her something nice in a T-shirt from Kansas City, Missouri. What a stupid name for a city. And where the hell is Chico?

To hell with it. To hell with everything. This is Devlin Tracy, crack investigator for Garrison Fidelity, signing off, unsuccessful and impoverished as usual. Crack investigator. Dat's the most ridiculous ting I ever hoid.

God, am I bored. Nothing ever happens anymore. Especially here.

4

There was no roommate and no dinner. Trace had had this expectation that he would walk in the door and find candles on the dining table, the silver set for a four-course dinner cooked by Chico's loving hands, Chico herself walking around in a French upstairs maid's costume, cut short, waiting on her man, a banner across the living room that read: WELCOME HOME, DEVLIN TRACY.

That was his vision. The reality was a note on the coffee table, written on a deckle-edged piece of note paper imprinted with the drawing of a teddy bear.

Trace.

I am getting tired of writing this note every day. But if you come home, I had to go out early tonight. Probably won't be home, Chico.

Trace crumpled the note and dropped it into the ashtray. The ashtray was a small piece of Italian leaded crystal, two inches across, and Trace looked at it unhappily, then went to a drawer in the kitchen and found hidden a nine-inch-across plastic ashtray. He put it on the coffee table, uncrumpled and read the note again, then squashed it up and put it in the big ashtray. With a large glass of vodka in one hand, a cigarette in the other, he lay down on the sofa and wondered what was happening with Chico.

They had been roommates for three years and they were about as good a three years as Trace could remember in his life. Chico made her living as a blackjack dealer at the

Araby Casino. She supplemented her living by doing occasional favors for the casino management and—she called it—"entertaining" high-rollers who were pushing a lot of money across the gambling tables.

She and Trace didn't talk about that part of her life. He didn't like it, but she never offered to stop it, so there didn't seem to be much to talk about.

Lately, though, it seemed that she was out "entertaining" more and more, and while he'd been away in that hellhole, Kansas City in freaking Missouri, he hadn't been able to reach her at night at all. Something was going on. Trace was sure of that, and it made him uncomfortable.

He didn't want to say it, even to admit it to himself, but the fact was that he kind of liked the way things were and the thought of their changing made him uneasy.

He drank a lot and smoked a lot and broke the stereo because he could never figure out how to work it and ignored the telephone when it rang because he knew it wasn't Chico and even if it were, he wanted to punish her so he wouldn't talk to her, and before he fell asleep on the couch, he got a pair of scissors from the kitchen and cut the T-shirt he had bought Chico into four separate pieces.

He was going to put the sections in the kitchen garbage, but if he did that, she might not see them, so he left the remnants of the shirt on the coffee table.

He wrote her a note. In the living room desk he found a pad of her note stationery with teddy bears on it. He drew a mustache and eyeglasses on the biggest bear, then wrote:

Dear Miss Michiko Mangini,

Mr. Devlin Tracy requests the pleasure of your company at dinner at 8 o'clock this evening. RSVP regrets only.

He sealed it in an envelope. He wrote her name on the front of the envelope, then scotch-taped it to the outside of the apartment door where she'd have to see it when she came home. If she came home.

Then he fell asleep on the couch.

Trace slept soundly only when drunk. When he woke up, he realized that he must have been drunk because he had slept hard and late and he saw that Chico had been home and had gone out again.

His invitation lay in the middle of the coffee table. Neatly printed under his note was her response:

Miss Michiko Mangini accepts. If you're buying. By the way, you got ripped off in Kansas City. This is some shitful excuse for a T-shirt. See you tonight. Chico.

5

"I don't mind that you're nothing. Less than nothing," Chico said. "What I mind is that you choose to be nothing. Less than nothing."

Trace looked at her across the table. The dining room was dark, and their table was lit only by a pair of candles in hurricane lamps. Which meant that Trace wouldn't eat. He didn't eat much anyway, but he especially ate little at restaurants that featured dim lighting because, while he knew it was supposed to be romantic, he was always afraid that the restaurants turned the lighting down just to make it easier to get rid of the leftover food from the kitchen.

In the soft diffused light at their table in the quiet far corner of the room, Chico's fine Eurasian face was fine indeed. Her lips were a full bow, her cheekbones high, and her skin smooth and healthy-colored, without looking as if she spent any of her free time "working on her tan." Chico had to work on nothing where her beauty was concerned; it all had come free, from God.

Her large brown eyes were staring at him with, he thought, a kind of sadness, maybe even loss. He wondered if that was the kind of look children had when they learned finally that there wasn't any Santa Claus. He tried to remember how his two children had looked when he had broken the news to them, but each of them had only been six months old when Trace had made the no-Santa-Claus pronouncement and neither had seemed to mind.

Chico was chewing. She swallowed, finishing her roll, and reached across the table for the one on his bread plate.

Apparently there was no emotional crisis deep enough to ruin Chico's appetite, he thought.

"What is this choose-to-be-nothing business?" he asked.

"Less than nothing," she corrected. "Just what it sounds like. You don't want to do anything. You don't want to be anything. You just want to drift along—"

"With the tumb-a-ling tumbleweeds," Trace sang. He tried a smile, but her eyes flashed without humor and he stopped smiling.

"That's it," she said. "It's a joke. Everything's a joke. Dammit, Trace, you're almost fifty years old."

"Hey, hold on," he said. "I'm forty years old."

"The blink of an eye," Chico said airily, waving her hand to dismiss the triviality of a mere decade. "In no time at all, you will be fifty and you'll still be nothing. Well, I don't want to be nothing with you," she said.

Trace looked around the room for a waiter. They were always hovering around, their big noses in the way between you and your coffeecup, except when you really needed them for something important, like refilling your drink. He lit a match, held it over his head, and looked at Chico again.

"I'm something," he mumbled lamely. "I'm me."

"Yeah. You're you and your you is getting less and less interesting. You know how much you drink nowadays?"

"Only half as much as I used to. Then I faw down, go boom."

"It's common with old drunks," Chico said. "Maybe you are drinking half as much, but you spend twice as much time doing it," she snapped.

"Oh, damn. I've been confusing drinking with sex again. I never can remember which one's supposed to go slow." He tried another unanswered smile which died a-borning.

She had finished his roll and now she grabbed his salad plate and started eating that too. With her mouth full, she said, unable to keep the disgust from her voice, "Always jokes. Maybe we should just write each other a letter."

"We'll talk," Trace said. "We've always been able to talk." The match burned his fingers and he dropped it to the table with a curse. He looked around again, caught the waiter's eye, and signaled for another drink.

Chico gulped and swallowed. "All right," she said. "Let's talk. I don't like things. I don't think I like you. I sure don't like much about you. You don't know what's happening in the world. You don't care what's happening in your life. Every day's just like the day before it: sodden, dumb, and dull. I've had it with that."

Trace raised himself to his full sitting height. "I resent that. Don't know what's happening in the world? Piffle. Piffle and rot. I know everything that's going on in the world. Ask me anything. Go ahead. Ask me about foreign relations."

"Tell me about foreign relations," she said, numbly, wearily.

"They're okay if they don't spend the night," he said.

"Fine," she said softly. "Good joke, Trace. But then your jokes should be good by now. You've had a lot of practice. Everything's a joke to you." Her dark eyes flashed, flooded with accusation. He thought of blowing out the candles on the table so he didn't have to look into her accusing eyes.

"That's not true," he said. "A lot of things are serious and I know it."

She gave back Trace's empty salad bowl. "Go ahead," she said. "Tell me something's that's serious."

"The Statue of Liberty," Trace said.

"Now I'm supposed to ask you why that's serious," Chico said. "Tell me, Trace. Why is that serious?"

"It's serious because it looks just like Sylvester Stallone," Trace said. "I think that's real serious. I think people come to America looking for freedom, like your folks when they escaped from Sicily and Japan with the cops after them, and then they get here and there's Sylvester Stallone standing in drag in the harbor, glaring at them. I think they raised all that money to fix the statue and they should have given it a nose job, and that's damn serious. Screw Lee Iacocca and Sergeant Slaughter. I've been thinking of starting my own fund to get the statue a nose job.

You don't think that's something a man can dedicate his life to?''

Again, she was not amused. Somehow dinner didn't seem to be going as swimmingly as Trace had planned. He had this vision that he would take Chico to dinner and he would wine her and dine her and find out what was bothering her and tell her a few jokes and get everything straightened out so that they could go back to being the way they had been. It didn't seem to be working out that way.

"That's exactly what I mean, Trace. You don't take anything seriously. Before you left for wherever the hell you were, you were talking about a foundation to cure AIDS.''

"I changed my mind about that," Trace said. "We've got to keep AIDS.''

"Why's that?" she said.

"AIDS is God's way of canceling the Phil Donahue show. I can't get involved with stopping that,'' he said.

Trace's drink—his third—came, and they took time out to order dinner. Chico ordered for both of them, one veal dish, one fish entree, and Trace knew they were both for her and he would wind up only picking at a baked potato. The rest of the food would vanish into the maw that was Chico's mouth. How could she eat like that and always weigh 105 pounds? A metabolic freak. If Trace could burn up alcohol the way Chico could burn up food, he would never leave the bar. Come to think of it, he considered ruefully, he rarely did. He had never told her, but that was one of the reasons he liked living in Las Vegas so much: the bars were always open.

When the waiter left, Chico drank half her glass of Perrier water and smiled sadly at him again. "You know, Trace, you told me once that there were horses for courses, different animals that run better on different kinds of track. Well, I think you were a pretty good horse for a short sprint but I don't think I want to be harnessed to you for the long run. You don't have any future.''

"And this explains why you're trying to turn more

tricks than anybody else in Las Vegas all of a sudden,"
Trace snapped. "That's your future?"

"I'm trying to put some money away. Trace," Chico
said. "I'm leaving this town soon. And you."

"After twenty years together?" he said.

"Three years. It just seems like twenty."

"I gave you the best three years of my life," Trace
said. He dabbed at his eyes with his napkin.

"You gave me grief, heartburn, and an overwhelming
desire to get away," Chico said.

"What are you going to do?" Trace asked. "Where are
you going to go? You're pretty old now to be thinking
about changing lives."

"I'm twenty-six," Chico said. "A lot of people are just
getting out of college at twenty-six. I'm going back to
Pennsylvania and start a business. Who knows? Maybe I'll
join the FBI."

"You'll never make it," Trace said. "The Restaurant
League of America will hand you up and tell them that you
steal food."

The waiter came. Their conversation had been slow,
stretched out, painful, taking longer than it should. Chico
stopped talking so she could concentrate on the food. She
started with the fish platter and allowed the veal to rest in
front of Trace.

"Maybe you can get a job as a professional taster,"
Trace said.

"I've had a large taste of misery," Chico said. "Does
that qualify me?"

"Eat and shut up," Trace said. He stuck a fork into a
baked potato, decided he wasn't hungry, and sipped at his
drink while he watched Chico eat.

Save for her part-time profession, Chico behaved like a
lady in every particular but one. She ate like Robinson
Crusoe must have when they got him back aboard ship,
head down, over her plate, total concentration on the food,
oblivious to everything else. Trace saw only the top of her
shiny blue-black hair.

Leaving him? She sounded serious this time, he thought.
Well, easy come, easy go. He had found her naked in a

hotel corridor one night and had taken her in. He had helped her get her job at the Araby Casino. How quickly they forgot. Everything good in her life had come from him.

But did she see it that way? Oh, no. What had she said? He gave her grief, heartburn, and an overwhelming desire to get away. Swell. Just because he had a drink once in a while. Was there anything in the world so selective of memory, so ungrateful for kindness, as a woman?

Good riddance to bad rubbish.

But what the hell would he do without her? A succession of warm bodies in his bed that he just wanted to vanish afterward? Who would he talk to? He thought for a moment and realized that, with Chico gone, the only people he would have to talk to were people who worked in bars and cocktail lounges.

What would he talk with them about? Bartenders wanted to talk about football and their bookies, and Trace had stopped finding that interesting years ago. Cocktail waitresses only wanted to talk about how the hostess was a bitch or the maître d' a bastard. Saloon singers wanted to talk about musicians in New York and the good hotels they had played that provided the best free meals for the help. Hat-check girls were always married and wanted to talk about their children.

And Trace didn't want to talk about any of those things. Not one.

The only person in the world, besides Chico, that he could talk to was his father, and Sarge lived three thousand miles away in New York. They could talk by telephone, but Sarge didn't like to talk on the phone any more than Trace did. But Sarge was all he had. Trace couldn't talk to his mother; he'd never been able to talk to his mother. His ex-wife spoke in grunts and snarls, and his two kids— What's-his-name and the girl—were still in diapers. Or in college. Or somewhere. Wherever they were, he didn't want to talk to *them*.

He waited for Chico to finish both their meals. It didn't take long.

"I think you're selling me short," he said.

"Tell me about it."

"Think about it. You've got to admit, I've had a lot of good ideas for inventions. Things that will make me independently wealthy. Make *us* wealthy."

"Sure," she said. Her voice was soft and, except for an occasional Pennsylvania-ism, as unaccented as a television news reader's. "Wonderful inventions. Great ideas. If you leave out the ones like making Tulsa into a parking lot. But some pretty good ideas. And you haven't followed through on any one of them, except when you bought into that stupid restaurant at the Jersey shore and lost your shirt. The rest of your inventions and schemes go nowhere. You know, Trace, I don't think I'd mind if you were some kind of lunatic inventor working on a bench in the back of our garage."

"We live in a condominium. We don't have a garage. Otherwise I'd be there right this minute."

Chico ignored him. "I wouldn't mind that," she said. "At least you'd be doing something. But not you. You just don't do anything. You don't even want to work when the insurance company calls you."

"I don't ever want to get to the point where in my own mind I believe that I work for an insurance company," Trace said. "That's why I just get a retainer and fees and don't go on their payroll."

"It's honest work," she said. "And it's work."

"It's disgusting and I refuse to have any part of it," Trace said.

They looked at each other across the table, eyes locked. Except for the soft, sad expression on Chico's face, they might have been gunfighters locked in a test of wills and courage.

"Well, it really doesn't matter to me anymore," she said finally. "You were yesterday. This is today and I'm thinking about tomorrow. And you're right, I'm not getting any younger."

"You get more beautiful every day," he said.

"I know. It's a bitch, isn't it? Every day I look in the mirror and say, 'Cheez-o-man, Michiko, you're better looking than you were yesterday. When's it all going to end?' "

"With death and decay, in the grave, the way all good things wind up," Trace said glumly.

She shrugged her shoulders in a gesture of "That's the way it goes." She said, "Everything dies. Except your mother."

He waited a long time, swirling the ice in his drink, and then said, "All right, what do you want? Lay it out, and whatever it is, if it's in my power to give without compromising my high standards, it's yours."

Chico giggled. "Standards? High standards? The only high standard you've got is that you never cheat on me with a homely woman."

"Everybody's got to start somewhere," Trace said. "Anything you want."

Chico shook her head, then leaned back in her chair and looked up at the ceiling. "They've got little luminous dots in that ceiling. Like little stars. We've been coming here for three years and I never noticed that before," she said.

"How could you when you're always looking straight down, diving into your stolen soup?"

She straightened back up and took a deep breath. "Trace, you don't understand," she said. "You've got this idea that I'm negotiating, that I want you to cut down on your drinking or your smoking or buy some new clothes instead of those rags you always wear." She shook her head. "That's not the way it is. I could put up with all that if I thought we were going somewhere, but we're not. You're not. I thought there was a chance when Sarge asked you to come into the private-detective agency with him."

"You'd be impressed if I were a private eye?" he asked.

"At least you'd be something." She twisted her mouth and did her Marlon Brando impersonation. "Instead of a bum, which is what you are. Something, Trace. Anything. It would have been good, but it's not there. What I want isn't in you to give."

"I'll join the CIA," Trace said. For a split second he meant it. He had seen an ad in the Sunday paper two weeks earlier advertising for CIA personnel. If they were reduced to advertising for spies, he could probably get in.

"They wouldn't have you. You'd sell America out for a drink," she said.

"Well, *they* don't know that."

"I'd tell them. This is my country too," she said.

"Yeah. This and Japan and Sicily," Trace growled. "All right. I'll join the FBI. I was an accountant. They'll take me. They take everybody nowadays."

"You look ridiculous in a trench coat. You always look like a flasher," she said. "You wouldn't make it."

Suddenly, she turned away from him and, head down, fumbled in her purse. She dabbed at her face with her handkerchief, and when she turned back, her eyes were wet.

"Let's stop it, Trace. Jokes and all, that's what we've had for three years. I don't have any more stomach for any more jokes."

His stomach seemed to settle lower in his body. He could smell the food scents from the tables around near them. The clinking of silverware and buzz of conversation seemed astonishingly loud and grew louder as he listened. He reached across the table and engulfed Chico's hand in his large hand.

"You're telling me there's no way?" he said.

"None that I see. You are what you are. I told you I would never try to change you and I'm not going to do that now. There's no point in it. Nobody can change anybody else."

"*I* can change me," he said.

"Sure. And it *can* snow in July. It's just not the way to bet," she said. She put her other hand on top of his.

"Go ahead, Trace. Have another drink."

"I'm going to cut down," he said stubbornly.

Chico shook her head. "It doesn't matter, Trace. It really doesn't matter." There were still tears in her eyes.

6

When the telephone rang, Trace decided not to answer it. It wouldn't be Chico; she never called when she was dealing at the Araby, so it was probably a bookmaker wondering why Trace hadn't been around. To hell with it, Trace thought. And besides, the answering machine would pick up the call on the fourth ring.

When it rang five times, Trace remembered that he had dropped the answering machine in the garbage pail the day before because he couldn't play back his messages. That was another thing. How the hell could Chico leave him? She was the only one who knew how things worked. She did something magic with the stereo to make it play when all he got was hiss. She was always able to get messages from the telephone tape when all he got were clicks and sounds like electrical sparks. She knew how to turn on the electric oven. He had tried to cook something in the oven once to surprise her when she came home from work. He turned the oven on to 450 degrees, and when she came home four hours later, everything in the oven was still cold. She tried to explain to him that you had to turn another dial also to actually turn on the oven. He thought that this was ridiculous and vowed never to use the oven again. Chico had agreed with this idea; in fact, she had gently suggested: "Keep your fucking hands off my oven."

What the hell was he going to do without her?

He answered the telephone finally, knowing that this was the way it was going to be. From now on, he'd have to answer the telephone to shut it up; he'd have to stand in front of the oven, hoping it would come on someday. He would have to listen to the radio because he would never get the stereo to play a tape or a record. How would he ever hear an opera again if he couldn't play a record? It was a certifiable fact that not once in the history of Las Vegas radio had an opera sound ever emerged from a radio receiver.

This was it, the end of his comfortable life as he had known it. From here on in, it was radio and cold canned beans—if he could figure out how to work the electric can opener. Answer your own phone all the way, no matter what detestable person might be on the other end of the line.

It was in a sour mood that he finally growled, "Hello."

It was his father. As usual, the easy seen-it-all voice of Retired New York City Police Sergeant Patrick Tracy made Trace feel instantly better.

"What's up, Sarge?" Trace asked.

"Just wanted somebody to share my misery."

"What happened?"

"Your mother won a cruise in some kind of raffle or something at the Hadassah."

"That doesn't sound so bad," Trace said.

"It's a cruise for two, son," Sarge said. "I've got to go."

"Oh. That *is* bad news. You have to go with Mother? You can't take somebody else?"

"No. I'm stuck. You know what's really rotten?"

"I don't know how anything can top taking a cruise with my mother," Trace said, "but try me. What's really rotten?"

"She won the damned thing a month ago and kept it a secret. She wanted it to be a surprise."

"Always the incurable romantic," Trace said.

"So yesterday I get this pretty good case and I go home last night and she's packing our bags. We're leaving on freaking Monday. God, I hate your mother's surprises."

"Did you try the old bad-back trick?" Trace asked.

"Right away. She wasn't buying. I guess I've gone to that well too often," Sarge said. "So I faked a coronary attack. She said if I died she'd bury me at sea. I even went over this morning to that old quack, Doc Johnson, to get him to write a report that I was allergic to sea air. You know what he told me? He told me I should stop complaining. That I should enjoy all these moments, that I should live in the present and learn to enjoy the present.''

"You ought to send *him* on the goddam boat ride," Trace said.

"I offered, but the quack turned me down. No use, son, I'm hooked. I've got to go."

"Where's the cruise to?"

"Puerto Rico or some other goddamn place where the sun's going to shine all the time."

"Might be nice," Trace said.

"Hey, I see enough Puerto Ricans around here," Sarge said. "If Puerto Rico's so nice, why the hell are they all living in New York?"

"They wanted to be close to you and Mother," Trace said.

"God, I hate this city," Sarge said.

"I know. More Puerto Ricans than San Juan, more Jews than Tel Aviv, more blacks than Kenya."

"Hell with that," Sarge said. "It's got your mother. Phooey. I didn't call to complain about my life."

"Sure you did," Trace said.

"Okay, so I did. Stop me before I wimp again. How's it by you?"

"Not so good, Sarge."

"What's the matter?"

"Chico's going to leave me," Trace said.

"She catch you in the sack again with somebody else?"

"Nope."

"You steal money from her savings account to buy liquor?"

"Not even that."

"I bet you rearranged the cans in her kitchen," Sarge said.

"Innocent."

"Then what's on her mind?"

"She says I don't amount to anything and probably never will," Trace said.

"Well, hell, she's known that for a long time," Sarge said.

"Thanks a lot, pal. That isn't exactly the reaction I wanted."

"Hey, son. The only good thing that ever happened to you in your life is that little girl. You're leading me one to nothing. Don't blow it."

"I don't know how to unblow it," Trace said.

"What do you have to do to keep her?"

"Change. Maybe get a job or something. Settle down a little bit. Try to make something out of myself."

Sarge whistled softly. "That's a lot to try to handle," he said, no trace of humor in his voice.

"You're not very encouraging."

"When I was bringing you up, I never told you life was going to be easy," Sarge said. "Now you have to pay your dues. Most of the time, all of us, we just drift through life and we don't have to do anything, and everything works out all right anyway. But once in a while, you have to punch the clock. This is one of those times, son."

"So you think I ought to change too?"

"I think you better not let Chico get away, is what I think. What you've got to do to do that is your business, not mine. She didn't ask you to stop drinking, did she?"

"No. Actually, she didn't ask me to do anything. In her mind, it's all over. She talks about us as if we were past tense. Like some old high-school sweetheart, you know, you think about once in a dozen years and you smile a little but you don't even ask yourself, I wonder what happened to old Glenda, 'cause you don't even care. It's just a nice memory but it doesn't have anything to do with your life anymore. That's the way she's treating us. Something dead and gone and once in a while remember it with a smile."

"You're in real trouble," Sarge said.

"I know. Aren't you glad you called looking for sympathy?"

"Let's think for a minute," Sarge said. He hesitated,

then asked, "If Chico could have anything, what would she want?"

"To be six feet nine inches tall."

"Why?"

"Because she'd like to kick the shit out of all the people who were rude or pushed her around because she was small or a woman or a half-breed or whatever."

"Shit, that's a tough one," Sarge said. "I don't know how we can make her six-foot-nine."

"Not without an operation," Trace said. "Maybe we can graft her and Mother together."

"Six feet nine tall, not wide," Sarge said.

"Then I guess we're lost," Trace said. "That's one of the reasons she's hung around with me so long, 'cause I'm big and people don't push hard against somebody as big as me."

"Wait. I got it," Sarge said.

"Quick, man. What is it? This is important."

"The great equalizer. I know how to make her six-feet-nine and make her stay with you."

"How's that?" Trace asked.

"Get her a gun."

"That's the dumbest idea I ever heard. The way she's feeling now, I give her a gun and she'll plug me between the eyes. Anyway, we've got a gun in the bedroom closet. I think it's there anyway. I don't take it out a lot."

"Not like give her a gun for a present," Sarge said, disgusted. "Sometimes you're as thick as shit."

"I'm all ears."

"Detective. You get your license here and work with the agency. Then we'll get her her license, and before you know it, she'll have a gun. That's what she wants, Dev. She wants power. Guns make everybody six-foot-nine. Why else do you think all those midget muggers carry them? If they were any bigger than four-foot-two, they'd carry chains and sticks."

"You think this'd work?" Trace said.

"I know it would."

There was a long pause before Trace said, "You're up to something, Sarge. When is that cruise anyway?"

"We leave Monday. For a week."

"Right. And you just happen to have a job that you would like me to keep an eye on while you're gone."

"I am hurt by your suspicious nature," Sarge said. "As I mentioned, yes, I do happen to have a case right now, but I'll have it done before I leave. You misjudge me totally."

"Sorry, Sarge. I want to think about this thing with Chico."

"Don't think too long. My idea will work. I guarantee it."

"I'll think about it. There's something else I want to try first. I'll get back to you tomorrow. And cheer up. You'll love the cruise."

"Not unless it goes down and only selected lifeboats sink," Sarge said. "Call tomorrow."

"I will. I just want to try this other thing first," Trace said.

7

"Birinci. Ikinci. Ucuncu. Dorduncu. Besinci. Altinci. Yedinci."

"What the hell are you doing?" Chico asked. She was standing inside the doorway to their apartment. Trace was sitting on the floor, facing a bare wall, his knees folded up in front of him, his back to her. He waved a hand over his head, as if gesturing for silence.

"Sekizinci. Dokuzuncu. Onuncu. On . . . Dammit, you made me lose my train of thought," Trace said as he lumbered to his feet.

"Please tell me what you're doing," Chico said.

"For your information, lady, I am improving myself."

"By mumbling at the wall?"

"That is not mumbling. That is Turkish. I am learning Turkish and I was counting. *Birinci, ikinci, ucuncu, dorduncu.* One, two, three, four. Hah! And you think you're so smart."

"Trace. Why are you learning Turkish?"

"Because I think unless people continually learn things and stretch their minds, they get stale, they get old, they get fat, and their women leave them. *Birinci, ikinci, ucuncu, dorduncu, besinci, altinci, yedinci.*"

"You're making that up, aren't you?" she said suspiciously.

"I knew you'd say that, but for your information, I am making nothing up. I am counting in Turkish for when I go to Istanbul. Actually it's very simple. You get to ten and then you start all over again. Nothing complicated like

48

a new word like eleven. See, one is *birinci* and eleven is *on birinci*. Two is *ikinci* and twelve is *on ikinci*. You just stick *'on'* in front of the numbers and that makes them ten higher. English should be so simple as Turkish. I'll have this language down in two, three days at the most.''

"Why?"

"I'm doing it all for you," Trace said.

"I'm still leaving," she said.

"Turkish won't do it? You mean, Turkish won't do it?"

"Not two days of Turkish so you learn just enough words to embarass me when we go someplace. It's like when you exercise and you promise one push-up a day for a year, except you forget to do them after the first day. Or you stop drinking vodka and you promise to drink wine, and you do it for a day and then you forget and you're back to vodka. Trace, you are a degenerate who cannot be trusted and that is that and why do we keep having this same conversation?''

"What can I do to make you stay?" Trace said.

"Nothing I can conceive of," Chico said.

"That's it. Conceive. I'll get you pregnant."

"Not as long as I'm in charge of that," she said.

She turned back to the hall, filled her arms with grocery bags, kicked the door shut, and brushed by Trace as she walked into the kitchen. With anybody else, so many groceries might have been a tipoff that she was planning to stay forever, but with Chico, it was just her usual precaution against hunger, famine, pestilence, plague, or worse yet, missing a meal. As she put the bags down on the kitchen counter, she saw a vase filled with the fresh flowers Trace had bought.

"The cleaning lady must have forgotten her flowers," she mumbled to Trace, who stood in the doorway of the small kitchen admiring her. He couldn't help admiring her. Even more than her face, than her form, there was something about her, something about the light way she moved, the way she seemed to command the air she moved through, that always touched his heart. It was time, he realized. Time to stop fooling around and to bite the bullet.

"All right," he said. He sat at the table in the kitchen,

and without being asked, Chico filled a glass with ice cubes from the freezer and poured over it from the bottle of vodka that Trace kept in the freezer compartment. The liquid, slightly purple, burbled out heavily over the ice. She set the glass on the table in front of him.

"Thank you. You like to see me crawl, don't you?"

"No, Trace. Just the opposite. I don't ever want you to crawl, but I don't want to crawl either. That's why I'm leaving."

"Don't lock yourself into fixed positions yet. It's too soon. You haven't heard my best offer."

"Go ahead." She turned away from the cupboard to look at him.

"You want a dollar?" he said, and winked.

"I'll pass. I've already got a dollar." She turned back and resumed putting groceries away.

"All right. Only kidding," he said. "I'm going to become a private detective. I'm taking the job with Sarge."

She turned back and said, "What's the catch?"

"No catch. And I want you to be a partner. Come into the company with us." Even as he said it, Trace thought this is a stupid idea. Sarge had his head up his ass from hanging around too long with Trace's mother.

"Do I get to carry a gun?" Chico asked.

"After you pass the licensing things, whatever they are," Trace said.

"I accept."

"And only when you learn to shoot with your eyes open," Trace said. "I've seen you shoot."

"I accept."

"Hold on. Just like that? You accept?"

"I accept." She came over and put her hands on his face.

"No negotiations?" Trace said.

She shook her head. "None necessary. You're joining Sarge's firm and you've got a place for me. Nothing to negotiate. I have reviewed your offer and find it acceptable."

"And you won't leave me?" Trace said.

"Not for the time being," Chico said.

"You can turn it on and off just like that?" Trace said.

"It's on again, pal. Don't knock it," she said.

"You always wanted to carry a gun, didn't you?" Trace said.

Chico nodded. She had that look on her face that comes to those who are speaking so basic and obvious a truth that it seems really unnecessary to have to say it at all, but if it made you happy, why not?

"If we're successful at this, you'll probably be busy," Trace said. "Have to give up your job at the casino."

"I'll walk away without ever looking back."

"No more boyfriends."

"Without ever looking back," she said.

"We might have to move to New York for a while, until we get a lot more business for the company. It'd take a while before we could justify an office out here."

"That's all right," she said.

"Just like that, you'd pick up and move to New York if we had to?"

"They haven't closed Bloomingdale's yet, have they?"

"We should leave right away," he said.

"I'll start packing."

"Give me a kiss," he said.

"Later," she said. "For now, practice your Turkish. In case you're a lousy detective."

"I hope you know what I'm risking for you," he said.

"What are you risking for me?"

"If we move east, we just move that much closer to my ex-wife and kids. I might have to see them someday."

"That's a chance you'll have to take," Chico said.

"The things I do for you," Trace said.

"I know. Ain't love grand?"

8

Except for the people, the only splash of color in the all-white room was a purple velvet cushion, as big as a car seat, on a platform at the front of the room. A lump of incense, the size, shape, and color of a vanilla ice-cream cone, burned on a white saucer next to the pillow, flooding the room with the treacly smell of sandalwood.

The room echoed with the *plink-plink-plink* of a stringed instrument that seemed out of tune, but if any of the fifty-two persons who sat cross-legged on neatly placed rows of white terry towels minded the sound, none showed it: they all stared straight ahead mindlessly, as if in trances, appearing not even to blink.

A redhaired woman in a long white gown rose smoothly in the front row and walked down the center aisle to a phonograph in the rear of the room and removed the needle from the record, halting the metallic sound of the sitar. With the music silenced, the faint sound of a portable television camera, operated by a young pimply-faced man in the back row, clicked in the room. He smiled at the redheaded woman, who nodded pleasantly and walked to stand behind him, in front of the room's closed and locked double doors. She clasped her hands in front of her waist and waited.

Then she smiled as the white satin drapes behind the platform parted. The people kneeling on the towels leaned forward and touched their foreheads to the floor as a tall brown-skinned man stepped onto the platform. He paused there as if posing for a painting of God. The man had a

neatly trimmed gray-flecked beard and wise-looking azure
eyes that seemed wisely to count the house before he
walked to the purple cushion and sat down. He spread his
long white robe neatly about him, smiled at the redhaired
woman in the rear of the room, looked around at the
still-bowed heads, and clapped his hands once, softly,
gently.

In unison, the bowed heads raised and the fifty-two cold
expressionless faces warmed into smiles.

"Om shanti," the man on the platform intoned in a
voice far more musical than the sound of the sitar.

"Om shanti," the people in the room mumbled in
answer.

"Welcome to the House of Love," the man said. His
voice was the singsong dialect of India, its cadence rising
and falling by some internal logic that seemed to escape
more Western minds.

"God is love. You are love. All is love. Do all here
believe that?" The man looked carefully around the room
at the fifty-two heads nodding agreement.

"Then rise, my children. Love thy neighbor, as it is
written."

The people rose from their white towels and the redhaired
woman stepped forward from the rear of the room and
placed her hand over the lens of the young man's television camera. She smiled at him and held her hand there as
the people in the room turned, each to his nearest neighbor, and embraced. Over their heads came the voice of the
man on the platform. "Love, love, all is love. Love,
children of love. Love. Love. Love. Love."

As his voice echoed, the embraces became warmer,
more ardent. It was a festival of wandering hands, between
legs, under blouses, inside pants. Men groped women,
men groped men, women groped women, as the man on
the platform continued to chant his one-syllable mantra:
"Love, love, love, love, love."

A young couple in the front row, apparently carried
away, began to undo each other's clothing. But suddenly
the man in the white robe clapped and all the activity
ceased. The people turned their faces to him, hastily rear-

ranging their clothing, and he spread his hands before him and gestured to them to sit again. Slowly, they sank back onto the towels on the floor. The redhaired woman removed her hand from the lens of the television camera and smiled again at the acned camera operator.

"God is love. Life is love. We are love," the man in the robe said. "Many have heard our message. Have you heard our message?"

There were mumbled cries of "Yes, yes."

"And will you live by our message of love?" the man said.

There were more yesses this time.

The man on the platform nodded his approval. "He who loves is never alone," he said. "Our numbers are thousands across this great land and will soon be millions around this earth. Many are on their way here now and next week we will begin our journey to our new home, the City of Love, even now being made ready in far-off Pennsylvania. Who among you will be with us in the City of Love?"

A dozen hands were shyly raised around the room.

"Very good, very good," the man on the platform said. "We welcome you who will join us in the City of Love and we welcome you who are here today to meet with us in this House of Love. Someday perhaps the rest of you too will give up worldly possessions and come to join us in far-off Pennsylvania to live a life of harmony with our fellow man, our fellow woman, our creator and our universe. We welcome all of you to our family today. A special blessing to all of you."

He clapped his hands again softly and the white drape at the rear of the platform parted and a young dark-haired woman stepped out. She was small and delicate and wore a long white robe. In her arms, she carried a dozen long-stemmed yellow roses.

Nervously, she moved forward and knelt before the seated man, touching her head to the floor of the stage. Then she carefully arranged the dozen roses about his feet, slowly and deliberately as if creating a sculpture. As she moved, a bell tinkled gently.

When she set down the last rose, she backed away from the platform and knelt on the floor, head down. The people in the room watched as the man picked up one of the roses. He held it before him, looking at it lovingly, his face set in a small whimsical smile, then lifted it above his head in both hands as if offering it up to God. He lowered the rose again to his face, inhaling deeply of its scent. Then he carefully plucked a petal from the rose in his lap and placed it in his mouth. He chewed the petal delicately, once, twice, swallowed, then peeled another petal and placed it in his mouth. Petal by petal, he denuded the rose. The young woman still knelt before him. The others in the room watched him reverently. The redheaded woman watched the actions from the back of the room and the television camera recorded the eating, the watching, the kneeling, and the waiting, all for posterity.

Slowly, the man on the platform rose from his purple cushion to his feet. He held the now-bare stem of the rose and lifted it skyward, over his head, looked upward, and then gurgled, deep down in his throat, a bubbling sound that seemed hard and gross in the still sanctity of the room, and then he coughed and choked and fell forward onto the floor, mashing his nose with a sharp crack of splintering bone.

Blood sprayed from his broken nose as his body lurched to the side, splashing the robe of the prostrate dark-haired girl. For a moment, the people in the room seemed rooted in their places by shock, looking at one another, then at the man who lay in a white crumpled heap, like a week's washing. The redhaired woman ran forward toward the platform. The kneeling woman looked up, touched the blood on her face, then screamed. The scream broke the tableau. People moved forward to the platform and milled about the fallen man. Others came from behind the white drapes to see what had happened.

In the confusion no one noticed the pretty dark-haired girl who had carried in the roses leave. Nor did anyone see the cameraman depart.

No one thought about the young woman until later when

a police doctor determined that the man had died from ingesting a huge dose of poison that had been sprayed over the petals of the rose. The other eleven roses contained enough poison on their petals to have wiped out almost the entire room of people.

9

Detective Ed Razoni was waiting in front of his seedy-looking West Side apartment building when Tough Jackson screeched his car to a stop at the curb.

Razoni clambered inside and Jackson took off with a complaint of rubber. Razoni dug his heels into the worn floormat of the car and covered his eyes with his hands.

"Tough, I know you're married, but I still got something to live for," he said.

"Captain says he wants to see us in a hurry. I'm hurrying," Jackson said.

"Hurry a little slower. Please. And isn't this some shit, getting called in to work on a Sunday? What the hell is this all about? Did the captain say anything?"

"He never says anything," Jackson said. "Just get in here or get out of here or go away. He never tells you anything."

Razoni grunted and fastened his seat belt. He finally relaxed sixty blocks later when Jackson skidded to a stop in a no-parking zone near police headquarters.

"What the hell is this?" Razoni said.

Through the windshield of the battered 1982 sedan, they saw a stream of people in white robes, silently walking in a single file around the entrance to the headquarters building.

"What do those signs say, Tough?"

"Avenge the death of Salamanda."

Razoni screwed up his face in bewilderment. "Somebody's lizard died? All this because somebody's lizard died?"

Jackson shrugged. "As long as it's not a Klan meeting."

"Maybe it is," Razoni said brightly. "Maybe it is. Maybe we're finally taking back control of the department from the pinkos and the communists and the fags and the bombthrowers. Tough, take me home so I can get my sheet."

"I think maybe we ought to see the captain first," Jackson said.

As they stepped onto the curb in front of the police center, Jackson was pushed from behind. He turned calmly to look down into the fuzzy eyes of the wiry-haired youth who had done it.

"Why did you do that, son?" he asked gently.

"The great Swami Salamanda is dead," the youth cried, his voice brushing the edge of hysteria. "If you're going in there, you got to be a pig. Are you going to get the killer of the great Salamanda?"

"Sonny," said Jackson, "I don't know who or what Swami Salamanda is, but if you call me a pig one more time, I'll use you for suet."

He turned and started up the five concrete steps to headquarters, Razoni one step behind him. There was a scream from within the crowd. Shrieking, a Brillo-haired girl in a white robe left the line and lunged toward Razoni with a kitchen knife in her hand.

Razoni turned at the scream, saw her coming, and darted behind Jackson.

"My suit, Tough. Don't let her get at my suit. It cost four hundred dollars." He cowered behind the big body of his partner.

The girl darted up the steps toward Jackson, the knife in front of her like a jouster's lance. Just when it seemed that the knife must find Jackson's midriff, he moved a few inches to the side. His giant right hand came down and closed around the girl's wrist. He squeezed. She screamed and dropped the knife.

Quickly, but without seeming to hurry, Jackson turned back toward the door and followed Razoni into headquarters, still holding the girl's wrist, pulling her along with him as easily as if she had been a stuffed toy. The door

closed behind them, just as the shouts of "Brutality"
began to rise from the crowd.

"Wow, that was a close call," Razoni said. "A four-
hundred-dollar suit and she goes waving a knife at it. You
ought to be ashamed of yourself," he said to the girl
angrily.

"Go fuck yourself," she snapped.

"Anything'd be better than you," said Razoni. He
marched toward the desk of the precinct, which shared
some of the space in the building with the headquarters
units.

"Prisoner for you, Sarge," he called out cheerily.

The bored-looking, middle-aged desk sergeant looked
up unhappily as Jackson dragged the girl along.

"What's the charge?" the sergeant asked.

"She assaulted Razoni's suit," Jackson said.

"Kill the pigs," the girl screamed. "Kill the pigs."

"No, sweetheart," Razoni said. "You've got it wrong.
This is the week we kill salamanders. Next week we've
got squirrels and the week after *that* it's pigs. You got it?
Sarge, we've got to see Captain Mannion. You got somebody to handle this dipstick?"

"Hunsburger," the sergeant called. A tweedy-looking
young detective with a beard came from an office. He
looked at the sergeant, who told him: "Book this one. She
assaulted Razoni's suit."

The detective nodded, then finally comprehended what
the sergeant had said, and looked up in surprise. "His
suit?" He looked at Razoni's plaid sharkskin suit. "It
might be justifiable homicide," he said.

"I hate cops who try to be smartass," said Razoni, who
took the girl's arm from Jackson and pushed her forward
into Hunsburger. "Watch yourself," he said. "She's a
killer."

Inside an office whose door announced PRIVATE, a uniformed sergeant with a thin pinched face looked up as the
two detectives entered.

"Hiya, Schultz," said Razoni breezily. "Jeez, it must
be important to drag you away from Sunday school."

"It's about time," the sergeant said. "He's been waiting for you a long time. You think when he said hurry, you'd hurry.''

Razoni had never liked Schultz and had absolutely detested him since he had been promoted to sergeant and Razoni had failed the test. He said, "Schultz, I want to get you something for your birthday. What does a weasel eat anyway?''

Schultz glowered. "Go inside. He's waiting for you.''

Captain Mannion sat behind a giant old wooden desk that always reminded Razoni of a coffin big enough to hold the bodies of an entire precinct basketball team. The varnish along the edges of the desk was scalloped with black parabolas where Mannion had let cigarettes burn themselves out.

The captain's face was shrouded in darkness. The only illumination in the office came from a gooseneck lamp and it was aimed toward them, toward the door, its hard light glaring angrily on a single red rose in a white milk crystal bud vase on the edge of the desk.

"Look at the flower," Razoni whispered to Jackson. "You think he's getting soft in the head?''

"Shhhh," Jackson responded.

Mannion, however, could not hear them, since he was too busy shouting into the telephone. Angrily, he waved to Razoni and Jackson, a wave that meant the two detectives should sit down. Their sitting down confirmed, in turn, that they were going to be given an assignment. When Mannion only wanted to chew them out, he made them stand.

"I don't care what your profit picture is," said Mannion into the telephone. "I don't want that goddamn place rented to those nit-nats.''

Razoni and Jackson slid into the hard-backed wooden chairs as Mannion listened quietly for a moment. The air in the office was shot through with stale cigarette smoke.

"This place smells like a burning dump," Razoni said.

"Shhhh," said Jackson.

Mannion was talking again and did not hear them. The captain took a deep breath and lowered his shoulders.

"This is it," Razoni said. "He's going to try to be reasonable."

"Now, now, now," said Mannion softly into the telephone. "I understand your problem, Mr. Macdonald. I truly do. Yes, I know how the economy is affecting your property rentals. Yes, sir, I certainly do. This sluggish economy is a terrible thing. Us police suffer from it too. Yes, sir. I guess you could call us fellow sufferers. But you see, sir, there is a different problem here. If you rent that loft to those people, it will probably serve as headquarters for whatever kind of disturbance they might take it in their mind to plan. It might lead to serious trouble. Yes, sir, it certainly could. It might even result in serious property damage to your building, and that is why the commissioner and I were hoping you would not rent it out." He paused. "I see. You're willing to take that risk. I see. You need the income from the building. Yes, I see. The public safety is not really your concern. Yes, I see. I can certainly understand that, Mr. Macdonald. Yes, yes. Oh, yes. Of course. May I just say one more thing, sir? Thank you. Let me just say that you are a tight-fisted prick and I hope those hairy scumbags tear your fucking building apart, and when they do, you cheap Scotch bastard, if you come whining around here, I'll throw you in the can and throw the key in the fucking river, now go fuck yourself, asshole."

Mannion slammed the telephone into its cradle with a crack that seemed to make the desk jump into the air.

"Now, what is it you two imbeciles want?" he shouted.

"Nothing, Captain," Razoni said quickly. "We just stopped in to see how your roses were doing. It looks all right, so we'll just be on our way." He stood up to leave.

"Sit down, Razoni. Sit down and, just for once, shut up, because I don't want to have to listen to you. Why me, God?" He looked heavenward, then back down, and his eyes shone black as coal as they glared at Razoni from under a pair of snow-white steel-wool eyebrows.

"Where the hell have you two been?" he snarled. "I called hours ago."

"We were checking out the white sale outside," Razoni

said, but before Mannion could respond, Jackson said, "What's going on, Captain?"

"A guru's been killed over in the East Village."

"That Salamanda?" asked Razoni.

"Right."

"See, Tough. I told you he wasn't a lizard," Razoni said.

"Shut up," Mannion bellowed. "This is important. Next Sunday, exactly seven days from today, this Salamanda was going to hold a national convention of the freaks that follow him. Right here in our fair city. And then they were all going to get into buses and drive out into Pennsylvania, where they are going to open, are you ready for this, the City of Love."

"Love is nice," Razoni said.

"Well, all these swami's followers are still coming and we're going to have trouble," Mannion said.

"How's that, Captain?" Jackson asked.

"These nutcakes are still coming. Dammit, Salamanda's body isn't even cold yet and already they're talking about protesting police inefficiency. That's just a taste outside. Can you imagine what it's going to be like next Sunday if this isn't cleared up by then?"

Razoni shrugged, then looked down and dusted the lapels of his suit jacket. "Put the killer in jail. That'll shut everybody up."

"Put the killer in jail," Mannion mimicked. "Put the killer in jail. Put the killer in jail. There's only one little thing missing from your plan, Razoni. To do that we have to find the frigging killer."

While Mannion was speaking, Razoni picked up the bud vase and sniffed it deeply. The rose had an outdoorsy smell that one could go years in the city without experiencing. Razoni thought it smelled funny.

"So let's find the killer," Razoni said.

"Good. Get right on it," Mannion said. He looked down at papers on his desk.

"It might help, Captain, if you told us a little bit about it," said Razoni.

"All I know about it is that somebody handed this guru a rose and he ate it and it was poisoned."

Razoni swiftly put down the bud vase. "He ate a rose?" he said.

"Right. He ate a poisoned rose."

"Why would anybody eat a rose?" Razoni asked.

"I don't know. Maybe he was hungry," Mannion snarled.

"I've been hungry," Razoni said. "I never ate any rose. Did you ever eat a rose, Tough?"

Jackson turned his head away, refusing to answer.

"Captain, you ever eat a rose?" Razoni asked.

"Oh, my God," Mannion said. "Is this what the rest of my life is going to be like?"

Razoni suspected that Mannion might be upset, so he asked brightly, "Who gave the swami the rose? The one that he ate?"

"Some girl. He was holding some kind of ceremony for just new members and the roses are part of the ceremony. He ate the goddamn thing and keeled over and died."

"Right after eating the rose?" Razoni asked.

"Right, Razoni. Right after eating the rose."

"No sweat, Captain," Razoni said. "We'll find the killer of this, er, guru for you."

"Please do, Razoni," Mannion said earnestly. "I would consider it a personal favor."

"Are the precinct bulls working on it?" Jackson asked.

"Yeah, and they've got to keep working on it. But they couldn't find cowshit in a pasture."

"Well, what do you want us to do?" Jackson asked.

"Go down and look around. See if you find out anything. Let yourself be seen. If they understand that the commissioner's office is hot on this, they'll work harder. You know what to do. Do what you usually do. Annoy people."

Jackson nodded. Razoni stood up, looking thoughtful. He walked from the office mumbling to himself, "Who'd eat a rose? Got to be damn hungry to eat a rose."

Razoni managed to knock over Schultz's coffeecup before leaving, ruining what looked like a freshly typed pile of correspondence. In the doorway leading to the hall,

Razoni said, "Tough, I've got to ask you something very important."

In the hall, with the door safely closed behind them, Jackson said, "What, Ed?"

"What the Christ is a guru?"

"You don't know? You live in this city and you don't know what a guru is?"

Razoni wrinkled his brow. "Somebody who eats roses?"

10

Sarge decided that someday, when he was old and writing his memoirs, he would write a special chapter for private detectives. And the first tip he would give would be: have a television set in the office and keep it turned on.

Since Friday, the retired New York City police sergeant had been working on Angelo Alcetta's wife. The first time Tracy had seen her, he had realized that neither Alcetta nor the photograph he had gotten of her lied. She was a breathtakingly beautiful woman. That was the good news. The bad news seemed to be that she was as straight as a tight clothesline.

Every morning, she went from her apartment to some Indian cult place called the House of Love down in the East Village. Sarge had thought that she was just some dippy follower, but that wasn't true. She was some kind of official there, in charge of membership and training. Angelo Alcetta apparently hadn't known that, but anyone who wanted to join up had to talk to Angelo's wife first.

The woman was at the headquarters all day every day and at night she called a cab and went to her West Side apartment and stayed there all night.

When he had first seen the name "The House of Love," Sarge had expected that the woman would be a little crazy, some bored housewife with hot pants and a cold husband, but that hadn't checked out. Everyone he had talked to who knew her had only kind words to say about her.

From the doorman of her apartment building, whose thirst was stronger than his sense of discretion, Sarge learned that Mrs. Alcetta didn't call herself Mrs. Alcetta anymore; she was now Gloria Charterman. She had no male visitors and only occasional female visitors, and as far as the doorman knew, no one ever spent the night and no one shared the apartment with Mrs. Alcetta-Charterman. Its rent was eleven hundred dollars a month and it was always paid on time.

Sarge hadn't ventured into the House of Love itself, but he had seen Angelo's wife a number of times as she went in and out of the health-food store next to the headquarters. She looked happy and smart, as well as beautiful, and not as if she were grieving for her lost love with her husband. And who, in her right mind, would? Sarge wondered.

As far as he could tell after only a day and a half on the job, she was what she appeared to be: an ex-housewife who had had a religious experience, left her boring stupid husband—and who wouldn't?—and was now ass over tea kettle in love with some swami's cult.

The swami was a different matter. Sarge didn't have much to report to Angelo Alcetta that he might care about, so he thought he would pad his report. He considered going to the New York City Public Library, but instead he stopped in at this dentist's office where every copy of *Time* and *Newsweek* for the past two years were kept and he looked through their indexes for anything on the Swami Salamanda.

There was plenty, and as he read the stories, Sarge had a growing sense of annoyance with himself, a feeling that he hadn't kept himself up to date with what was going on in the world. Was that a sign of getting old? he wondered. When you cut down on the number of things you paid attention to and stayed interested in?

Salamanda was called the Guru of Sex. As best as anyone could tell, he was forty-five years old and had come to the United States from India about two years earlier. His message, which had made an immediate hit, was simple: "More sex, with more people, is the way to break the psychic bonds that trap us in lives of misery.

One will only be truly fulfilled and enlightened when he makes himself as one with the greatest pleasure the great creator has given all of us—sex." The swami went on to say, "There is no unwholesome sex, just unwholesome attitudes on the part of people who are afraid of sex."

Salamanda had toured the United States preaching his message, and the converts came by the hundreds. *Newsweek* pointed out that it would be easy to think these converts were kids, teenagers rebelling at their home life and the restrictions placed on them by their parents. But, the magazine said, while it was true that the Salamanda movement had a full complement of pimply-faced nerds who joined up hoping to score sex, the real core of Salamanda's strength was older people—the parents, not the children—which led the magazine to believe that there were a lot of unhappy people out there.

"And only one of them married to Hilda," Sarge mumbled under his breath, thinking of his wife and her damned stupid surprise plan to take him on a boat cruise.

As for the rest of his message, Swami Salamanda didn't seem to have one. He talked about a couple of breathing tricks, meditation, hyperventilation, what *Time* magazine called "the same mixed bag of take-a-deep-breath-and-smile philosophical techniques." The core of everything was sex. It was the be-all and end-all of Salamanda's movement.

Both magazines indicated there was no way to tell if Salamanda was getting rich on his movement. He stayed in hotels when he traveled, and when he was in New York, he lived in a small apartment in the same building as his House of Love headquarters. But he was building. Near the small town of Butler, Pennsylvania, Salamanda was building a commune that would be called the City of Love. The area was sealed off and not open for inspection, but a couple of flyovers in a rented helicopter had convinced *Newsweek* that this would be the commune to end all communes, with a central mansion with minarets, swimming pools, tennis courts, stables, a private air landing strip, a warehouse-size garage that already held seven

Rolls-Royces, and small apartment units that looked as if they could house more than a thousand people.

Who would live there? *Time* pointed out that many hundreds, perhaps thousands, of people had already pledged to turn over all their worldly goods to the People of Love, as Salamanda's movement was known, and take up residence in the new city devoted to pleasure.

Salamanda's own city, built with the donations of the faithful. This raised some eyebrows, but the swami was not reluctant to defend himself. He appeared on one popular morning talk show whose moderator had a reputation for being a tough interviewer, and wound up tying the moderator in knots. Where the moderator was smirking and smarmy, the swami was direct, caustic, and unfazed.

"Don't you find the emphasis on sex in your love-is-all movement . . . well, unhealthy and unreligious?" the emcee asked, rolling his eyes as if sharing a deep secret with the members of his audience.

Salamanda, wearing a white robe and sitting on a cushion on stage, said, "The greatest expression of physical pleasure given to us by God is the sexual act. We see nothing wrong in partaking of God's provided pleasure through that act. We pity all those who are so repressed, so dried up of body, soul, and mind that they cannot so participate. And we pity them even more because in their frustration, they try to stop others—those who can believe and can practice that love is all—these ineffectuals try to prevent others from believing and practicing, and we pity them and we pray for them to the great god who gave us all, including the act of love." He paused and looked at the emcee. "We pray for you too. And for your wife."

"You mentioned God. Who is God?" the emcee asked.

"Who would you want him to be?" Salamanda said.

Smugly, the emcee said, "There are many views of God in our Judeo-Christian world. Jesus, Jehovah, Brahma, Buddha. Which is your god?"

"You omitted some," Salamanda said. Then, for five minutes, he recited the names of other gods, as if to underscore the ignorance of the TV-show host. When he was done, he looked up and smiled.

"Whichever of these names you choose to give to God, that name is pleasing to us. But know you this: that each of these gods has followers and that, we think, must please that god. But for a god's followers to carry on, a god's followers must procreate. Therefore, does it not mean that all these gods approve of the sexual act, and of sexual congress? Because if they did not, they would be saying to the man who follows them: no more, stop, cease, stop living, be gone and be dead. That is not a living god who speaks to living people. We share with everyone's view of god the idea that god is love and his people are love and he has made them to love. And we practice what god preaches."

According to the magazines, it was no contest. The talk-show host was reduced to falling back on the fear of spreading AIDS to discredit Salamanda. *Time*'s television critic pointed out that in Swami Salamanda America was seeing a new kind of guru. In the past, he said, the gurus who had come to America to shill their wares—most of them from India—were a decidedly foreign commodity. They looked funny. Most were bearded, short, and squat. They spoke funny, some of them with such heavily accented English that it couldn't be understood by anyone but Peter Sellers. Salamanda looked like the start of the second wave. His English—which had an Indian accent only when he chose to use one—was better than most Americans', and instead of looking like a foreigner, he looked like a handsome British actor wearing tea stain and doing a remake of *Four Feathers*. This was a guru who used television for his own ends instead of being victimized by it the way most were.

A final paragraph in one story wondered about Salamanda's own sex life and a reporter was able to ask him about it in a written question. He got a written reply: "I have always held that we should do sex, not talk about it," Salamanda wrote. The reporter conceded that there was not even a hint of sex scandal about Salamanda personally but pointed out that if the urge ever hit him, there was certainly no shortage of beautiful, willing female disciples standing by.

Sarge borrowed the copies of *Time* and *Newsweek* and took them to the stationery store on the corner, where he photocopied the stories about Salamanda for twenty-five cents a page. He had found out in life that good reports weren't really as important as thick reports.

Sunday morning, he had followed Gloria Alcetta from her apartment to the House of Love, where a sign was posted on the front door: CLOSED MEETING TODAY.

He had returned to his office over Bogie's Restaurant and had called the Salamanda headquarters and asked to speak to Gloria.

"You mean Sister Glorious?" a male voice asked.

"Yes."

"I'm sorry. She is working today with new members. She will not be available until late this evening."

"Thank you." Sarge hung up, feeling sure that Gloria Alcetta wouldn't be leaving the House of Love, and started to typewrite—with two fingers—a report for Alcetta. He doubted that the young moron would ask him to keep following his wife when he had obviously found nothing of any worth. But who knew? Maybe all the talk about the Swami of Sex might get Alcetta mad enough to pay Sarge some more good money to follow his wife from apartment to office and back to apartment again.

One thing he suspected. The fact that Gloria was now using the name "Charterman," instead of Alcetta, would make him furious. He made that one of the cornerstones of his report.

He finished it up with a few large questions:

Does Salamanda approve of bizarre sex practices as has often been alleged?

Does the woman who now calls herself Charterman participate in these dangerous practices?

Are there other criminal activities under way at the Salamanda headquarters, and if so, does the woman who now chooses to call herself Charterman know anything about them? Or is she just a dupe?

It is impossible to answer these questions at this time. More surveillance work might, however, produce the answers.

Sarge snapped the manila folder shut, after rereading, with a certain literary pride, his last couple of sentences. If that didn't get Alcetta to say continue the investigation, he didn't know what would.

He locked the file in a drawer in his desk, and to celebrate its completion, he went downstairs to Bogie's to drink and to await the arrival of Trace and Chico from Las Vegas.

And that was when he decided he had to get a television set for his office.

Bogie's had no television, but playing softly over the stereo system was music from one of the soft mush-music stations that abounded in New York City. At the stroke of the hour, the news came on, and the first item reported that Swami Salamanda, the controversial sex guru who had been attracting thousands of followers nationwide, was poisoned today in his East Village headquarters.

Police called the death an apparent homicide and said that Salamanda appeared to have been killed by an exotic poison that had been painted on some roses. Salamanda traditionally ate the rose petals as part of a welcoming ceremony for new members.

The news report said that Salamanda's movement had been preparing for a nationwide rally in New York City the following Sunday. From there, as many as a thousand were expected to drive in caravans to Western Pennsylvania, where Salamanda's new national headquarters—the City of Love—had been completed and was ready for occupancy.

Sarge cuffed down his beer and left, annoyed at himself for not having a television set so he could have heard that news bulletin earlier. How stupid would he look if he had called Alcetta and said he had completed the report on the man's wife, and somehow forgot to mention that his wife's guru had just been murdered.

He got into his rusty old black Ford sedan and drove
downtown toward the Salamanda headquarters. With luck,
he would be done and back in time to meet Chico and
Trace at his office.

11

It was just the way Chico had feared it would be. The meal on the plane was shish-kebab, and after it was placed in front of Trace and he had examined it, he called the stewardess over.

"This is a pretty poor excuse for shish-kebab," he said.

"It's one of our most popular meals, sir," she said. "Perhaps you should try it before you decide you don't like it." She was a statuesque blonde who had always been pretty and so had always been used to giving orders.

"I'm sure it'll *taste* all right," Trace said, "but . . ."

"Yes?"

"It only has *altinci* shishes on the kebab. I think to be a real shish-kebab, it ought to have least *yedinci* shishes on the kebab."

The stewardess looked at the plastic dinner plate in front of Trace, then questioningly at Chico, who was busily eating.

Chico gulped and swallowed. "Turkish," she explained. "He's counting in Turkish for you."

"That's right," Trace said. "Turkish is like my second skin, a language I'm so familiar with. What I said was that there are only six shishes on this kebab and there ought to be at least seven. That's what it means, *altinci* and *yedinci*. When I first started flying, stewardesses knew a lot of languages. Almost every one of them knew Turkish."

"That's 'cause when you started flying, one of the scheduled stops was the Tower of Babel," Chico said.

73

"I'm sorry, sir," the stewardess said. "I don't know Turkish."

"Want to learn?" Trace asked. "It's easy. Just repeat after me. *Birinci, ikinci, ucuncu, dorduncu, besinci*. That'll get you up to five. Basically that's all you need in Turkey. Except Istanbul. You have to go up to seven or eight in Istanbul. Unless you're buying a woman. Then it's back to five. If you pay more than *besinci* for a woman, you've been taken."

"Thank you very much, sir," the stewardess said, backing away nervously. "Let me know how you enjoy the meal."

"On a scale of *birinci* to *onuncu*, I'd make it a *besinci*," Trace said.

"Will you stop?" Chico said.

"All right," Trace conceded. The stewardess left. Trace took a piece of meat from the shish-kebab, chewed it for a while, and said, "I overrated it. It's only a *dorduncu*."

"Good. More for me," Chico said, and switched her empty plate with his.

"Listen," he said. "I'm changing my whole life for you. Don't you think you can change your eating habits for me?"

"Sure. What do you want me to change?"

"Eat less."

"Why? Is America running out of food?"

"Any day now, if you keep going," he said.

Chico patted his arm reassuringly. "Don't worry about a thing. When America goes empty, we'll just move to Turkey. With your extensive knowledge of the language, I'm sure we'll get along. And it *is* the perfect language for you, Trace, because you are a real turkey. Are you sure Sarge knows we're coming?"

"I told you, didn't I?"

"You did. That's why I'm asking you again."

"Sarge knows we're coming. He is delighted. He is doubly delighted that I may join his firm. He is triply—is triply a word? or is it triplily?—anyway, he's delighted threefold that you may also join the firm. He says you provide the missing ingredient to our success as a detective agency.''

"Brains?'' she said.

"No, money.''

"Fat chance,'' Chico said, "that you two ding-dongs will ever see a penny of mine. Did he really say that?''

"No. He said you'd provide the female touch. Those little feminine wiles that disarm a suspect without ever letting him know that he's a suspect, and then you finally have his head on your shoulder and he's blubbering, telling you how he stove in Aunt Dilys' head with an ax just to get his hands on her collection of stuffed mice.''

"But I get to carry a gun, right? Can I shoot the fucker?''

"Is he our client?'' Trace asked.

"Yes,'' Chico said.

"Did he pay his bill yet?''

"Yes.''

"Shoot the fucker,'' Trace said.

12

Razoni and Jackson learned, from Detective Gault and Gorman at the local precinct, that more than fifty persons had watched Swami Salamanda eat the poisoned rose and that the other eleven roses brought out to the stage were also poisoned. The young dark-haired girl who brought in the roses had vanished after Salamanda collapsed; no one knew her name or where she lived, and no one had yet come up with a line on her.

Additionally, Razoni and Jackson learned that Detectives Gault and Gorman were not especially pleased about having two other detectives intruding on "their" murder investigation, even if those two other detectives did work right out of the commissioner's office, because this was a page-one case and a chance for Detectives Gault and Gorman to get some publicity and perhaps get a leg up on the ladder toward promotion.

In return, Detectives Gault and Gorman learned that Detective First Class Edward Razoni did not give a shit about their feelings, because how did he feel being dragged out of his house on a Sunday, and that if he were running the police they would both be promoted the day after the last of the new police cadets had made deputy chief inspector, and even this would be too soon because Detectives Gault and Gorman had made "the worst mistake detectives can make" and did they ever think of finding a new line of work?

"Ed," said Jackson later in the car, "what's the 'worst mistake detectives can make?' "

Razoni shrugged. "I don't know. I just made that up to make them feel rotten."

"Do you know that for the rest of their lives they're going to be wondering what terrible mistake they made?"

Razoni covered his eyes with both hands as Jackson slalomed his way through a busy intersection against a red light. When he heard no crash, he uncovered his eyes and said, "Serves them right. Anybody stupid enough to be a cop deserves misery in his life."

"You're a cop," Jackson said.

"That's right, and I've got you for a partner."

"That's misery?"

"That's right. Misery. Who ever heard of a black detective? Who ever heard of a black who wasn't a criminal? And here I get one who thinks that a guru's a person who eats roses," Razoni said.

Jackson swerved around three pedestrians stepping from between parked cars. They were crossing the invisible dividing line into Alphabet City, a particularly degenerate sprawl outward from the eastern part of Greenwich Village.

"Who drives like a maniac," Razoni said.

Jackson laughed and stepped hard on the gas.

"And who's arrogant."

Jackson drove faster.

"And pushy."

Jackson skidded around a corner.

"And arrogant."

"You already said arrogant," Jackson said.

"Did I say pushy?"

"Yeah, you said pushy too."

"Shit," Razoni said. "Drive slow and give me a chance to think of something else."

"Nobody drives that slow," Jackson said. "We're here." He skidded the car into the curb in front of a fire hydrant and turned off the motor.

"We're where? The city dump?" asked Razoni as he lowered the window and gazed down the garbage-bedecked street.

"The scene of the crime," Jackson said.

"I've got to go to the bathroom."

"They'll have one inside."

"Why should they? When they've got the whole outdoors?"

Two young uniformed policemen stood near a wooden barricade in front of the heavy planked door of one of a pair of matching long, low buildings. The building on the left seemed to be some kind of food market; the one on the right had old-fashioned glass store windows, but covered with heavy draperies. Jackson waved his badge at the two police officers as he and Razoni went into the second building, where a young man sat at a table just inside the door, dressed in a white robe.

"Welcome to Salamanda Ashram," he said.

Razoni moved from side to side like a little boy trying to control his bladder by making it seasick.

"Good afternoon," said Jackson, moving up to the table, which was covered with a white cloth. The young man looked past him at Razoni, who stood rocking in place.

"Is there anything wrong with your friend?" he asked pleasantly.

"Just tell me where the men's room is," Razoni growled. "Emphasis on men."

The young man pointed to a door at the end of a small corridor. Razoni brushed past Jackson, whispering loudly, "Don't give this twerp any money."

As Razoni vanished down the corridor, the young man at the table looked up expectantly at Jackson.

"We're here to see Mr. Gildersleeve," Jackson said.

"Brother Gildersleeve is busy inside with Sister Glorious. Your business is . . . ?"

"We're detectives."

"You're too late. Detectives have already been here. The press too."

"I know. We're just following up a few things," Jackson said.

Razoni reappeared. "Hey, Tough," he whispered. "This is a junk joint, I think."

"Why?"

"There's a whole bunch of guys in the men's room and

they've all got this retarded look on their faces. Like they're on something.''

"I think that's called peace," Jackson said. "Could you call Brother Gildersleeve?" he asked the young man.

"Brother who?" Razoni said.

"Brother Gildersleeve should be free any moment," the young man said. "Please—"

He was interrupted by a bustling sound behind him as double doors that led to a meeting room were pushed open. A small man wearing a conservative brown suit strutted through the door. He had slick black hair and the chesty walk of a bantam rooster who had just demolished the barnyard's last virgin hen. Under his arm was a thick roll of paper. A half-dozen young people straggled after him.

Without looking toward Razoni and Jackson, the little man walked toward one of the walls of the anteroom. He put his pile of paper down upon a desk where it rolled itself flat into a stack of heavy paper posters.

"That's Brother Gildersleeve," the young man told Jackson.

Gildersleeve held one of the posters against the wall with his left hand as if measuring its location, then slid it upward a half-foot and anchored it there with masking-tape strips that he tore from a roll of tape with his teeth.

In the center of the poster was a color photograph of Swami Salamanda. Atop the picture, the poster screamed in black, still-sticky end-of-the-world type: SWAMI LIVES!!!!

Under the picture, the legend read:

> TRUTH NEVER DIES.
> LOVE NEVER DIES.
> THE MESSAGE OF LOVE
> OF SWAMI SALAMANDA
> WILL CONTINUE.
> NATIONAL RALLY SUNDAY.
> JOIN THE CARAVAN
> TO THE CITY OF LOVE.

Gildersleeve backed off to inspect his work. He smiled, baring oversized discolored teeth spaced like loose Chiclets.

"That guy doesn't look like he belongs here, Tough," Razoni said.

"I think he tried to sell me swampland in Jersey once," Jackson said, moving toward Gildersleeve. He touched the small man on the arm, gestured toward the poster, and asked, "What's that all about?"

"The Swami Lives," Gildersleeve said in a vibrato voice that sounded as if it belonged to the town crier of Munchkinland. "His voice shall not be stilled."

Young people drifted out of the meeting room behind him toward Gildersleeve and the two policemen. From the corner of his eyes, Gildersleeve saw them. "The Great Swami Lives," he said, louder this time. "His work shall never die."

One young woman brushed past him to the poster and kissed its face. She began to sob gently. More and more people poured through the double doors, wearing white robes with black patches pinned to the sleeves. Many wept; soon the room was filled with the sound of choked crying. Gildersleeve kept barking: "The Swami Lives. This weekend. The Swami Lives."

"This is like a goddamn carnival," Razoni said. He watched disgustedly as two young women, weeping, put their arms about each other. Two young men embraced and cried openly on each other's shoulder.

"I told you this was a fag joint," Razoni told Jackson.

"They're just expressing themselves," said Jackson. He looked down onto the shiny top of Gildersleeve's head.

"We're detectives, Mr. Gildersleeve. Could we talk to you?"

"I guess so," he said. He raised his voice to a shout. "All right, everybody. Take a poster. Put them up around town. We'll have more tomorrow. The Swami Lives. The work goes on."

The downtown streets were always crowded and Sarge had to park his old Ford relic two blocks away from the

House of Love and walk to Salamanda's headquarters. He
noticed that it was appropriately enough located in an area
of the city dedicated to love, of the rough-trade kind. He
passed a handful of leather bars with names like Bull's
Pizzle and Tunnel Traffic and Coal Chute.

As he approached the building, passing the almost empty
food store alongside it, he saw a group of young people in
white robes exiting. Most held posters, many were weeping, some mumbled, "The Swami Lives."

His old gold badge from the New York police got him
past the two patrolmen who were lounging around at a
barricade out front. He passed the empty desk just inside
the front door and walked into what seemed to be a large
meeting room. There was a purple cushion on a low stage
at the front of the room and on the floor was a chalked
outline of a body. This was where Salamanda had died.

There were twenty young people kneeling around the
room, humming to themselves, eyes fixed and glazed as if
they were in trances. The sound they made was like a
low-intensity dentist's drill. Sarge walked to the side of the
room and then approached the platform where Gloria Alcetta
and a small man in a conservative suit were talking to two
other men who were obviously detectives. Once again,
Sarge was impressed by the woman's beauty. Her figure
was lissome and full, her hair flowed softly about her face,
and she had that rare ability to look smart and nice at the
same time. That the other two men were detectives Sarge
knew beyond dispute. One was a black giant with a gentle
face and soft eyes; the other was not quite so tall, not quite
so burly, but big enough to justify his face, which seemed
all angles and wedges. There were scowl lines by the side
of his mouth and his suit looked very expensive.

Sarge took a seat up front, close, and heard the white
man say, "I'm Detective Razoni and this is Detective
Jackson. Christ, it's noisy in here."

"Why are you detectives here after the other detectives?" the small man said. "Does this go on forever?"

"Just talk to us," Razoni said wearily. "See, we're like
Hallmark."

"What's that?" the little man said.

"When the department cares enough to send the very best, they send us. Tough, show them now good you are. Whistle or something."

He turned to the tall redhead. "Who are you?" he said.

"I am Glorious," she answered.

"No, lady. Just your name, not description."

"Sister Glorious," Gloria Alcetta said with a sad smile. "I am . . . was the Swami's assistant."

"If she's the assistant, Gildersleeve, what do you do around here?" Razoni asked the small man.

"I am the national director for the City of Love," Gildersleeve said.

The humming in the room grew louder.

Razoni said, "Do you have someplace else where we can talk? All these June bugs are making me nuts."

"We can go to one of the offices in the back," Gloria Alcetta said.

"Lead the way," Razoni said.

The four started toward the white drapes at the back of the platform, and Sarge got to his feet and tried to look busy in case one of them should glance his way and wonder who he was. He waited a minute, then walked across the platform and into a corridor lined with rooms on each side. He could hear voices coming from one of the rooms at the end of the hall, and he latched on to a push broom that leaned against the wall and with it walked quietly to the end of the corridor.

He heard Razoni say, "Okay. This is more like it. Tough, are you taking notes?"

"No. I'm writing my autobiography."

"Well, interrupt it for a while and take notes," Razoni said. "Now, Gildersleeve, this girl who slipped the lizard the mickey, what do you know about her?"

Sarge peered around the corner of the door. Gildersleeve looked pained. "As I told your colleagues earlier, I know nothing about her. There are many people in here all day long, seekers of truth. One girl does not stand out."

"You must have her name on a record somewhere. Doesn't she pay dues or something?"

Gildersleeve looked at Gloria Alcetta, who shook her

head. "We charge no dues; we keep no records. The Swami's movement is open to all."

Sarge noticed a faint crack in her voice.

"No records?" Razoni said disbelievingly.

"No, dammit, no records," Gildersleeve snapped. "Sister Glorious just told you that. This isn't the FBI, you know."

"Would either of you recognize her if you saw her again?" Razoni asked.

"I wouldn't," Gildersleeve said. "You, Sister?"

Gloria Alcetta shook her head.

"Damn curious," Razoni said. "The other detectives talked to everybody that was here. Nobody knows nothing, nobody knows anybody, nobody ever saw that broad before."

"She was a new member," Gloria Alcetta said. "No one had a chance to know her."

"How'd she happen to bring in the flowers, then? Who picked her for that?"

"That, Officer, is part of our custom," Gildersleeve said. "Each Sunday, a new group of followers goes into meditative discipline. One of them is picked, usually by the Swami himself, to handle the roses for the initiation ceremony."

"The initiation ceremony. That's what was going on when the lizard ate the flowers, right?" asked Razoni.

From his vantage point in the hallway, Sarge saw Gloria Alcetta's lips tighten in anger. Gildersleeve snapped angrily, "I will not have you calling the Swami any such obscene name."

"But he ate the rose at the ceremony, right?"

"Yes," Gildersleeve said.

"Tough, I hope you're getting all this down," Razoni said. "Now, Brother Throckmorton—"

"Brother Gildersleeve," the small man corrected, his face reddening.

"Right. Let's take it from the top. What's your full name?"

"John J. Gildersleeve. I told that to the other officers earlier."

"Just tell me again," Razoni said. "You live where?"

"I live in western Pennsylvania, on the site where the City of Love is being built. I am staying in town at the Hotel Palmer."

"Why'd you come to town?" Razoni asked.

"To handle some financial matters. To assist the Swami in next Sunday's rally. This building is really too small and I was arranging the rental of a theater. I got here just around the time the Swami was stricken."

"When was the last time you saw him alive?"

"Last night."

"Where?" Razoni asked.

"In his apartment here."

"What were you doing?"

"We were discussing plans for the conference," Gildersleeve said. "Really, do we have to go through all this again? I told it all to the other detectives."

"Good. Then you won't have any trouble remembering all the details. Was anybody else here?" Razoni said.

"As I told them too, no. Wait. For a while, there was a girl there."

Razoni winked at Jackson broadly. "Now we're getting somewhere. Was this girl the one who took a powder?"

Gildersleeve looked off into space. "No," he said after a pause. "The girl you are seeking was new. This girl was around here for quite a while. She brought in tea last night."

"Well, who is she?"

"I don't know. I told you they all look alike," Gildersleeve said. "She was tall."

"That's a terrific description," Razoni said. "Tough, put out a thirteen-state alarm for her. Be sure to let everybody know she's tall so they don't make any mistakes." He turned back to Gildersleeve and asked, "Is that all you remember about her?"

Sarge, from the hallway, could see Gildersleeve visibly thinking. "Tall," the small man said. "Blond, I think. Yes, blond. I don't know."

"You remember her name?"

"I don't know. Kara or Kuri or . . ."

"Or kitchee-koo?" Razoni said.

"Her name is Keri," Gloria Alcetta said. "She is a follower and she is often working here."

"Why don't you stop asking all these questions," Gildersleeve said, "and find that girl who killed the Swami? Really. After all I have heard about the efficient New York police. What a laugh."

"Is that why you have pickets down around police headquarters?" Razoni said.

"I have removed the pickets," Gildersleeve said. "I spoke to a Captain Mannion in the commissioner's office. I told him that the followers of Swami Salamanda will wait until the end of the week for the police to do their duty. If they have failed by then, we will return and call attention to their inadequacies. This Mannion said he would assign his best men to the case."

"He has," Razoni said.

"You?" said Gildersleeve.

"Him," Razoni said, jerking his thumb toward the huge figure of Tough Jackson, who leaned against a wall, taking notes. "He counts as two."

After lighting a cigarette, Razoni asked Gloria Alcetta, "Now what's your name again?"

"Sister Glorious."

"And before you were Sister Glorious, you were?"

"Gloria. Gloria Charterman." Without being asked, she gave Razoni her address on the Upper West Side.

"How long have you been with this carnival?"

Sarge saw the lovely redhead bite her lip before answering. "I have been with the Swami for three months."

"And what's your position?"

"I was the Swami's assistant," she said.

"That's pretty fast moving for someone who's been on board for only three months," Razoni said. From the corner of his eye, he saw Gildersleeve nod, almost imperceptibly, but a nod nevertheless. Sarge saw it from the hallway too.

"Length of time is not the only consideration," Gloria said. "From the time I first met the Swami, I devoted my life to him."

"And you say this girl with the tea was Keri?"

"That's right."

"You have a last name for her?"

"No. We don't deal in last names here," she said.

"And you don't know anything about the girl with the roses?" Razoni asked.

"Nothing. I never saw her before."

"Would you recognize her if you saw her again?"

"Yes. I think so."

"Do you people draw a salary?" Razoni asked. He looked at Gildersleeve, who nodded and said, "Yes, and the amount is none of your business." Gloria said, "Only expenses. It was an honor to work for the Swami. There wasn't anyone else like him."

"I imagine not," Razoni said. "You said the Swami had an apartment here?"

"In the back of this building," Gildersleeve said.

"Let's see it."

Gildersleeve started for the door and Sarge turned his back to the doorway and started pushing his broom down the hallway. He heard their footsteps moving away and peeked over his shoulder. Gildersleeve and Gloria were leading the two detectives down the hallway, past the men's room, past the women's room, past a storeroom. They passed a refrigerator and Razoni opened it and looked inside, then slammed the door in disgust.

Sarge heard him grumble, "Nothing but roses in this joint."

Razoni and Jackson followed the two officials through a door with a heavy-duty lock on it. When they were out of sight, Sarge opened the refrigerator door. It contained only a bouquet of yellow roses, tied together loosely with string, lying on their side on an otherwise empty shelf. It was a funny place to leave evidence, Sarge thought, and without knowing why, he slid one of the roses from the bunch and slipped it, stem first, into his inside jacket pocket.

When he heard a sound at the end of the hallway, he turned and started pushing the broom again. He heard the door close and then Razoni's voice: "Nothing to see in there."

"No. Hey, was there any beer in this refrigerator?" the black detective's voice asked.

"No. Just some more frigging roses. This place is like a flower shop," Razoni said.

Jackson opened the refrigerator anyway and looked at the flowers.

They passed Sarge and walked toward the end of the hallway, which led to the curtains separating this area from the large meeting room.

As they passed through the curtains, Sarge heard Razoni say, "She was sleeping with him, you know."

"I know," Jackson said.

"What the hell do you expect in this massage parlor?" Razoni said.

And then they were gone.

Sarge put down the broom and glanced into the two offices, but he knew it was a senseless formality because there was nothing to be seen. When he stepped out into the hall, Sister Glorious came from Salamanca's apartment.

"Those two men who were here?" she said to Sarge. "Did they leave?"

"Detectives Razoni and Jackson?" Sarge said. "Yes. I'm working with them. Can I help?" He pulled his wallet from his back pocket and showed her his badge. "Sergeant Tracy," he said.

"Oh, good," she said. "I just remembered something that I thought they might be interested in. I didn't think of it, they asked so many questions."

"I understand, ma'am," Sarge said. "What was it?"

"There was a young man here today recording the ceremonies on television tape. He might have film of the young woman they're looking for."

"Well, that's very good. Who's the young man?"

"I don't really know," Gloria said.

"Was he a follower of the Swami's?"

"I don't really think so. But he came here quite a bit and said that he would shoot pictures for us and someday make a documentary. He seemed harmless enough and nice, so I gave him permission to do some photographing here. As I say, he might have pictures of the girl with the flowers.''

"Well, that's very helpful, Sister," Sarge said.

"You'll pass it along to the other detectives?" she asked.

"I certainly will," Sarge said.

13

To Trace, New York was a dentist's drill of a city, a kind of throbbing noise that came at him from all sides and gave him a headache. He found it bearable only at times like these, Sunday evenings, when the traffic was light and the city's population seemed magically to have been halved.

Riding in the cab from the airport, he kept looking out the back window, until Chico said. "What are you doing?"

"Keeping an eye out for the ex-wife. She may have gotten word from her spies that I'm in town."

"All right, knock it off," she said. "We just got here and I don't want you to start complaining right from the git-go."

As they drove through Manhattan, Trace said, "What is this crap? I've been out of the city only a couple of months and already everything's changed."

"Like what?" Chico said.

"All the women are wearing sneakers, for Christ's sake. What's that all about? Look at them all. This damn city looks like a girl's gym."

"It's the new fad," Chico said. "Women wear sneakers on the street; they carry their shoes in their purses. Then, when they get where they're going, they put on their shoes."

"That's stupid," Trace said.

"It's comfortable. Why should only men be comfortable?" Chico asked.

"If women want to be comfortable, they don't have to wear sneakers. They should wear comfortable shoes."

"There are no comfortable shoes for women," Chico said. "Not unless you have a face like a horse, wear a nubby tweed suit that could sand wood, and live in Paddlington on the Puddlington."

"Women are dopes as human beings," Trace said.

"Fortunately the level of competition is real low," Chico said.

"That's right," the cabdriver said. "Women are dopes."

"Hey, pal, watch the road, huh?" Trace said. "We want to get there alive. And today if you don't mind."

"Sorry," the cabdriver said. "I just thought you'd want to know somebody thinks you're right. Women are dopes."

Chico said, "Drive the freaking cab before I put a bullet between your eyes."

Trace sighed. Chico with a gun was going to be something to deal with. The world would never be the same.

Nothing much had changed since the last time Trace had been to Sarge's office, a second-floor walkup over Bogie's Restaurant. The "C" had again fallen out of the sign on the door making it TRA Y DETECTIVE AGENCY.

There were still *Playboy* centerfolds on the walls, still a ratty old velveteen couch, two metal folding chairs, an old wooden burn-scarred desk that might have once belonged to a bookkeeper for a gambling syndicate who worked in the cellar of an olive-oil warehouse.

An improvement was the calendar on the wall behind the desk. Sarge was watering plants by the windows that looked out over the street when Trace and Chico entered. Chico looked around and said softly to Trace, "What a dump."

"Improving," Trace said. "Last time I was here, the calendar was three years old. Now he's got a new one. Hello, Sarge," he called out.

Sarge turned and smiled at them. He was a big man, not as tall as Trace but broader and bulkier. His face was ruddy, but it looked like outdoor living and not whiskey had caused that. He was a little thicker around the middle than Chico remembered him, but he was a formidable-looking man, not for sixty-seven but for any age. He had a large brush of snow-white hair that made him look a little like Spencer Tracy with a mean streak. His hands were big and powerful-looking and the little metal sprinkling can, the kind children used to use on the beach before plastic enveloped the world, looked like a drinking cup in his mitt.

"Here they are. Nick and Nora," he said. "Ready to go to work?" He came forward and embraced Chico.

"Sure," Trace said.

"When do I get my gun?" Chico said.

"Soon, soon," Sarge said.

"Not safe to walk down these mean streets without a gun," Chico said.

Sarge nodded, agreeing with her. "That's right, and you'll have a gun mighty soon, little lady."

"He's jerking me around, Trace," Chico said. "I can tell that tone in his voice, he's jerking me around."

"Not me, Babe," Sarge said. "You've got my promise. You want some coffee?"

"Did you teach Trace how to make it?" Chico asked.

"Yes."

"I'll pass," she said.

"When are you and Mother leaving?" Trace said.

"Tomorrow morning. Seven days of fun and frolic in the sun. Do you know your mother gets seasick?"

"Just what she needed to make her perfect," Chico said.

"Exactly," Sarge said. "Seven days of watching Hilda barf. I bet you both think this is going to be fun, don't you?"

"Maybe if she gets sick enough, she won't spend her time complaining," Trace offered brightly.

"She's never been that sick," Sarge said. "Hey, I'm sorry. Sit down, make yourselves comfortable."

Chico looked at the shabby chocolate couch, once brown, now the color of chocolate that had aged in the open air. "Must I?" she said.

"I vacuumed that couch especially for you," Sarge said with a hurt expression.

"Turn down the suction. You pulled off all the nap," Chico said.

"Very funny. Is she always this funny?"

"Always before she eats," Trace said.

"We're having dinner tonight at my house," Sarge said. "Mother's cooking. So you can get the lay of the land."

Trace looked at her, then took her arm and led her to one of the folding chairs and elaborately helped her sit down.

"Can the manners," she said. "What lay of the land?"

"So you know where everything is in our house," Sarge said.

"Why should I want to know where everything is in your house?" Chico said.

Sarge shrugged puzzlement and looked at Trace, who told Chico, "I forgot to tell you something."

"Tell away. I know I'm going to love it."

"I told Sarge that you and I would stay at their house until they got back," he said.

Chico made a growling sound in the back of her throat.

"It's not that bad," Trace said. "My mother's not going to be there."

Chico growled again.

"Look at the bright side," Trace said.

"There *is* no bright side," she said. "You watch. Your mother's going to have a list made of everything she owns in that house. Every junk spoon-rest she ever bought in Winston-Salem, North Carolina. Every plastic ashtray from Miami Beach. She's going to make us sign an inventory. And when she gets back, she's going to check every item on the list before she releases our bags. I know it, I can feel it, I can see it coming."

"The bright side, the bright side," Trace said.

"I'm waiting," she said.

"I'm going to try to get a job out of the insurance company. What I figured I'd do is tell them we're staying in a New York hotel while we're on the job, see, and then make them pay for the hotel. And all the while, we'll be in the lap of luxury out at Sarge's house. In a week, I'll be able to beat the company out of a thousand dollars or so."

"Let's spend the thousand and stay in a hotel," Chico said.

"We're starting out in business," Trace said. "Every dollar counts."

"I don't want to count a dollar. I don't want to beat the insurance company out of money and I don't want to be in your mother's house. Excuse me, Sarge, nothing against you, but that woman doesn't like me."

"I wouldn't say that," Sarge said.

"It's not true," Trace said. "She doesn't not like you. She hates you."

"Much more accurate," Sarge agreed. "It'll work out, you'll see."

"I hate it," Chico said.

Sarge went to his jacket, hung on a hook screwed into the plaster wall, and when he turned, he held a yellow rose. He stepped forward and handed it to Chico.

"Sort of a welcoming gift," he said.

"How nice." She sniffed the rose and Sarge said, "Smell but don't taste. It may be poisoned." When Chico looked up, he said, "The case I'm working on."

Anxious to change the subject from the question of where they were spending the night, Trace looked at Chico and said, "If we're going to be partners and all, I think it's a good idea for Sarge to tell us about his cases, don't you?"

"I don't want to stay at your mother's," Chico said.

"Come on, Sarge," said Trace. "Let's talk money."

"If we're going to be partners here," Chico said, "we ought to see the books. Make him show you the books."

"Show me the books," Trace said.

Sarge tapped his forehead. "I've got it all up here."

Trace tapped his mouth. "Make it all come out here."

Sarge sat down heavily behind the desk. "You have to realize that getting this furniture was a cash deal."

"How much did they pay you to take it?" Chico asked. "That should be listed under miscellaneous income."

"Very funny. She's very funny, isn't she, son?"

"Don't 'son' me. You only 'son' me when you're trying to run a con. We're waiting for an accounting.

We're going to cast our lot in with you in the detective business, we ought to know if we're going to have bread on the table.''

"We're family," Sarge said with a grin. "What is all this accounting stuff?"

"It's one of the things I learned in the restaurant business," Trace said.

"What was that?"

"Don't invest money with friend or family unless you're holding a hostage."

"I don't understand this attitude," Sarge said.

"You're suggesting that we invest money in this so-called firm," Chico said. "You're suggesting that we temporarily uproot ourselves from our very comfortable life . . ."

"In the desert," Sarge said. "With the snakes."

"At least the women don't wear sneakers all the time," Trace said. "You're asking us to possibly move to New York—New York, for God's sakes—and we're not buying a pig in a poke. The accounting, please."

"All right. This is it approximately," Sarge said. "I didn't know you two were going to audit me today or I would have had Touche Ross send in the four accountants I keep on retainer."

"Go ahead," Trace said.

"All right. Approximately. Since January first, the firm has taken in about eleven thousand dollars. I've paid myself about seven thousand dollars in salary. Expenses have been almost three thousand dollars. A thousand dollars left for profit or operating, and that's in the bank. Satisfied?"

"No," Chico said. "Your expenses are too high. From now on, you're going to have to find a better class of people to give you money to take their old furniture away. And spend less money on blondes with legs from here to here."

"Tell us about your pending cases," Trace said.

"Actually it's a pending *case*," Sarge said.

"It better be a big case if it's going to support all of us," Trace said.

"Poisoned rose, right?" Chico said, waving the yellow

rose in the air. "Murder, right? Danger, intrigue, shoot-outs in alleys. I'll take it, just as soon as you give me a gun."

"Well, actually," Sarge said, "all I'm handling is the possible divorce end of it."

Trace and Chico were silent. She slowly jabbed the pointed end of the rose stem into her palm. Finally, Sarge told them the story of how Angelo Alcetta had hired him to check out his wife and how her religious leader had been murdered that very day.

"You say this is one of the roses?" Chico asked.

Shrugging, Sarge said, "I don't know. I doubt it. This was in the refrigerator and I don't think even today's cops are stupid enough to leave evidence in a refrigerator at the scene."

"So what about your report to this Alcetta character?" Trace asked.

"I just finished it up before you arrived. Tomorrow ends the three days of surveillance, so I was hoping you'd call him and give him the report."

"Think there's any hope there that he might ask us to keep watching her?" Trace asked.

"Damned if I know. Who knows what Italians think?" Sarge said. "Oh, this is the wife, by the way." He opened the folder on the desk and took out the wallet-sized picture of Gloria Alcetta.

Trace looked at it and passed it to Chico. "I'll get right on it," he said.

"Not with me in town, you won't," Chico said.

"How much of your business does Mother know?" Trace asked.

"Nothing. I don't tell her what I do or what I make. She doesn't want to know. She just doesn't want me to ask her for money, so I don't."

"Okay. We'll keep it that way, then. No talking business in the house," Trace said.

"We talk business now, though," Chico said.

"Sure."

"Talk away," Sarge said.

"Okay. First thing is you don't do enough business here

for us to invest money in it. That's just sensible from my standpoint. And from Trace's standpoint, he doesn't have any money, 'cause he never does."

Sarge started to speak but she silenced him by raising the rose over her head like a sword.

"So scratch us as investment sources. What we *can* do is try working here for a while to see if we can expand the business. If we can, then we can do something about salaries and ownership and like that. How does that sound?"

"It sounds all right," Sarge said, "but I don't want you to downgrade the business. Just remember, nobody ever went broke taking a small profit."

"And you remember, nobody ever got fat eating three from one dish," Chico said.

"Speaking of which, let's go home and eat," Trace said.

"Good idea," Chico said. "And then we'll talk about getting me a gun."

14

Razoni was speaking to the Sunday bartender at the Red Horse Tavern, a man with black hair, a shocking-pink face, and nose pizzaiola.

"You got the order wrong," Razoni said. "I asked for bourbon and soda."

"That's what you got. Bourbon and soda."

"No, no," Razoni said. "What I got is bourbon and soda and dirt. Now take this back and make me a drink in a clean glass. Clean. That's without dirt in it."

The bartender looked annoyed but picked up the drink and put it on the sink counter below the bar. Noisily, he began looking through a tray of glasses, occasionally selecting candidates, then rejecting them after holding them up to the light for inspection.

Razoni shook his head in disgust. Sitting next to him, Jackson sipped his drink quietly and tried to concentrate on the television news, but Razoni kept interrupting with a running commentary on the sexual preferences of the newscasters.

"That guy Barnes is a fag, Tough. Look at him."

"Shhhhh," said Jackson.

"Yeah, but look at his nostrils. Fags always have noses like that."

"Shhhh," Jackson said. "There might be war in the Mideast."

"Good," said Razoni. "Let all those assholes kill each other, then the winners can come over here and start working on these TV fags. Look at them. You think with all the money they make, they could at least buy good clothes.''

Jackson sighed. "Maybe they don't all want to look like dance instructors.''

"Shhhh," Razoni said. "The sports is on. Don't you ever shut up?'' He cradled his newly arrived drink in his hand and sipped it without looking at the glass. The television sportscaster was showing the highlights of the afternoon baseball games.

"Why are you watching this?'' Jackson said. "You don't even like baseball.''

"I watch this because baseball is a great American institution,'' Razoni said smugly.

"What do you know about great American institutions?'' Jackson asked.

"What I know is that at least in baseball, the players keep their own names. You never heard of no Reggie Muhammad. Not like football or boxing where everybody sounds like they ought to be riding a camel. That's why I'm beginning to like baseball. 'Cause it isn't stupid. You ain't ever going to see any player named Peewee Abdul Jabbar, not in a baseball uniform. We real Americans think of things like that," Razoni said.

"I was thinking of changing my name, actually," Jackson said.

"To what?''

"To Mustapha. I thought it would be good for my son to be named Mustapha for when us blacks take over the world.''

Razoni searched his face. "You do that, Tough, and I'd never talk to you again.''

"That was another reason I was thinking of doing it.''

"Go scratch your ass.''

"It doesn't have to be Mustapha," Jackson said. "Hell, maybe something else. How about Cavatelli? Detective William Cavatelli? How's that sound?''

"Why not?'' Razoni said. "If football players can make believe they're freaking Ay-rabs, you can make believe you're a human being.''

"Do you think I'll pass?" Jackson asked. "Noodles Cavatelli, the great Eye-talian detective."

"I wouldn't let you marry my sister," Razoni said.

"I wouldn't want to." Jackson said.

Razoni, thinking of his sister, said, "I don't blame you. You know, you've ruined everything now. The sports report is over."

"Good. Then we can do some work. What are we going to do about the guru?" Jackson asked.

"Stuff him and keep the party going." Razoni said. "I hate to admit it, but it looks like the precinct bulls are covering all the bases. I didn't see anything they left out."

"Neither did I," Jackson said.

"I called Pat up at the *Times*. She's going to see what she's got in the files on the Lizard and Gildersleeve and get back to us."

"You still seeing her?" Jackson asked.

"Once in a while," Razoni said. "She's a freaking liberal like all the rest of them but she's . . ."

He stopped and jumped off the stool as the telephone rang. "I bet that's her now."

He waved the bartender away from the telephone, picked it up, and said, "Hello."

"If you're not drinking coffee, you're drinking booze," a voice growled in his ear.

"Who is this?"

"Captain Mannion."

"Oh, hi, Captain. You've got me confused with my partner, Detective Jackson. He's the one with the drinking problem. Remember? I'm the good-looking one."

"That's right," Mannion said. "He's the smart one." Razoni did not answer and Mannion asked, "How's it going with the Salamanda investigation?"

"I can't tell you a lot about it now, Captain, but we're right on the verge of a major breakthrough."

"Good," Mannion said. "Let me talk to Jackson."

"Sure. By the way, Captain . . ."

"Yeah?"

"How're your roses?"

"Put Jackson on the fucking phone," Mannion screamed.

Razoni shrugged and dropped the receiver. It hit against the wood-paneled wall with a thud. He walked back along the bar and got back into his seat.

"Who was it?" Jackson asked.

"I don't want to talk about it," Razoni said.

"Why? Who was it?"

"Not was, is," Razoni said.

Jackson looked past him at the telephone dangling at the end of its cord.

"Who is it?" he said.

"It's the captain. He wants to talk to you."

"Oh, you evil fucker, you," Jackson said, jumping to his feet and running toward the telephone.

"Be careful, Tough," Razoni called. "I think he's pissed at you."

"Hello, Captain," Jackson said into the phone.

"Took you long enough," Mannion grumbled.

"Sorry, Captain, I was in the men's room."

"All right, all right. Razoni says you may have a break-through on the Salamanda case."

"I think that's a little overoptimistic," Jackson said. "We don't have anything yet."

"Okay. Just let your flea-brained partner keep after it. I've got something else for you to do."

"Alone?" Jackson asked.

"Of course alone," Mannion said.

"But Ed's my partner."

"I know *that*. But I just want you to check something out and it's a little delicate." Jackson was silent and Mannion said, "Are you still there?"

"Yes, sir."

"Anyway, do you know who Theodore Longworth is?"

"Sure. He's the guy who runs United Broadcasting."

"That's right. I want you to go up to his place and talk to him. His daughter may be missing."

"Missing? How old is she?"

"I don't know. Twenty. I don't know. Longworth thinks something may have happened to her."

"Something?" Jackson said.

"Jackson, I don't want you to mention this to anyone. He thinks maybe kidnapping."

"Why us? Why not the FBI?"

"Because probably she hasn't been and he doesn't want any publicity on it. Will you just go up there and see what you can do?"

"And then what?"

"Fill me in and stay on the case if you have to," Mannion said.

"What about Ed?"

"Leave him with the Swami. Tell him to eat a rose."

"But, Captain, we're partners."

"Jackson, get up to Longworth's right away. And report to me when you're done. And listen, I know you guys are working on a day off. I'll make it up to you. It's just been one of those days. Get moving."

"Yes, sir."

The telephone clicked off in Jackson's ear. He replaced the receiver slowly and returned to his seat.

"What'd he want?" Razoni asked.

"He was just wondering when you were going to solve the Swami's murder."

"What'd you tell him?"

"That I didn't think you were cut out to be a detective."

"Me neither. I'm a lover."

"Then you'll love this," said Jackson. "He wants to split us up."

Razoni had his glass to his lips. He froze in position, then put his glass back down and turned slowly toward Jackson, "Split us up? Split us up?"

Jackson nodded. "Not permanently. Just for a while."

"What while?" asked Razoni.

"He wants you to stay with Salamanda. He's got another job for me."

"Oh, bullshit. After I've gone to all this trouble to train you? What other job?" Razoni demanded.

"He wants me to go to talk to Theodore Longworth. You know, the guy who heads UBC."

"I know who he is. He's a fag."

Jackson looked around cautiously, then lowered his voice. "Well, his daughter may be missing."

"No good," Razoni said. "Absolutely no, no, no way, no goddamn good. You'll go up there to see him and you'll be shuffling around, holding your hat in your hand, and you'll embarrass the whole department."

"I don't wear a hat."

"You should always have a hat when you go to see the president of a television network. When do you have to see him?"

"Right now."

"Let's go." Razoni drained his drink and stood up, then waved the bartender over with an imperious crook of his finger.

"I'm leaving now," Razoni told him, "so you can throw away that drink you were hiding under the bar in the dirty glass to slip back to me when I got drunk."

The bartender smiled uncomfortably.

"There's a girl may call here or stop in. Her name's Pat. She's good-looking. If she's got a package for me, you just take it and I'll pick it up. And make sure none of these slobs go pawing her." He turned back to Jackson. "You ready yet?" he asked, and without waiting for an answer, he headed toward the door.

15

"It's a good thing I'm going along," Razoni said as they drove uptown.

"Good," said Jackson. "Keep the reason fresh in your mind so you can tell the captain all about it."

"Stop worrying."

"Promise me one thing . . . that you're not going to punch Longworth's face out if he says something you don't like."

"I'm the soul of discretion," Razoni said. "It's just nice to be on a case again with real people instead of some half-assed sheet-wearing lizard. Even if Longworth is a fag. There's one thing I can't understand, though."

"What's that?" Jackson asked.

"Who'd want to steal his daughter away? She's probably a fag just like him. Watch out for that dog!"

Jackson swerved the car to avoid a lonely scraggly dog dragging himself across the street.

"That's probably the only dog on the East Side," Jackson said.

"If you don't count the women."

"How do you know Longworth's a fag?" Jackson asked as he tromped down again on the gas pedal.

"Anybody could tell," Razoni said. "First of all, he owns that TV station, UBC, right?"

"Right."

"And anyway, he still does all those editorials for them."

"What does that have to do with anything?" asked Jackson.

"Why does he do those editorials if he doesn't have to? Why does he go out at eleven o'clock and read the news when he owns the freaking station and he doesn't have to? Did you ever hear those editorials? Did you ever hear him read the news? If I hear about one more goddamn homeless person, one more complaint about cutting the welfare budget, I'll throw up. He's a fag."

"I give up," Jackson said.

"Speaking of fags, what's that awful smell?"

"I hope you're not talking about my aftershave," Jackson said. "Sara gave it to me."

"Throw it away. I'll give you some of mine."

"I don't think I'd look right wearing Calabrian Nights of Revenge."

"Oh, shut up," Razoni said. "Up there. That's his house. Look at the size of that house. That fag bastard. Start slowing down. Slower. Slower."

Jackson hit the brake hard and swerved the car into a long cobblestoned driveway lined with evergreens. The house was well-known as the only one on the East Side of Manhattan with land around it. When they opened the car doors, a tree smell permeated the air. Jackson smiled at the freshness he rarely encountered anywhere in the city. They walked away from their car, parked behind a big Cadillac limousine, and Razoni breathed deeply as they walked up the marble steps to the entrance of the old Victorian mansion.

"What an awful smell," Razoni said. "It smells like trees."

"That's what it is," Jackson said.

"I thought so. He's a fag."

"Please, Ed," said Jackson as he rang the doorbell. "No nonsense."

They waited ten seconds before hearing a fumbling with the door latch. Slowly, the door opened wide to reveal a butler in formal uniform. Razoni jumped back in mock fright and Jackson gave him a look that would wilt a lawn.

"Good evening," said the butler, holding his head up so that it seemed he was bouncing each word off the underside of his large British nose.

Razoni quickly said, "Mr. Longworth's expecting us."

"Very good, sir," said the butler. "Whom should I announce?"

"Detectives Edward Razoni and Noodles Cavatelli," Razoni said. "He's Noodles."

"Would you please step inside." He stood aside to let them enter, and Jackson said, "That's Detective Razoni and Detective Jackson."

The butler nodded. "Please wait here."

Out of his hearing, Jackson cautioned Razoni with a kindergarten wagging of a finger. "Now I warned you," he said.

"Sorry, Tough, I thought he was Count Dracula. He scared the hell out of me."

"No more, Ed. Please. I mean to collect my pension someday."

"Aaaah, you got no sense of humor anymore."

They spent the minute the butler was gone inspecting the large center hall, its vaulted ceiling with a central crystal chandelier, its curved and hand-carved wooden staircase at the far end. Razoni tried loudly to estimate the price of the furnishings, but since he had never owned a piece of furniture more expensive than the $119 foam-rubber sofa on which he slept, he was inadequate to the task.

"Why is it that expensive things are always ugly?" he asked Jackson.

The black detective reached out his right hand and carefully fingered the broad lapel of Razoni's suit. "That's what I keep asking you, Ed."

The butler came back and led them through a broad sliding door into a wood-paneled study. Sitting in a tan leather chair on the far side of the room, in front of a stained-glass bay window, was the patrician face they had seen so many times on television—Theodore Longworth, who was high on Razoni's list of those whose liberal policies had led to the disintegration of the city. Longworth looked up and his face brightened. The butler slid the door closed behind them.

"Hello, men, I'm glad you're here," Longworth said.

He rose and walked to them, extending a very nervous hand for them to shake.

Jackson gripped it with a normal squeeze but Razoni let his own hand go limp and Longworth reacted as if he had just squeezed a lump of gelatinous ham-packing.

"Good to meet you. Sit down. Would you like a drink?" Razoni looked at Jackson, who said quickly, "No, thanks. Not on the job."

"What's the problem?" Razoni said, noticing how golden Longworth's hair was. It never looked that light on television. Fag hair.

"My daughter, Abigail," Longworth said, pouring himself a Scotch from a sterling-silver-and-glass decanter. It was a fag of a whiskey bottle, Razoni thought, but somehow suitable for a man whom most considered the most important man in New York City. Longworth was the sole owner of the United Broadcasting Corporation, by far the largest television network headquartered in New York. He ran it with an iron hand, some calling him involved, the rest calling him a meddler. His reputation was that he personally approved each piece of film used on the network and local news shows; he hovered around the studios like a sorority mother, often on a whim chasing one of his regular anchormen from behind the desk and delivering the news himself. He kept to himself the job of delivering all the network and local-station editorials, concerned, earnest, thoughtful pieces that Razoni thought sounded like they'd been written in the Kremlin. Razoni welcomed the chance to examine him at first close range, this man who had been spoken of as a possible president of the United States.

Longworth took a large gulp from his whiskey glass, then turned slowly around, smiled, and stuck out his pinkie, holding the glass as if he were at a cocktail party of the Junior League. A fag, Razoni thought. Longworth sat in a Queen Anne chair, in front of Razoni and Jackson, and put his drink down on the table next to him.

"She didn't come home," he said.

"Home from where?" asked Razoni.

"From school yesterday. She had some morning classes and she left at the usual time, but she wasn't there when my driver went to pick her up in the afternoon.'' He picked up his drink and sipped it in a genteel but efficient fashion that emptied two-thirds of the liquid.

"What school?'' asked Jackson

"Uptown branch of the city college,'' Longworth said. He sipped again. "I believe in public education. We're not going to make it better by sending all our brightest students to private schools.''

"And she didn't call you after school? To tell you she was staying out?''

"No. And, besides, she never stays out.''

"So the last person we know who saw her was the chauffeur?'' Jackson said.

"That's right. Jenkins,'' Longworth said. Razoni noticed that Longworth's light-blue suit matched his eyes perfectly. His tie was a Pierre Cardin.

"Who's Abigail's boyfriend?'' Razoni asked.

Before answering, Longworth finished his drink and got a refill from the decanter.

"No boyfriend. She's a good girl. Never goes out, comes straight home from school. She knows how vulnerable she is, being the daughter of a public figure, and how her mother and I worry.'' He finished pouring the drink and sipped it before turning around. Razoni had an urge to bite off the extended pinkie. "No, no boyfriends. She doesn't run around at all,'' Longworth said.

"Okay. Any girlfriends?'' Razoni said.

"There's a girl she knows from school. Karen Marichal. Her parents are artists. They live across the park on the West Side. But I called and they haven't seen Abigail.''

"Where could we find this Jenkins?'' Jackson asked.

"He's at home. I spoke to him earlier and he'll be home all night, in case you should want to talk to him.'' He gave them an address in the West Side, midtown, not far from Razoni's apartment.

Razoni saw a framed eight-by-ten photo of a pretty dark-haired girl with slanted brown eyes on the mantel over the unused fireplace.

"Is that Abigail?'' he asked.

"Yes," said Longworth without looking away from his glass.

"She's pretty. A pretty girl like that *must* have some boyfriends," Razoni suggested.

Longworth's patrician face turned into a scowl and he said in a less smooth voice, "No. No boyfriends."

Jackson glanced at Razoni, but Razoni was too interested in the changed expression on the television executive's face to notice Jackson.

"But a pretty girl whose father is so rich must have plenty of boys banging on her . . . door,"

"Abigail is a good girl. She only has a girlfriend," said Longworth, his voice rising to tenor.

Razoni looked at the picture. "Beautiful eyes," he said. "Boys should come running."

Longworth drained his new drink too. "No, no, no," he said. "No boys. She always tells me I'm the only man in her life." He stopped as if realizing he might have said something odd. He corrected his posture, crossed his legs, and slid back into an impeccable Ivy League accent. "What are you men going to do about my daughter?"

"You understand, Mr. Longworth," Jackson said, "that we have to consider every possibility. Have you heard anything from anyone about her absence?"

"You mean, a ransom demand or something like that? The answer is no."

"Then we have no real reason to believe that there has been any foul play?" Jackson said.

"No. Except that my Abigail is never away from home. She wouldn't be out overnight without letting her father know."

"I see. May we have this photograph?"

"I have a copy." Longworth extracted his wallet from his jacket pocket and took out a picture that he handed toward Jackson. Razoni intercepted it. He looked at the picture, a wallet-sized duplicate of the one on the mantel. On the back of it was written, "To my Daddy, my only man, Abigail." Razoni smirked as he put the picture inside his jacket.

"If you or Mrs. Longworth can think of any other

names of friends Abigail might have mentioned, it might be helpful," said Jackson. "And, of course, if you hear anything, you should let us know immediately. In the meantime, we'll go speak to Jenkins."

"You understand, of course, the need for discretion here," Longworth said. "First of all, it'd look ridiculous if it appeared in the press that my daughter was missing, particularly if she was just detained somewhere for some simple reason. Second, after she does come home, it might give some other lunatic ideas . . . kidnapping ideas."

"We understand," Jackson said. He rose to his feet. So did Razoni. Longworth was a shaky third.

The TV man extended his hand. Jackson took it but Razoni turned his back, casually, as if looking over the room.

"I didn't get your names."

"I'm Detective Jackson and that's Detective Razoni."

"The mayor had the police commissioner call me. The commissioner said he would send up his best men."

"That's us," Razoni said.

Longworth led them to the study door. "You can find your way out?"

"Yes, sir."

At the door, the man clapped Jackson on the shoulder. Razoni noticed moisture in Longworth's eyes.

"Find my little girl," he said.

"We will," Jackson promised.

As the sliding door closed behind them, Razoni heard Longworth mutter to himself: "You'd better."

The two detectives sat in the car for a minute before Jackson started the motor.

"I don't know why I let you drag me up here," said Razoni. "Can you imagine two detectives wasting taxpayer's money because sweet old Abigail is late for supper or something?"

"Poor bastard," Jackson said.

"Disgusting," said Razoni. "He's not only a fag, but he's got the hots for his own daughter."

"He's just a father," Jackson said.

"Bullshit," said Razoni. "He's disgusting. And you'll

see, Abigail's going to be disgusting too. And did you see the way he was guzzling?''

"Let's go see Jenkins."

"All right, but it's a waste of time."

"Why?"

"Because you know what happened as well as I do. She met somebody yesterday at school. He's a dancer at Chippendale's or something. She fell in love with his neck muscles and she went to the movies with him and now she's been in bed in some motel for the last eighteen hours. And Daddykins just doesn't want to face the idea."

"Probably," Jackson said. "But we better talk to Jenkins anyway."

Razoni slumped back into the seat. "I can't get over it. The city's in the hands of a drunken demented fag who's in love with his daughter. Disgusting."

16

"I thought you'd be staying in a hotel," Hilda Tracy said.

"Naaah," Trace said.

"You'd probably be a lot more comfortable in a hotel," his mother said.

"We thought that too, at first," Chico said sweetly. "But then we thought about your house being unoccupied for a whole week. Burglars could get in and take everything. That lamp over there with the clock in the lampshade, for instance. We know you'd be crushed if anything happened to that treasure. That's when we decided to stay."

"Good thinking, girl," Sarge said. He turned away from his wife and winked at Chico, who was still smiling sweetly, looking at Trace's mother, her own smile up as a shield to deflect the waves of hatred that came from the older woman.

"Neighbors could always watch," Mrs. Tracy said sullenly, knowing she was losing this discussion.

"Would they care about that lamp with the clock in the lampshade as much as we do?" Chico said softly. "I don't think so. Honest, Mrs. Tracy, we don't mind. That lamp's new, isn't it?"

"Yes. I bought it in Atlantic City last month when our club went down on the bus."

"It's a real treasure," Chico said. "It captures the flavor of the real Atlantic City."

Trace stepped on her foot under the table.

They were at the dinner table in Sarge's house, and for

the occasion, Mrs. Tracy had taken out her box of best paper napkins. The food was pot roast, so overcooked that the meat had turned gray, mashed potatoes that had been punished with an electric mixer for so long that they resembled semen, and green beans that were so stringy the residue could have been used to weave rope.

Trace noticed that none of this seemed to matter to Chico, who still ate as if this were the award-ceremony dinner for the Cordon Bleu cooking school in Paris.

"Yes, it's a nice clock," Mrs. Tracy said. "And we'd feel terrible if anything happened to it."

"I personally would be shattered," Sarge said. "I don't know where I'd muster up the strength to go on." He poured beer from a can in front of him into a water tumbler, surprisingly made of glass, not plastic.

"There are a lot of little treasures around here," Mrs. Tracy said. She sat at the end of the table, as far away from Chico as she could possibly get without calling in a surveyor. "You're going to stay and watch them for us? That's definite?"

"Yes," Trace said. "Definite."

"I've made up a little list of things around the house." She glared at Chico, then looked at her son. "So you'll know where to find everything." She reached into the pocket of her shapeless house dress and pulled out a sheaf of papers. From the end of the table, Chico could see typing on the pages.

Mrs. Tracy handed the list to Trace, who opened it up and pretended to peruse the contents of the four typewritten pages.

"That's real good, Mother," he said. "I'm sure it'll come in handy if we have to find . . . well, say, the ashtray with the roulette wheel in the base. Never know when we might feel like playing roulette." Chico stepped on his foot this time.

"Exactly," Mrs. Tracy said. "That's why I made up that list. So you'll know where everything is."

"And you'll know if anything is missing," Trace said.

"Or broken," his mother said. "Sometimes things get broken." She glared at Chico, who swallowed her mouthful of food and said, "And stolen too. I bet that ashtray with the roulette wheel in the base would bring a pretty penny with some fence." She gestured with her fork. "You haven't told anybody you're going out of town, have you? I wouldn't be surprised if the street outside is lined with burglars, just hoping they'll find this house unprotected." She smiled at Trace. "Good thing we're staying here, Trace."

"Sure is," he agreed. "I think maybe one of us ought to be on guard all the time. Maybe we can take shifts doing guard duty." He folded the papers and stuck them into his pants pocket. "It's not just the ashtray with a roulette wheel in the base. There's a lot of stuff. A ceramic Indian head matchbox holder from Honesdale, Pennsylvania. A collector's item if ever I saw one."

"I'll take the first shift," Chico said. "Maybe we should rent a guard dog?"

"A pair of them," Trace said. "Killer Dobermans."

Hilda Tracy didn't quite understand what was going on around her, but some instinct told her it was time to change the subject. "It's nice having dinner like this, Devlin. Do you remember the nice times we used to have at dinner with Cora and your two children?"

"You've got a better memory than I do," Trace said, "especially pertaining to my ex-wife. The last time I remember us eating here, she threw a knife across the table at me."

"No, no, no," Sarge said. "You've got no memory at all for the high points of your life. The knife was the time before the last. The last time was when she put the sour-cream dip in your coffee."

"That's right," Trace said. "How'd I forget that?"

Mrs. Tracy looked at the small Eurasian woman at the other end of the table. "Don't listen to them," she said. "We were a close-knit family then. There was a lot of love at this table."

"A lot of hate, too," Trace said. "Bruno, my ex-wife—"

"Her name is Cora," Hilda Tracy said. "I wish you wouldn't call her names that aren't hers."

"I've got a lot of names for her and they all fit her exactly."

"I'll bet," Hilda said.

"Bet red or black and you can use your roulette ashtray," Sarge said.

Trace and Chico went for a walk before dessert was served, after Chico warned Trace that it was his mother's special cheesecake, made of spackling compound, and they had forgotten to bring a chain saw with them from Las Vegas.

They walked down the quiet shadow-dappled street of Sarge's neighborhood in Queens, just a few miles from the bridge to Manhattan.

"Didn't I tell you she'd have a list?" Chico said. "She thinks I'm going to steal her collection of plaster statuettes."

"You don't deserve this, Babe, you know," Trace said. "I've been thinking . . ."

"Oh, oh. Sounds like trouble to me," she said.

"Listen to me. I'm doing this for you and you're doing this for me, right? Well, I wouldn't blame you if you did pack it all in and just take a powder. First, we're supposed to be partners in Sarge's business and he doesn't have enough business to matter a damn. And then you put up with this bullshit from my mother. Chico, you don't need all this and I'd understand if you took off."

"Are you trying to get rid of me?" Chico asked.

"No, but . . ."

"No buts. First of all, maybe we can make something out of Sarge's business. Who knows? Let's try. Second, your mother is the least important person on earth to me. My mother's Japanese, and if your mother thinks she can lay Jewish guilt on me, she's off the wall. My ancestors were spreading guilt when your mother's were wandering the desert in search of sugar diabetes. Forget her. Third, Trace, I want you to do this. I think working with Sarge might be just the thing to get you off the dime and back into the real world. I don't expect you to stop drinking and I'm not expecting miracles. But I think maybe something good will come out of it. And fourth, and most important,

I want to do it. Because *I want a fucking gun!* When do I get it?''

"I talked to Sarge about that tonight," Trace said. "Being a private detective isn't as easy as we thought. First of all, there are forms and investigations, and you've got to own property, and fingerprints and bullshit. The easier way to go is to be operatives with Sarge's firm. That just costs six bucks and get your prints taken. Only thing is, then, we can't be officers in the firm."

"Screw all that. How do I get my gun?" Chico asked.

"It's the same in either case. Fill out some forms, send in some money, tell them we protect people and property, and then wait for six months until the cops get off their butt and send you the license to carry. Sarge says he can probably get them to speed it up."

"If that's the best we can do, that's the best we can do," Chico said. "Maybe I'll carry one illegally in the meantime. But we're staying and that's that."

"If you say so. Should we move into a hotel?"

"No. What the hell. Let's stay here. It'll give your mother something to think about while she's on the cruise. Let her think I'm redecorating like she did when we let her stay in our place."

They stopped at a tavern three blocks from Sarge's house and Trace drank vodka while Chico, who could not drink, sipped at a ginger ale. When they got back to the house, Hilda was wearing a nightgown that looked as if it had been commissioned for Mother Goose.

She said to Chico, "You'll sleep in the guest room." And to Trace: "And you'll sleep on the sofa."

"Yes, Mother," Trace said.

"Sneak up later," Chico whispered in his ear. "We'll do loud boom-boom and make her nuts."

"She already is nuts," Trace said.

17

Jenkins, chauffeur to Theodore Longworth, lived in a third-floor walkup in a neighborhood heavily populated by streetwalkers and the people who lived off them: pimps, pushers, and police.

Jenkins was a sixty-one-year-old former city policeman who had retired a year ago and was now collecting his pension as well as his salary for working for Longworth.

His room was filled with whiskey bottles, littered, and with racing forms, neat piles. He greeted Razoni and Jackson warmly, offered them a drink, which they turned down, and with no real display of loss condescended to drink alone. Jackson wondered how many bottles of whiskey it had taken to paint the road map of purplish veins on Jenkins' bulbous nose.

"Mr. Longworth called and said you were coming," Jenkins said as he waved the two detectives to seats in the sparsely furnished living room of his apartment. "He sounded upset."

"Shit-faced is more like it," Razoni said.

"Worried about his daughter," Jackson said. "You saw her last?"

"Right," said Jenkins, who seemed to straighten himself as if undergoing a roll-call inspection at headquarters. "I dropped her off at the college, usual place a block away."

"Why a block away?" Jackson said.

"She's self-conscious about people seeing her arrive in a limousine."

"Then you didn't see her go inside?" asked Jackson.

"Sure I did. I always wait awhile, then drive past the school. I always see her go in." He left the sentence hanging up in the air.

"That sounds like you see her come out too," Jackson said.

"Well, once in a while. Sometimes I leave the car parked and go for a walk and a couple of times I saw her go out the back door of the school."

"You follow her? Where'd she go?"

"I followed her last week. Kids are nuts. She went to some kind of health-food place down in the East Village."

"You ever tell Longworth about it?"

"No," Jenkins said. "I wouldn't rat on the kid."

"Maybe she did that yesterday?" Jackson said.

"She went into the school and I hung around. I didn't see her come out."

"She say anything strange? Anything that'd make you think she was going to run away or anything?"

"No. Same Abby. Quiet. Doesn't say much at all," Jenkins said.

"What's the address of the health-food place?" Razoni asked.

Jenkins told him the street. "You can't miss it. It's next to this meeting hall or something, and there's plants all over the place and pictures of yogis with beards."

Jackson looked at Razoni, who nodded. "We know where it is," Jackson said. "You don't seem as worried as her father does," Jackson said. "You've been around, Officer Jenkins, what do you think happened to her?"

"Just between us guys on the job," Jenkins said, "I don't think anything bad. She probably went off to a meeting or something and ran into some school friends and stayed over and forgot to call. Kids do that."

"I guess so," Jackson said. "By the way, how does Abigail get along with her folks? No chance that she ran away?"

"No. Her father's crazy about her."

"We noticed," Razoni said. "Is she crazy about him?"

"I guess so. She doesn't talk much, like I said."

"What about boyfriends?" Razoni said.

Jenkins shook his head. "Never saw or heard of any."

"Okay," Jackson said. "You working tomorrow?"

The burly old man snorted. "If I don't work, how will I support the ponies?"

"If we need you, we'll call," Jackson said, and rose from his chair.

Jenkins stood up along with him. "Tell me," he said. "How is it in the department these days?"

"I don't know. How is it, Ed?" Jackson asked.

"Same old shit," Razoni said. "A lot of liberal faggots running it."

"Yeah. I guess it never changes," Jenkins said. "You two work for Captain Mannion?"

Razoni nodded.

"Give him my best. We came on about a year apart and I used to run into him. Never thought he'd get anywhere. Worst-tempered man I ever saw."

"He's changed now," Razoni said.

"Yeah? Mellowed?" Jenkins said.

"Right. He grows roses now."

"You know, this day has sure come up zero," Razoni said.

"Gee, and I thought it was about the seventeenth best day of my life," Jackson said.

"That's because you're with me," Razoni said. "But look at me, here it is, one of my few days off and I get called in to work and then I've got to spend the whole day with you, and first it's find out who killed some goddamn flower-eater and then it's forget the flower-eater, go see where the fag's kid is, and I'm really getting tired of this day."

"It'll get worse," Jackson said.

"It can't," Razoni said.

"If that girl Pat from the *Times* is still waiting for you at the Red Horse Tavern, it can."

"I'm ashamed of you. You forgot all about her," Razoni said.

"*I* did?"

"Yes. And I know you're going to blame it on me," Razoni said.

"True. So, since you're going to take the blame anyway, we'll just let her wait a few minutes more and go to that health-food store. Recognize the address?"

"Sure. It's right next to where that dippo rose-eater got killed. Maybe all the nuts in New York have decided to move to one street. You want I should call a moving company for you?" Razoni said.

They parked again in front of the fire hydrant. The police barricade and the uniformed officers were gone from the front of the House of Love, but the side of the building was plastered with all the signs that they had seen Gildersleeve with earlier: THE SWAMI LIVES. He had told the young people to take the signs out and plaster them everywhere and apparently all of them had taken them outside and put them up on the front of the same building.

The store was in the building next to the House of Love. There was a big wooden door, also plastered with the poster that proclaimed Salamanda still lived. On either side of the door were windows, filled with plants and displays of dried fruits and burlap bags of granola.

"I figured out the crime," Razoni said. "The lizard didn't die from eating the roses. It was trying to eat that cereal that tastes like fish-tank gravel."

An overhead bell tinkled when they pushed open the door of the store. Two young women stood at a counter in the back. One of them, a blonde almost six feet tall, fixed a large smile on her face and stepped forward to the two men.

"*Om shanti*," she said in a deep, smooth voice, almost British-sounding.

"*Om shanti*," said Jackson.

"In old Shanty Town," Razon muttered.

"How may I help you gentlemen?" The girl was close to them now. Her perfume was sweet and seemed to give off warmth. Her teeth were brilliant white and even.

"Do you have a box of Cap'n Crunch?" Razoni asked.

Smile fixed in place, the girl shook her head.

"Sugar Snacks? Crispie Twinkies?"

"This must be your first time in the House of Love food shop," the young woman said.

Jackson nodded.

"Then I must show you around." She turned. A bell tinkled.

Jackson touched her arm and said, "That won't be necessary." He handed Razoni a plastic bag from a stack at the end of the aisle. "Here. Indulge yourself."

"Only when I buy a horse," Razoni said.

"That is our heaven-sent mixture," the girl said. She pointed to another pile of packages. "And that is spiced cracked wheat." She waved her arm toward a large display case of frozen food. "And there are our wonderful fresh vegetables straight from the earth." She seemed delighted at the thought until Razoni said, "From where else? The clouds?"

"All pure," she said, looking into Jackson's eyes. "Organic. Grown with no chemicals, just with pure manure from our beloved cows."

Razoni gasped. Jackson silenced him with a look.

"And these are pure herbal medicines. Balsa bark for colds. Devil's smile, for cuts and wounds."

"You got anything for headaches?" asked Razoni.

"You're a follower of the Swami's, aren't you?" Jackson said.

"Yes."

"And you're Keri?" he said.

She looked surprised. "How do you know me?"

"We were at the mission earlier," Jackson said. "We heard your name. We're detectives." He extended his hand toward Razoni for the picture of Abigail Longworth and showed it to the blonde. "Have you ever seen this girl?"

The girl raised her eyes to meet Jackson's. "No. Does she come here?"

"We were told that," Jackson said.

"Well, I am here every day and I have not seen this person. I would know."

Jackson put the photo of Abigail in his jacket and took a

card from his wallet. "It is very important that we locate this girl. If you see her, will you call me?"

The girl read the card. "Yes, Detective Jackson. I certainly will. Perhaps you can tell me. Have the police solved the killing of our leader?"

"I don't think so," Jackson said. "But it's not really our case. I understand you served tea to the Swami last night."

"Yes," she said.

"Who else was there?"

"Sister Glorious, Brother Gildersleeve," she said.

"Did you notice anything unusual?" Jackson asked.

"No. Nothing. I told all this to the other policemen," she said.

"I'm sure you have. What is your name?" Jackson asked.

"Keri. Keri Ellison."

Jackson nodded and delicately touched a small gold bell at the girl's throat.

"Lovely," he said.

"Thank you. It is a gift of love," she said.

He met her eyes again. "You will call me if that girl comes here?"

"Yes."

"Ed, pay the girl for your granola."

"No," Keri said. "That is all right. Accept it as an introduction to our way of life."

"Thank you, Miss Ellison," Jackson said.

Outside the door, still holding his bag of cereal, Razoni said, "Stop at the park. I want to poison the pigeons. And don't think I didn't see you hitting on that big blonde. I'm thinking about telling your wife on you."

"Do yourself a favor. Don't," Jackson said.

Pat, Razoni's girlfriend from the *Times*, had decided to wait along with her report, but she had not suffered in the Red Horse Tavern for want of company. When Razoni came through the door, she was seated in the middle of the bar with a man on each side, each trying to talk to her at the same time. The rest of the bar was empty.

Razoni stood behind her and put a hand on her shoulder. She wheeled angrily on her bar stool, then smiled when she saw him.

"Hi, sourpuss," she said.

"All right, you two, beat it," Razoni said.

The man on Pat's left shrugged, picked up his drink and change, and moved down the bar. The man on the right hunched himself over his drink even more intently.

"Friend," said Razoni, "I just invited you out. Move."

"Go screw yourself. This is my seat," the man growled without turning.

"One more time, friend. Beat it."

"One more time, friend," the man mimicked. "Go screw yourself."

"Ed," the young woman cautioned.

"Now, now," he said. "Do you think I would lose my temper over something like this?"

He tapped the man on the shoulder and felt Jackson move up behind him.

The man turned slowly, as if reluctant to give Razoni the thrashing he deserved. "What do you want?" he sneered.

"My brother here wants your seat," said Razoni, nodding toward Jackson. The seated man looked past Razoni at Jackson, looming black and huge in the darkness of the bar.

The man swallowed hard. "Well, if you really are a group. I mean, I didn't know. I thought you . . ."

"Yeah, we know, friend. Up, up and away."

Moving with more haste than seemed possible, the man had his drink and change and was moving toward the far end of the bar. Razoni and Jackson took the two vacated seats on both sides of the young woman. Pat was a short, pert, frizzy-haired brunette who looked as if she had been the cutest member of the high-school cheerleading team, all boobs and bounce, smiles and sunshine. She patted Jackson's hand as Razoni said, "I don't know what there is about you, Tough, that frightens people."

"I don't either," Jackson said.

"It's not your face 'cause you got a face like a pail of mush. You think maybe it's because you're big?"

"No. A lot of people are big. You're big. Maybe I carry a voodoo curse or something."

"You don't scare me," Razoni said.

"The curse doesn't work on Italian detectives."

"That's because when I was young, my folks took me to the zoo a lot and I got used to seeing gorillas," Razoni said.

Pat giggled.

"Did they let you feed ravioli to the pigeons?" Jackson asked.

Pat giggled again.

"Right. Ravioli and granola," Razoni said. He looked hard at the young woman. "If you don't want company, sit at the end of the bar. Sit in the middle and you're either lonely or a drunk or a hooker. Nice girls sit at the end when they can."

"Who says?" she demanded.

"I says. Everybody knows that."

"That's right, Pat. Listen to Ed. Everybody knows that."

Razoni ordered drinks for them while Jackson filled in details in the notebook he always carried in his jacket pocket. He tried to concentrate, it being his habit to jot down everything: phrases he had heard, things that he didn't understand but that seemed a little out of place. Often, later, they turned out to be important in a solution to a case. He found it hard to keep his mind on his work, though, when Razoni began to question Pat in intimate detail on the quality, frequency, and duration of her love life, so he excused himself to call Captain Mannion.

"Give him my love," Razoni said. "Tell him I'm taking charge of everything."

"He'll be so pleased to hear that," Jackson said.

As he walked away, Razoni demanded of the young *Times* reporter, "Did you find the clippings?"

She reached down to her brown leather bag, which was on the floor, its strap hooked around her ankle to discourage pocketbook thieves, and took out a manila envelope. Onto the bar she emptied from it photocopies of news clippings.

Razoni held them up one at a time and read just the headlines:

SALAMANDA PLANS WORLD TOUR

AMERICA FINDS NEW GURU

THE NEW MESSAGE IS LOVE

SALAMANDA PLANS CITY OF LOVE IN PA.

SALAMANDA PLANS NATIONAL RALLY OF FOLLOWERS

"How come this guy's so popular and I never heard of him?"

"Because you can't find him in the sports pages," Pat said.

"Very funny. I read the paper," Razoni said.

"What's today's big story?" she asked.

"Something about war coming to the Mideast," Razoni guessed.

"How did you know that?" she asked.

"I told you. I read the paper," said Razoni, who did not even know where the Mideast was and who thought the problem of war there had been resolved years ago with the bombing of Hiroshima and Nagasaki.

Jackson came back and Razoni asked, "What did he say?"

"He said that I was the next to stupidest person in the world. You can fill in the blank. But he said you weren't in the case long enough to do any harm and we're off it anyway because Abigail called home just a few minutes ago, so that's that. Back to Salamanda."

"This is getting to be a pain in the rectum," Razoni said. "First this, then that, then this again."

"Who's Abigail?" Pat said.

"Some fag's kid was missing, but Tough and me got her home, so that's that." He pushed the photocopies of the news stories along the bar to Jackson. "Here, read these."

"Did you read them?" Jackson asked.

"Yes," Razoni lied.

"No," said Pat.

"I did read them. Speed reading," Razoni said.

"To an Italian, that means moving his lips in a blur," Jackson said.

"Will you read the goddamn clippings?" Razoni yelled. "Do I have to do everything around here?"

Jackson sipped his drink and read the clippings while Razoni drummed his fingers in annoyance over Jackson's slowness. Finally, the black detective looked up.

"What do you think?" Razoni asked.

"Nothing here that we didn't already know," Jackson said.

"That's just about how I figured it," Razoni said, relieved that he didn't have to read the stories.

"No sign yet of who the girl was who poisoned the Swami?" Pat asked.

"Nothing that we know of," Jackson said.

"But you'll be the first one we tell," Razoni said. "It's only a matter of time before we break this case. Now that we're allowed to concentrate on it."

And that was that, and later they drove Pat to her posh East Side apartment, and Razoni, surprisingly, declined her hospitality, swore her to secrecy about everything they had talked about, and drove with Jackson to the small frame house out in the suburbs where Jackson lived.

18

Sarge and Hilda were going to the ship. Chico had arisen early and cooked them breakfast, which Mrs. Tracy had refused to touch, clearly fearing it was poisoned. Sarge said, "More for me," and dug in with both hands. Hilda said, "You never eat breakfast like that when I cook it." Sarge said, "Perhaps there is a lesson to be drawn from that, Hilda."

Trace woke up on the couch just as they were at the front door, ready to go out to the waiting limousine.

"So long," he called out.

Sarge came back and stood over the sofa where Trace had slept under a flannel blanket so thin it looked as if it had been used to keep cannonballs warm on the *Mayflower*.

"You know our ship," Sarge said. "If you have any trouble, call me."

"What trouble? With a divorce case?"

"Well, if you get in a big new client, you call me."

"Not likely we'll get in a big new client," Trace said. He didn't really want to talk in the morning. Why was Sarge talking at him so much?

"Well, if anything comes up that's really important, you let me know," Sarge said.

"Like what?" Trace said.

"Never mind," Chico said. "Sarge, if anything big comes up, we'll call or wire you right away so you can come home. Maybe grab a plane if you have to."

"Smart girl," Sarge said.

"What are you two talking about?" Hilda called from

the doorway. "Patrick, we've got to go. We'll miss the ship."

"It doesn't sail for four hours," Sarge said.

"If we don't get there soon, we won't get a good table for dinner," she said.

"Coming, Hilda," Sarge said with a sigh. He jammed his big hands into his pockets so hard that Chico felt sorry for any change he might have been carrying.

He patted Trace's forehead and kissed Chico's cheek, and then the two of them were gone.

Chico said, "That poor man."

Trace said, "Poor man? What about me? Sleeping on a couch at my age when there's a nubile little Eurasian upstairs, all liquored up on ginger ale and all hot to trot." He reached for her wrist, but missed.

Chico said, "I'll make breakfast."

While Trace picked desultorily at the food on his plate, Chico wolfed down her second breakfast of the day. Between chews, she said, "Good news."

"My mother's decided to stay in Puerto Rico forever?" he said.

"No, not that good. I called our apartment and checked the phone messages."

"No good ever comes of that," Trace said.

"Maybe, maybe not. There was a message from Walter Marks. He has a case for you. Name of Dundee or something."

"Why is Groucho calling for me ever good news?" Trace asked.

"Because it's a case for the firm," Chico said. "You do remember the firm, don't you? You and me and Sarge?"

"Don't get smart, woman. Of course I remember. I remember every dumb thing I've ever agreed to in my life."

They parked Sarge's car in the lot across from the office and Trace gave Chico the keys to go upstairs first. "I've got a couple of errands to do first," he said.

When he came into the office a half-hour later, he was carrying a paper bag with two leaking coffee containers, and a small box containing a seven-inch black-and-white television set.

Chico cocked an eyebrow at the television set and Trace said, "Sarge said to buy one. He said no office should be without a television."

"Why?"

"I don't know why," Trace said. "Maybe he likes to watch the old folks on *Wheel of Fortune* call all the letters that have already been called. I don't know why. Why does this office already look better?"

"That's called clean," Chico said, gesturing at him with a dustcloth. Trace was afraid to ask her where she had found a dustcloth in this office. "And those stupid centerfolds are gone," she said.

"You're taking all the character out of this place," he said.

"When we're cooking, Trace, we'll have real women like that in here, not just their pictures from some magazine. We'll be stars."

"I've already got a real woman like that in here," Trace said gallantly.

"How nice of you," she said.

"Want to trick on the couch?" Trace asked.

"I'll pass," she said. "Call Walter Marks. Get us an insurance case and make us some money."

Trace sat behind Sarge's desk and sipped at one of the coffees. "Not so fast," he said. "You just can't go charging ahead when you're dealing with Groucho. I've got to think this through."

Chico glanced at her watch. "Think it through fast. You've got five minutes. Then get on the phone."

19

"Hello, Sarah. I kept him out of trouble all night," Razoni said. Sarah Jackson was as feminine and shapely as her husband was masculine and muscular. She carried herself like all women who know they are beautiful.

"Coffee's on, Ed. Come on out."

Razoni nodded, and when Sarah went back into the kitchen, he rolled off the living-room couch, picked up his clothes, and made his way to the bathroom.

In the kitchen, he sat down at the round butcher-block table across from Randolph, the Jacksons' eight-year-old son, who tried to stare him down. Razoni commandeered the copy of the *Times* from Jackson's chair and put it between his face and Randolph's.

Jackson came into the kitchen straightening his tie. " 'Morning, all. 'Morning, Ed."

"Shhhh, I'm reading the paper," said Razoni, who was glancing at the baseball scores.

"Did you say good morning to Mr. Razoni?" Jackson asked his son.

"No."

"Why not?"

"He didn't say good morning to me," the boy said.

"That's right, Tough, I didn't," said Razoni. "I was afraid to. He was looking at me real mean. Look at him. He's still looking at me real mean."

"Randolph, don't stare at Mr. Razoni," said Sarah Jackson.

"All right, Ma," the boy said. He looked at Razoni

and, when he was sure his parents were not watching, stuck out his tongue. Razoni saw him and stuck out his own tongue. Just as he did, Jackson turned to his partner and saw him with his tongue protruding from his mouth.

"No wonder he doesn't say hello to you. You stick your tongue out at him."

Randolph Jackson smirked.

Under the table, Razoni kicked him in the ankle.

The boy's yelp was interrupted by Sarah Jackson shoveling scrambled eggs from a huge skillet onto the four plates on the table. This was followed by quarter-inch-thick slices of scrapple, then by toast, then by homefries, until each plate was a heaping mound of food.

They ate themselves full. Randolph Jackson continued to stare at Razoni. Razoni gave Jackson the newpaper, and Jackson read the page-one story about Salamanda's death, occasionally reading sentences aloud. Razoni seemed surprised that the paper would print such inconsequential drivel.

"Drivel it may be," Jackson said, "but it's our case."

"That's this minute," Razoni said. He turned to Sarah. "Did he tell you about yesterday? First of all, a day off, we've got to go in. Then it's who killed the Swami, then it's forget the Swami and go find the fag's daughter, then it's forget the fag's daughter and go look for the Swami's killer again. I don't know what they want from us."

The telephone interrupted his soliloquy. Sarah Jackson answered it, then handed it without comment to her husband. He said, "Yes, sir," then listened a lot. "Okay, Captain."

"What'd he want?" Razoni said.

"Guess what?"

"What?"

"Abigail didn't get home last night."

"Who cares?" asked Razoni.

"He does. We're back looking for her."

Razoni groaned and Jackson got up to kiss his wife. Razoni stood and slowly waved his hand in front of Randolph Jackson's eyes to see if the boy would blink. He didn't. He jerked forward with his mouth and tried to bite Razoni's fingers.

Razoni retreated to the door of the kitchen, where he nodded toward Jackson's wife and son and said to his partner, "You sure it's safe to leave her alone with him?" Jackson snorted and Razoni shrugged, then called out, "So long, Sarah. Don't worry about anything. I'll make sure he doesn't get into trouble."

"I can't tell you how secure that makes me feel," she said, sharing a wink with her husband before walking the two men to the front door.

When his terror at the way Jackson drove had subsided to a steady level of fright, Razoni said, "Where are we going anyway?"

"Better talk to that Karen Marichal. Abigail Longworth's friend."

"What happened to the little twit anyway?"

"She called last night and told her father she was all right and she'd be coming right home. That's when we got pulled off the case. Then she didn't show."

"So now we forget the lizard again?" Razoni said.

"Looks that way," Jackson said.

"I swear to God Captain Mannion's getting as nuts as the rest of the fags who run this department," Razoni said. "Take me home before we do anything else. I want to change my clothes."

When he came back out of his apartment, Razoni was wearing a dark-blue suit, "To match my mood," he explained.

Jackson peeled away from the curb. Five minutes later, he ran two turning-red lights, barely missed a bus as it pulled from the curb, and parked in front of a fire hydrant.

As he got out of the car, Razoni was told by a street sweeper, "You guys can't park here."

"Why not? You see any fires?"

"You're going to get a ticket for interfering with firemen."

"Good," Razoni said. "They want the same pay as cops, let them work for it."

Jackson led the way up the stairs to the front doors of a

renovated brownstone. The light-tan doors were so heavily varnished that Razoni could see his reflection in them, and he carefully arranged his dark wavy hair. Then he straightened his tie. Then he looked down at his shoes.

"Are you finished?" asked Jackson.

"Yeah. But as soon as we leave here, we go back to my place so I can change my shoes. These are scuffed."

Jackson pushed the bell button. It sounded out with the first line of the chorus of "With a Little Help from My Friends."

No one answered.

"Ring it again, Tough. See what they do for an encore."

Jackson hit the bell again. It played the same notes, but this time the door opened. A uniformed butler stood there, a huge man with a shaggy head of blond hair that reached to his shoulders.

"Yes?"

"We'd like to see Karen Marichal," said Jackson.

"Whom may I say is calling?"

"Mr. Razoni and Mr. Jackson."

"Wait here, please." The butler closed the door on them.

"I guess everybody has a butler these days," Razoni said.

"Everybody's who's too lazy to open his own door."

"Maybe I'll get one."

"Just what you need in a one-room apartment," Jackson said.

They waited until the door opened again and the butler invited them inside. They followed him toward a pair of French doors at the right side of the entrance hall. The butler pushed open the doors. The two detectives began to step inside, then stopped short.

The doors had opened on a long elegant room with tall and narrow stained-glass windows. Hanging from the twenty-foot ceiling was a cut-crystal chandelier that looked as if it belonged in a theater lobby. Suspended from the ceiling, next to the ornate light, were a pair of ropes. Tracing them down with their eyes, they found the ropes ended with a pair of gymnastic rings. A man wearing gymnast's leotards was reaching up for the rings.

They turned back to the butler, but he had gone. They stepped into the room.

Along the far wall was a twelve-foot-long satin white couch. It was splattered with paint of many colors. Next to the couch was a woman standing in front of a painter's canvas. The canvas was eight feet long and six feet high. She was slapping red paint onto the canvas with a housepainter's brush. Large globs of it bounced off and dropped onto the couch.

"Let's get out of here," Razoni whispered.

"Where's your guts?" Jackson said.

The man was swinging on the rings now, back and forth, picking up speed. Finally, he let loose, turned a somersault in the air, and landed with feet together in an Olympic dismount position. There was a little thudding of applause from the corner of the room to the detectives' right. They looked in that direction and saw an old woman, wrinkled, wearing pink aviator glasses and a formal satin gown in powder blue, clapping. She clapped by slapping one hand down onto the oak table at which she sat. Her other hand held grimly onto a crystal goblet filled with red liquid, apparently from the gallon jug of Gallo burgundy that sat on the table in front of her.

The man from the trapeze stepped forward to the two detectives.

"Hi there, old buddies. How are you?"

"Fine," said Jackson. The man grabbed Jackson's right hand and pumped it. He advanced upon Razoni, who thrust his right hand into his jacket pocket.

Nothing daunted, the man gave Razoni a bright smile. He was perhaps in his early sixties, but only his lined face and bald head showed that age. His body had the long stringy muscles of a teenage gymnast.

"I'm Ferenc Marichal. That's my wife, Charmaine," he said. The woman at the mural-sized canvas did not turn around but waved the big red paint brush over her head in a sign of greeting.

"And that's Mother," said Marichal, pointing to the woman in the corner. She did not look at the detectives because she was busy shaking the gallon jug over her goblet. When only a few drops trickled out, she yelled, "Shit," reached over her head for the bell rope, and began to yank it angrily.

"Well, Mother's occupied," Marichal said blandly.

The old woman kept yanking on the bell rope. Resounding throughout the house, Razoni could hear the *bong-bong-bong* of a heavy bell. If there were a hunchback in this house, he was leaving.

He heard a voice behind him.

"Beep, beep. Coming through."

Razoni moved aside, and the uniformed butler skidded past him, almost on a run, carrying a full jug of wine. He brought it to the aged woman, filled her glass, put the rest of the jug on the table, and removed the empty bottle.

"About time," the woman said.

"Yes'm," the butler said.

"I think you're getting too old for this work," she said.

"Yes'm."

"You're fired, asshole," she said.

"Yes'm."

"Don't worry," Marichal whispered to the detectives. "She fires Igor several times a day. What can I do for you, now?"

"We don't want to bother you," Razoni said. "We'll be glad to come back during visiting hours."

"Nonsense," said Marichal. "We're always at home to visitors. *Mi casa es su casa.*"

"We've come to see Karen," said Jackson.

"Karen?" Marichal said. He looked puzzled. "Oh, yes. Karen. My daughter," he said brightly.

"Yes. We understand she's a friend of Abigail Longworth."

"That's right. Close. Close. Very close." He stopped and waited. After a few seconds, he said, "Now it's your turn."

"My turn?" asked Jackson.

"Yes. Your turn to talk. I said close, close, very close. Then you were supposed to say something. That's how conversations go, first one, then the other."

"Oh, I see. May we see Karen?"

"I don't know. How are your eyes? Hah! A joke. Mother, did you hear that? He said, may he see Karen and I said, how are your eyes? Charmaine, did you hear that?"

"Oh, go scratch your ass, Ferenc," said Mother Marichal from the corner. Across the room, Charmaine Marichal waved her paint brush over her head. A large glop of red paint fell in the middle of her hair. She didn't seem to notice.

"Very funny," Jackson told Marichal.

"Look, we want to see Karen," said Razoni.

"You can. If you've got good eyes," Marichal said. He seemed about to say something more, but instead went over to a column that stood in the middle of the floor. Atop the four-foot-high column was a mound of clay that was slowly being sculpted into some sort of head. With his thumb, Marichal smoothed out a spot over the left eyebrow. He cocked his head and looked at the mound of clay, then picked it up from the pedestal and threw the head against the far wall. The soft moist clay hit with a splat, stuck against the deep wood paneling for a second, then trickled down toward the floor.

Marichal turned back to Razoni and Jackson. "I'll take you to see Karen. But don't be surprised if she doesn't want to talk. She's been depressed since her guru died."

"Her guru?" asked Jackson.

"Yes. Poisoned. Very guru-some." He giggled.

Razoni felt something brush the back of his legs. He turned, just in time to see a spider monkey hopping up onto his shoulder. It put its face next to Razoni's ear.

Jackson laughed.

Razoni screamed. "Get this son of a bitch off me. I ain't no banana."

"Come here, Percy," called Mother Marichal from the corner of the room. "That gentleman isn't your friend. He isn't even a gentleman. He's just a plain ordinary dork."

The monkey jumped down from Razoni's shoulder and skittered across the floor, hopping into a chair across the table from the woman. When she pushed her wineglass forward, it stuck its face close to the wine and began lapping it with its tongue.

Razoni rolled his eyes. Jackson kept laughing. Ferenc Marichal, suddenly all business, brushed by them and led the way to the stairs. At the top of the stairs was a red door with a yellow-and-orange sunburst painted on it. Marichal knocked, then opened the door a crack.

"There are gentlemen here to have a word with you, Karen," Marichal said. He stepped aside to let the two detectives into the room, then closed the door behind them and left.

The room was illuminated only by a small votive candle in a glass saucer on an end table at the far side of the room. Over the candle hung the poster of Salamanda with the legend: THE SWAMI LIVES. On the end table near the candle were two framed photographs, but in the darkness their subjects were not visible. Next to the candle was also a bowl of fruit, looking like an offering to the darkness.

Razoni reached for the light switch on the wall beside the door. He flipped it but the room remained dark.

"Pleathe," came a voice. "I am thenthitive to the light."

The voice was a soft lisping breath of a woman's voice. The two detectives turned toward its source and saw the girl, sitting in lotus position, atop the couch in the corner of the room farthest from the candle. Her head and entire body were draped and veiled in some kind of dark gauze. Not even her eyes were visible through the gauze.

"Karen?" said Jackson.

"Yeth."

"I'm Detective Jackson and this is Detective Razoni. You're a friend of Abigail Longworth's?"

"Yeth."

"Have you seen her?"

There was a pause. "Why?"

"She hasn't been home and her family is worried," Jackson said.

"Oh. I thaw her on Thaturday at thchool."

"Not since then?"

"No."

"Did she give you any indication that she might be

thinking of going away for a while?'' As he spoke, Jackson gradually moved closer to the candle.

"No," the voice answered.

"Do you know the name of any of her other friends?" Jackson said.

"Abigail hath no other friendth. Jutht me."

"He means boyfriends," Razoni said.

"No boyfriendth," answered the voice.

"Do you know where she might be staying away from home?" Jackson asked.

"No."

Jackson took his business card from his wallet, walked to the end table, and put the card on it. "I'm leaving my card here," he said. "If you hear from Abigail, please call us."

As he put the card down, he picked up one of the photographs on the table. It was a snapshot of Swami Salamanda. He replaced it and picked up the other photo. It was a duplicate of their photo of Abigail Longworth. There was a message written on it, but Jackson couldn't see it in the dark. He fished a cigarette from his pocket and lit it with his lighter. In the light, he read the message:

"Dearest K., The beauty of love must always be our guide, A."

"A beautiful sentiment Abigail wrote you," he said.

The girl was silent.

Jackson replaced the picture and his fingers brushed against something metallic. It was a small gold bell. He looked at it, then put it back down.

"We'll be going now," he said. "We're very sorry about your guru."

"Life alwayth endth in death," the girl said.

"Right on," Razoni said.

Jackson turned, cigarette lighter still burning in his hand, but he could not see past the girl's veil. He put out the lighter as Razoni opened the door and light from the hallway leaked into the room. Jackson continued to stare at her, but she seemed, under the veil, to turn her face toward the wall as if to avoid the light.

Jackson followed Razoni out into the hallway and closed the door behind them.

Razoni hissed, "If we've got to fight our way out, I take the old lady."

"I thought you'd want to plug that monkey."

"No, monkeys I leave to you. They're more in your line," Razoni said.

But they went downstairs and let themselves out without anyone wishing them good-bye or noticing their departure.

20

"Hello. This is Devlin Tracy. That's T-R-A-C-Y. May I speak with the honorable Mr. Walter Marks, please?"

Would wonders never cease, Chico thought as she sat on a chair in the office and listened to the telephone conversation. Trace being polite to the secretary of Walter Marks. The poor woman was probably rolling on the floor, holding her chest.

"No, of course I do not mind telling you what my business is," Trace said. "I have decided to accept an assignment that Mr. Walter Marks has so graciously offered to me."

He winked at Chico and covered the telephone with his hand. "You can catch more flies with honey than with vinegar," he said. Quickly uncovering the phone, he said, "No, of course not, madam. It's Devlin Tracy. T-R-A-C-Y.

"My company? Of course. My company is that noble institution for which you work. The Garrison Fidelity Life Insurance Company. And I have news that will delight the right honorable Mr. Walter Marks."

Trace winked at Chico again.

"The name is Tracy," he said. "Devlin Tracy. No, not Stacy. Tracy. T-R-A-C-Y. What? You don't know me? Well, I know you, you stupid twat. You are the latest in a long line of morons to hold that job. Now, put Groucho on the phone before I come up there and kick in your homely insipid face." He covered the mouthpiece and shook his head sadly.

"Honey," Chico reminded him. "I think that was a little vinegary."

"Screw her," Trace growled. "That's what I get for trying to be nice. Just watch me charm Groucho."

"Hello, Walter," Trace said. "Ho, ho, ho, it's good to hear your voice again."

"What are you up to, Trace?" Marks said. He was a small man with a voice to match: a small, pinched, suspicious voice that sounded as if he were being charged by the vowel. He was also the vice president for claims of the insurance company, and thus Trace's boss on those occasions when Trace chose to work.

"Why are you always in such a hurry to talk business?" Trace said. "Ho, ho, ho. How's the family?"

"The family's fine," Marks said. "What do you want?"

"Glad to hear it," Trace said. "Ho, ho, ho. Dorothy's fine? The boy . . . Walter Junior . . . is fine too?"

"My wife's name is Gladys and she's fine. There is no Walter Junior. My son's name is Paul and he's fine. Everybody's fine but me. You know why I'm not fine?"

"I'm sorry to hear it, Walter. Why aren't you fine? Ho, ho, ho."

"I'm not fine because I'm wondering why the hell you're calling me only one day after I called you and I'm wondering why you're doing this Santa Claus impersonation. Ho, ho, ho. What do you want, Trace?"

"Remember that assignment you mentioned on the telephone?"

"Right. The Dundee matter."

"Right," Trace said. "Exactly correct, Walter. How you do get right to the heart of things? The Dundee matter. Exactly. Well, have I got exciting news for you."

"I'm listening," Marks said.

"I'll take the case, you see. I know that's what you wanted me to do."

"Yesss," said Marks, suspiciously, stretching the word out, as if waiting for Trace to say something so he could withdraw the word without ever having finished it.

"But I've set up a new venture, Walter. I wanted you to be the first to know."

"I'm not investing in it or buying stock in it," Marks said. "That's that."

"No, Walter," Trace said. "Ho, ho, ho. It's not like that at all. What it is is that I'm entering the private-investigation business and Garrison Fidelity now is going to be one of our corporate clients. You won't have just me on your cases now: you'll have a whole team of top-flight investigators at your disposal."

"Who's on this top-flight team?" Marks said.

"We've started out with Sarge and Chico, but already we're looking for staff, good staff. Sarge has just got more work than we could possibly handle. But I . . . well, I just wanted you to know, Walter, that no matter how big or how busy we get, we'll always have time for Garrison Fidelity and its piddling little piss-ant cases. And when we get more staff, we'll be able to help even more. Maybe young Walter Junior would like a job. What do you think?"

"Paul is my son's name, and if he were ever to be associated with you in any way, I would know that all the money I spend on his education has been wasted," Marks said.

"Well, if you ever change your mind, you just let me know. Ho, ho, ho. We can always use another good man," Trace said. "Now about our fees."

"I'm listening," Marks said sourly. "Somehow I knew it would get to this."

"Commerce rears its ugly head. Ho, ho, ho," Trace said. "Since you're going to have a whole agency now at your disposal instead of just one operative, of course we're going to have to charge more of a fee. But even though we've got three people now servicing your account instead of one, we're not going to triple your fees. No, sir. Ho, ho, ho. We're just going to double the fee. Just double my present retainer, Walter, and that'll be the new annual contract with the new detective firm. You can't ask for a better deal or more consideration than that, can you?"

"Ho, ho, ho," Walter Marks said. "Double your fee? Ho, ho, ho, *and* ho."

"Which means exactly what?" Trace asked politely.

"It means exactly, Trace, that I don't care if you bought

the Pinkerton agency with Wells Fargo thrown in. There is no way your fee is being raised. If you have not three but a million operatives, if you con the KGB into working for you, there will be no change. Your fee is the same. Period. End of story. Next.''

"But the company . . .'' Trace protested.

"I don't care about the company. I don't care about you, if the truth be known. You and your precious company just work for the same number. No more. Not a penny more.''

"I think you're making a mistake, Walter. I think a little incentive increase would have inspired us all to work harder for good Old Garrison Fidelity.''

"Tough titty, pal,'' Marks said.

"Well, just for you, Walter, we're going to give you a break. The firm is going to take this case, what is it . . . ?''

"The Dundee matter.''

"Right. Dundee. We're going to take this case and we're going to do such a good job on it that you're going to say . . . Because you're a big man, Walter; inside that shrunken body beats a giant heart and you're going to be big enough to say, 'Trace, old buddy, I was wrong. Your firm is a wonderful new improvement and I want to raise your fees.' You'll say that, Walter. You'll see. You'll say it.''

"Right after I say, 'Look, Ma, I can walk on water.' Don't hold your breath,'' Marks said.

"No need to be like that, Walter. No need to be testy. We'll pick up the file on the Dundee case and get right on it and we'll do our regular top-notch job. Don't you worry.''

"I—'' Marks began.

"No, don't you worry. Same rates, just more staff. For our very best client, the right honorable Walter Marks. Ho, ho, ho. I'll be talking to you, Walter. Give my best to Dorothy and Walter Junior.''

Trace hung up.

"Ho, ho, ho,'' Chico said. "Doesn't sound like your suggestion went over real well.''

"Ho, ho, ho, to you too,'' Trace said. "We got everything we wanted.''

"Don't forget," she said. "I was listening."

"You'd better pay attention because I'm about to teach you some of the facts of life," Trace said. "Now, do you really think I'd ask that backbiting little bastard Groucho for a raise? If it was time for a raise, I'd go talk to the president of the company, not Groucho. I threw that in so he'd have a chance to turn me down and feel good about himself."

"Well, what did you want that you got?" Chico asked.

"From here on in, the company—this company—is handling the Garrison Fidelity Account." He smiled at her. "Groucho could have said no, you know."

"I'll be damned, Trace. Every time I think you are a hopeless dimwit, you do something that totally surprises me."

"Here's something else that will surprise you. Get on over to Gone Fishing's offices and see Groucho. You're handling the Dundee case."

"Cheez-o-man," Chico said. "My first job in the big time. Wow." She stood up, snatched up her purse, and started for the door. "I'm on my way," she said.

Trace called her at the door. "Hey."

She turned and he said, "Be careful out there." As she left, he turned on the new television set.

21

Their car had been ticketed while they were in the Marichal home.

Razoni ripped the ticket from the windshield, crumpled it, and threw it into the gutter. "See, you did it again," he said.

"Don't worry about it," Jackson said.

"No, don't worry about it. But if I don't worry about it, who will? You people don't worry about anything. But I'm the one—"

"Will you shut up and get in the car?"

Inside the car, Razoni kept going.

"Another thing. Nice place you take me to."

"Just wanted you to see how a real American family lives," Jackson said.

"Yeah. Especially the monkey. A monkey named Percy. Good Jesus."

"Will you disengage your mouth and put your brain in gear for a minute?" asked Jackson as he lurched away from the curb.

"I'm thinking, I'm thinking."

"Are you thinking about how it's kind of unusual? These two cases keep turning in on each other?"

"That's just what I'm thinking about," Razoni said.

"And?"

"Well, first, the lizard is done in by some chick. But nobody knows who she is. Then we find that the mayor's daughter used to go down to the lizard's cereal shop. But nobody there ever saw her. Shit. I can't make head or tail out of it. You think about it for a while," Razoni said.

"You forgot about the bells," said Jackson as he headed crosstown.

"What bells?"

"That's what you get for not reading reports. The girl who slipped the Swami the mickey was wearing a bell. And the girl last night in the health-food store was wearing a bell. And this Marichal kid was wearing a bell."

"And Elsie the Cow wears a bell," Razoni said. "So what? Maybe all these House of Love nut cases wear bells."

"No, they don't."

"Why do *you* think?" Razoni asked.

"I don't know yet," Jackson said.

"For Christ's sake," said Razoni in exasperation. "You get me all worked up with bells and things and then you don't know. I don't want to think about it anymore. Let me know if you decide anything. Where are we going?"

"To Abigail's school."

"What for?" Razoni asked.

"See if anybody knows anything about her."

"I know all you need to know. Her old man's a fag who's in love with his kid. He's nuts, her friends are nuts, including that frigging monkey, and she's nuts."

"You're sure of that?"

"What else could she be?" Razoni said.

"What about Jenkins?"

"I don't trust anybody who takes a job as a chauffeur for a fag. And besides, he's a horseplayer and all horseplayers are nuts."

"And Gildersleeve?" Jackson asked.

"I don't trust him," Razoni said.

"Why not?"

"He's a little guy. Little guys are always sneaky," Razoni said.

"Sister Glorious?" Jackson asked.

"Obviously a nut case. A woman who looks like that, why is she jerking around with some swami and all those sappy people with big asses or pimples that hang around there?"

"What about the Marichal family?" Jackson said.

"I don't trust any of them," Razoni said.

"Why not?"

"Because they look like liberals. All liberals are nuts."

"Is there anybody you do trust?" Jackson said.

"Yeah. Three people. Me, myself, and I."

"What about me?" Jackson said.

"*Om shanti* in old shanty town," Razoni said.

The only person in the registrar's office at the uptown college was a long-haired T-shirted youth behind a desk, feet up, reading *Screw* magazine.

"Hello," said Jackson politely.

"Yeah," answered the youth noncommittally, glancing at Jackson, then looking disdainfully back to his reading.

"I want to know the schedule of a friend of mine and the names of her instructors."

"Oh, you would? Well, we're not allowed to give out that information," said the youth, pleased at telling off a man a foot taller than he was.

Jackson showed his badge to the youth. "We're police officers," he said.

"So what?"

"We need the schedule of Miss Abigail Longworth," said Jackson. "Now, either direct us to someone who can give it to us or get up off your fat ass and get it yourself."

"The registrar is out to lunch and I don't have the authority to look in the files and I'm not going to break the rules because establishment lackeys tell me to."

Razoni inhaled deeply. He held a hand up to Jackson. "Let me reason with him, Tough," he said mildly.

Razoni grabbed the youth by the pigtail that hung down the back of his neck and jerked him across the room, back to the desk. He picked up a pair of scissors and cut off the first inch of the pigtail.

"Now, little man, I'm going to cut off your hair inch by inch until you learn some manners. And if that doesn't work, I'm going to turn very mean and frisk you for the stash you're carrying in these beautiful jeans and then I'm going to bust your bald fucking head." Snip. Another inch. "Are you getting the message from this establishment lackey?"

"Stop it, stop it," the young man yelled, and Razoni released his death grip on the boy's hair. The youth scurried to a file cabinet. "What's her name?" he asked Jackson, glancing back over his shoulder at Razoni, who held up the scissors as a reminder.

"Abigail Longworth," said Jackson. "Don't you have all that stuff on computer?"

"Yeah, but I don't know how to work the computer," the young man said as he began looking through the cabinet.

"Try looking under L," suggested Razoni.

"Right, right. Under L," the youth said. "Here it is. Longworth, Abigail." He looked up with a smile that pleaded for approval.

"What's the schedule?" asked Jackson.

"Every day, she's got creative writing with Professor Foley in the morning and then illustrative art with Dr. Mack."

"Where do we find Foley and Mack?"

"They're in this building. Foley's in Four-A. Mack's in the seventh-floor workshop."

"Thank you," said Razoni. "You're a credit to your race, whatever that is."

As the two detectives walked away, the young man fingered his raped pigtail, then bolted toward the office restroom so he could inspect the damage in a mirror.

In the elevator riding up to the fourth floor, Razoni said that kids weren't what they used to be.

"What did they used to be?"

"Damned if I know, but it wasn't what we just saw."

Professor Foley's creative-writing group was on a break. The professor was a long-haired man in his forties with hair that seemed electrically charged and a flowered shirt open at the throat.

Through the open classroom door, the two detectives saw Professor Foley seated at his desk reading some typewritten papers. To his right stood a tiny buxom brunette, whose sweater celebrated her bust and whose short skirt celebrated her legs. She leaned over Foley's right shoulder. He seemed intent on reading the paper, but his right hand seemed intent on keeping busy under her skirt.

"Professors aren't what they used to be either," Jackson said. He called from the doorway: "Professor Foley?"

The man at the desk looked up. His right hand dropped casually out from under the skirt.

"May we have a word with you?"

"Sure. Why the hell not? Everybody else is always bothering me when I'm trying to read my assignments. Why should you be different? Come on in, come on in. Beat it, Monica. I'll talk to you later."

The brunette smiled at him worshipfully. She passed Jackson in the doorway without a look. She gyrated a little passing Razoni and gave him lots of teeth.

He smiled back at her.

Professor Foley pushed away the paper in front of him and turned in his chair to look at the two men. Razoni noted with disgust that the professor wore brown leather strapped sandals and no socks.

"We understand Abigail Longworth is one of your students?" Jackson said. As he stepped closer to the desk, he could smell the powerful reek of alcohol emanating from Professor Foley.

"That's another thing," Foley said. "How can I teach writing when the people I'm supposed to teach writing to don't show up? Here I am, one of America's very finest uncelebrated writers and—"

"You mean Abigail misses your classes?" Jackson said.

"She's not here today, is she?"

"When was the last time she was here?"

"I don't know. Last week. Wait a minute, I'll tell you. She turned something in." He began rooting through a pile of papers on the side of the desk. "Here it is. Saturday. She was here on Saturday."

"May I see that?" asked Jackson.

Foley shrugged and pushed the paper forward. Jackson looked at it. It was covered with tight lines, neatly handprinted in a calligraphic style.

"It's awful," Foley said. "I'm warning you. It's terrible."

As Jackson looked at it, Foley opened a desk drawer and took out a Styrofoam coffee container. It reeked of alcohol too. He took a large sip and put it back in the desk.

Jackson skimmed the paper, reading some of it in a soft mumble. "From A to Z with a stop at K . . . let our bodies touch . . . let our breasts form one jealous mountain . . . let your warm lips ignite my essence . . . please violate me with your kindness. . . ." The big detective looked up. "Very interesting."

"That's what people always say when they don't like something or don't understand it. It's not interesting at all," Foley said. "It's shit. That's what it is. That's what all these are." He pulled up the pile of the papers on his desk. "Shit." He threw them in the air and they fluttered to the floor. "All shit. Why am I wasting my time here?"

"God knows," Razoni said. "You should be in Hollywood. Let me see that." He took the paper from Jackson and began to scan it. "Ummmmm. Ummmmmm. Ummmmmm. Just what I thought," he said.

"What is just what you thought?" Jackson asked.

"Never mind. It's for me to know and you to find out."

"Does Abigail always write like this?" Jackson asked.

"Just about. Maybe worse," said Foley. "Poor thing."

"Why poor thing?" asked Jackson.

"No talent. Dippy and no talent. Talks funny. And small tits. Hardly any tits at all."

"Do you have any of her other papers?"

Foley grimaced. "God, no. It's bad enough I have to read this shit once without keeping it around. Do you realize that I've spent ten years wallowing in shit?"

Razoni muttered something about water always seeking its own level, but Foley had never heard that statement before and gave no indication that, now having heard it, he had any idea what it meant.

"Does Abigail have any close friends in class that you know of?" asked Jackson.

"No. Shy too. She never talks to anybody. When she's here. She hasn't been here since Saturday. How can I teach people when they don't show up?"

He had the Styrofoam cup in his hand again, even before the detectives reached the classroom door.

In the hallway, waiting for the elevator, Jackson said, "Why are you smirking?"

"Because I called it right again. That Abigail's as big a freaking fag as her father. You read that poem. Let's put our boobies together and make a big tit mountain. She's a fag."

"You don't call girls fags, Ed. It's not polite. Lesbians or gay, but not fags."

"I don't see anything gay about being a fag," Razoni muttered.

Dr. Madeline Mack was another professor who wasn't what teachers used to be either.

She appeared to be no more than twenty-one and her face was scrubbed bright, shiny, and flawless without makeup. Her eyes crinkled at the corners all the time, as if hearing a secret joke. She wore blue jeans that encircled her smooth buttocks like a pair of firm hands and a red silk almost-see-through blouse with something to see through to.

She insisted upon bringing Razoni and Jackson into her classroom where twenty students were standing at easels painting. Their backs were turned to the front of the class and their attention was fixed on a slim curly-haired man who sat on a stool at the far end of the room, one hand behind his head, the other resting atop his left thigh.

"He's naked," Razoni whispered to Jackson.

"Right. He's a model."

"Yeah. But he's naked."

"You never heard of a nude model before?"

"Not a man," Razoni said. "That's disgusting."

Dr. Mack had perched her buttocks on the edge of the desk. She leaned back and extended her fine long legs. Her tennis shoes touched the toes of Jackson's feet.

"Now what was it you gentlemen wanted to talk about?" she asked.

Razoni was staring at the students. He took a few steps forward to look over the shoulder of one middle-aged woman at an easel. She was painting the model, ringlets and all—including a Homeric member jutting out from his loins. She felt Razoni's eyes on her back and she turned to him. She was a pudgy little gray-haired woman.

"Do you like it?" she asked with a hopeful smile.

Razoni leaned forward with a smile of his own. "It's disgusting, Mama. And so are you."

She giggled, thinking Razoni was joking. Jackson asked Dr. Mack about Abigail Longworth.

"A nice girl," Dr. Mack said.

"Is her attendance regular?" Jackson asked.

"It isn't really customary for me to talk to strangers about my students."

"We're police officers," said Jackson softly so the class would not hear. "This is business."

"Oh, my. Abbie's not in trouble, is she?"

"Not that I know of. This is a confidential thing for her family," Jackson said vaguely.

"I see. Well, yes, Abbie's very good about her attendance." She shrugged. "But she missed today."

"You saw her Saturday?"

"Yes."

"You're sure? With so many students, you can remember?"

Dr. Mack smiled at him. "Sure," she said. "Saturday was the first day Freddy down there was modeling for us. Abbie seemed to be a little upset at the idea. Like your friend there."

"Strange attitude for an art student, isn't it?" asked Jackson.

"Perhaps. Different strokes for different folks." Her eyes locked on Jackson's for a moment, then she turned her head away. "There," she said. "That's one of Abbie's." She pointed to a pen-and-ink sketch that hung on one of the cork panels that surrounded the room.

The drawing was of a young blond woman, done with delicate loving strokes. The blonde was nude, except for a small gold bell that hung about her neck.

Jackson stepped forward to examine the sketch more carefully. At the bottom was the title: *Keri.*

"Was this one of your models?" asked Jackson.

"No, that was just a free memory exercise one of the classes did. It's very good, don't you think?"

Razoni had rejoined them in front of the paper sketch. "Well, it's sure a lot better than these disgusting things they're doing now," he said.

"The human form is never disgusting," Dr. Mack said vigorously.

"Yours isn't," Razoni said. "That one isn't," he said, pointing to the drawing. "That one at the end of the room is."

Dr. Mack looked at Jackson and shrugged.

Jackson said, "Has Abigail seemed upset lately?"

"No," the young professor said. "Just the opposite. She's seemed very happy."

"Does she have any special friends in the class here?"

Dr. Mack shook her head. "Abigail's a very shy girl. She hardly ever speaks to anyone, much less have friends."

"I see," Jackson said. He pointed at the drawing of the blond woman and said to Razoni, "Recognize the model?"

Razoni looked at the drawing carefully, then nodded.

When Jackson asked for the drawing, Dr. Mack declined, but made him a photocopy of it on the class copying machine.

Jackson folded the copy and put it in his pocket. "Thanks, Dr. Mack," he said. "You've been very helpful."

"My pleasure. If you two ever want to come back and model for our class, we'd be glad to have you."

"What's it pay?" Razoni asked.

"Four dollars an hour."

"To sit naked in front of all these Peeping Toms?"

"Yes."

"That's disgusting," Razoni said.

22

After Chico left the office, Trace read again the report Sarge had prepared for Angelo Alcetta on his wife. Basically, it said that the agency had found out nothing about the woman, and Trace thought it was depressing.

From the center desk drawer, he took out the four lined pieces of paper ripped from a notebook that constituted Sarge's business records and learned what depression was really like.

So he called Angelo Alcetta's number. Alcetta wasn't there, but some male of indeterminate species took the message that Trace wanted to see him in Sarge's office that afternoon. After hanging up, Trace read the report again. It didn't contain anything, except a lot of leading questions that it didn't answer, but Trace thought he could fake his way through it.

The telephone rang.

"Tracy Agency."

"Hello, Devlin." Suddenly Trace knew everything else that had happened in his life was just a warm-up for this feeling of really being depressed. The voice was his ex-wife.

"Better talk fast, Cora. I was just leaving to catch a plane."

"Don't give me that, Devlin. I know that you're going to be in town for the whole week and you're staying at Hilda's house. I suppose that floozie is with you?"

"What do you want, Cora?"

"What I want is for you to visit your two children.

That's what I want. Do you know how long its's been since you saw them last?''

"Let's see. The last Ice Age ended in 15,000 B.C., I think. It's been since then."

"Very funny. Really, Devlin. Don't you think you could spare a few minutes to see your children? They need you."

"Why? Did you go and buy them target pistols again?" Trace asked.

"I don't know how you can ignore your own flesh and blood," she said.

"I pay great attention to my flesh and my blood," Trace said. "It's just my kids that I ignore. Let's face it, Cora. They're yours. You spawned them and you raised them and I don't even know What's-his-name and the girl, and they don't know me. Why ruin something that's working perfectly?"

"Devlin, I am cooking dinner at this house on Saturday. Seven P.M. Your children and I will expect you here."

"Good-bye, Cora."

"Don't forget. Seven o'clock Saturday."

Trace hung up, feeling sweat starting under his arms. She might call back, he realized with panic. He had to go out. He smiled when he realized he had a perfectly valid business reason. He would go and take a look at Gloria Alcetta. Call it background information for when he delivered his report to Angelo later that day. He could honestly tell Angelo that not one, but two operatives had been working on his case.

From the desk drawer where he had stashed it, Trace took a small tape recorder. He locked the office door, then removed his shirt and taped the recorder to the right side of his back. He donned his clothes again and threaded the microphone wire through a shirt buttonhole and attached it to a tie clip in the shape of a golden frog. The frog's mesh-covered open mouth covered a very powerful microphone. Trace tested the tape device, satisfied himself that it worked, then turned off the television set and left the office. Time to go see Sister Glorious.

*   *   *

"Next stop, Cap'n Crunch's cereal shop," Razoni said.

"Absolutely kee-rect," said Jackson as they drove away from the uptown college.

"I can't understand why the girl in the store lied to us about not knowing the Longworth kid," Razoni said.

"Maybe she thought she was protecting her," suggested Jackson.

"Yeah, but from what? All we did was ask her if she knew her."

"I don't know," Jackson admitted. "They're close enough that Abigail draws nudes of the blonde. Maybe she thought Abigail was in some kind of trouble."

"Probably just trying to keep her away from us. Dirty fags," said Razoni.

"Not just the two of them either," said Jackson.

"What do you mean?"

"The Marichal kid. She's got a picture of Abigail in her room with a little love message on it too."

"What is this?" Razoni said. "Everybody in this town is turning queer. Lesbian Fagola City. It's all that Longworth's fault. As soon as that pinko came to town and started ruining all the television, everybody's turning swish. He won't rest until he gets this town renamed San Franswishco."

"Everybody's favorite city," Jackson said.

"Aaaaah, bullshit," Razoni said. He was quiet for a while, then asked, "Did the captain say how those two precinct morons—what's their names, Gault, Gorman—how they were doing with the Salamanda investigation?"

"No break yet," Jackson said.

"Well, at least we're not involved in that one anymore," Razoni said.

"That's not exactly correct," Jackson said. "The captain told us to keep an eye on it."

"What?" Razoni yelled. "How the hell can I investigate a missing lesbian and a lizard's murder all at the same time? Why the hell doesn't he get a broom for my butt and I can sweep the floor on the way out of the office?"

"He probably didn't think of it yet," Jackson said.

"You're a fine one, Jackson. You don't care how much work gets laid on me."

"I don't know anybody else who could handle it all with such grace."

Trace had this idea that Indian holy men were interested in nothing so much as the bottom line. So as he walked down the street toward the Salamanda ashram headquarters, he knew that in Nirvana somewhere the Swami would be pleased to know that his fruit-and-nut factory was doing a land-office business selling granola and birdseed.

Trace picked his way through the crowds of people in the store and asked a young man at a back counter, "Where's Sister Glorious?"

"I suppose you're another one of them from the press," the young man said with great disdain.

"Had a lot of press around?" Trace asked.

"Yesterday. Gawd. We had everybody but the *National Enquirer*. Who are you?"

"I'm with the *National Enquirer*," Trace said. "Jerome Falwell. Were you one of the Swami's disciples?"

"With all my heart."

"What do you say to people who said his message wasn't one of love, but just a call to free indiscriminate sex. What do you say to them?"

"I say they should go fuck themselves," the young man said with a grin.

"Well-phrased, well-phrased," Trace said. "Is Sister Glorious here?"

"She's next door at the ashram," the young man said.

"Thank you very much."

"Have a nice day, Mr. Falwell."

Razoni and Jackson went into the food shop and asked the man at the counter in the back, "Where's Keri?"

"Keri?"

"Yes. The tall blonde that works here."

"I don't think I know her," he said. "Who are you?"

Razoni ignored the question. "We were in last night. She waited on us."

"You know, we don't really have people who work here," the man said. "Anybody who's here will work here. That's the way it works under the Swami."

"Maybe somebody else here knows her," Jackson said.

The young man shrugged. "Janelle," he called out. A fat young woman pushed her way through a beaded curtain that separated the store from a back room. "They're looking for a Keri," the young man said. "Said she was working last night."

Razoni had turned to watch the people milling about the store. Without thinking, he dipped his fingers into a bucket of grains, pulled out a few, and started to chew them. They were good. Surprisingly good. He had a few more.

"Yes, Keri was in here last night," the fat girl told Jackson.

"But she's not here now?" he said.

"No."

"Do you know her full name?" Jackson asked.

"No, I don't. We have all given up our old names, we who serve the Swami."

Jackson fished the photocopied sketch from his pocket, unfolded it, and placed it on the counter. "This is the girl we're talking about, right?"

"That's her," said Janelle.

"Damn," the young man said, scanning the nude drawing carefully. "I knew I should have worked last night."

"Think she might be next door?" Jackson asked.

"She is there a lot," Janelle said. "She might be there now."

Behind him, Jackson heard the sound of crunching. "You almost finished fooling around?" he asked Razoni.

"Anytime, Tough. I just want to get a bag of this stuff." He poured a scoopful of the grains into a clear plastic bag and brought it to the counter. "How much?" he asked.

The young man put the bag on the scale. "That'll be four dollars."

"What?"

"Four dollars. It's eight dollars a pound and you've got half a pound."

"For cereal?"

"Special natural grains and kernels," the man said.

"Special natural rip-off," Razoni said. He took the bag and poured it back into the bin. "Let's go, Tough."

"Cheapskate," the young man muttered.

"Thief," Razoni muttered.

In the street outside, Razoni said, "Well, the blonde knows something about the lesbian's disappearance. That seems to be pretty sure. But I wonder. Did she make us last night as cops? Is that why she lied to us?"

"Maybe somebody told her we were at the headquarters," Jackson suggested.

"Yeah," said Razoni. "Somebody with a bell. Everybody's got a bell. Stand aside for Tough Jackson, who knows all about bells. Ring dem bells, won't you ring dem bells, dey is ringing out de glory of de land."

"Go soak your hand in granola."

"Not at eight dollars a pound," Razoni said.

Walking next door, it was decided that Jackson was too nice a person to be a policeman. It was also decided that Razoni would handle the case from here on in.

These decisions were made unilaterally by Razoni, who took Jackson's silence for agreement.

There were new signs in front of the Swami's headquarters.

WHEN WILL THE POLICE DO JUSTICE?

NATIONAL CONVENTION THIS SUNDAY.

JOIN THE TREK TO THE CITY OF LOVE.

"Brother Gildersleeve's not kidding," Razoni said. "He's going to stuff that lizard and prop him up and go ahead with that convention."

"Well, that's the way it goes," Jackson said blandly.

There had been nobody at the reception desk inside the Salamanda building, so Trace had wandered into the large meeting room—obviously the place where the Swami had died—and sat quietly in the back, looking around and wondering.

He was wondering what he was doing here, what he could do that Sarge hadn't already done. It wasn't likely that he could just walk up to Gloria Alcetta when he saw her and say, "What are you doing that your husband ought to know about, so that when you sue him for divorce he can cut you to ribbons?" No, not that. How about "My father thinks you were sleeping with the Swami. Were you? If so, was it any good?" No. He got up to walk around, hoping he'd think of something.

He was looking down a hallway leading from the main meeting room when he saw Gloria Alcetta. She had stepped from a small office, followed by a small man in a shiny-fabric suit. That must be Gildersleeve, he thought. Both persons looked angry, and as Trace watched, they stopped, turned toward each other, and seemed to be arguing.

Just then, two men, big men, one black and one white, entered the hallway and walked up to Gildersleeve and the woman. Trace was not close enough to hear what they were saying, but he didn't like the looks of the men. Mob guys if he had ever seen them.

Gildersleeve stopped talking to Sister Glorious when he saw Razoni and Jackson coming toward them.

"Are you here to tell me that you've solved the brutal murder of our leader?"

"We're not here to tell you anything," Razoni said. "We're here to ask. Where's the girl named Keri?"

"Keri?"

"This is like a record. We say 'Keri' and somebody else says 'Keri'? Yes, dammit, Keri. The tall blonde who served you and the lizard tea on Saturday night."

"I don't know," Gildersleeve said. "And I don't know why I should have to do your work for you. I'm very busy. And I just want you to know that if you incompetents don't solve this murder promptly, you're going to have a lot of trouble on your hands.''

"Trouble has a way of leaking," Jackson said softly. "Sometimes everybody's feet get wet."

Gildersleeve snorted and stomped away, leaving Gloria Alcetta alone there.

"I know Keri," she said softly.

Jackson pulled the sketch from his pocket. "This girl?" he said.

Sister Glorious looked at the sketch and nodded. "That's her," she said.

"Keri Ellison," Jackson said. "That's her name?"

For a moment, Sister Glorious looked confused. She shook her head. "No," she said. "That's not the name I know."

"What is her name?" Jackson asked.

"Keri is the name she uses here. I've never heard the Ellison name before. We spoke once. Her real name is Karen. Karen Marichal. She lives up on—''

"We know where she lives," Razoni said.

Sister Glorious stepped closer and put a hand on each of the detective's arms. "Is there any indication of who killed the Swami?"

"Nothing yet, ma'am," Jackson said, "but we'll find out."

"Somehow I'm sure you will," she said.

Mob guys, pure and simple, Trace thought. The white one looked hard and mean, his suit was too expensive, his features whittled too sharp for him to be up to any good. The black man was softer-looking, almost gentle, probably a kind of Lenny from *Of Mice and Men*, the kind who would kill anything or anyone the other one pointed him at.

Why was Gloria Alcetta talking to the mob? This might be a home run, he realized, a piece of information important enough for him to con Angelo Alcetta into keeping the firm working for him for weeks more. Maybe months.

The two big men were leaving and Trace decided Gloria

Alcetta could wait. He had to follow these two and see what they were up to.

Walking to their car, Razoni said, "I knew that family was nuts. I guess we'd better go talk to her, but I'm surprised at you, Tough. Not figuring out that the big blond chickie was the looney hiding in the dark in the monkeyhouse."

"I did figure it out," Jackson said.

"Oh, sure."

"Remember I told you about the bells. Karen had one on her dresser when we went to see her. I knew there was something to that. And she disguised her voice when we talked to her there so we wouldn't recognize her as the girl in the cereal shop."

"Right," said Razoni. "How come you're always so smart after I solve the case?"

They got into the car and drove off, but Jackson stopped at the corner and walked into a small store at the end of the block. He came out minutes later and got back behind the wheel.

"I knew I didn't like this case," said Jackson.

"Why not? Now that I have it all solved."

"I just talked to the florist there. He sold this joint the roses for their ceremonies."

"And?"

"And somebody came in every Sunday morning and bought a dozen yellow roses. All for the initiation ceremony."

"So what?"

"The last batch, the ones that killed the Swami, were picked up by two girls."

"Oh, no," said Razoni.

"Oh, yes. Karen Marichal and Abigail Longworth. He positively identified them from the pictures."

"Shit. Does that mean—" Razoni began.

"I think that's just what it does mean," Jackson said.

"Oh, Jesus. The captain's going to love you when you

tell him that Theodore Longworth's daughter killed the lizard,'' Razoni said.

"What makes you think *I'm* going to tell him?"

"Who else?" demanded Razoni.

"You. Remember? The Swami's murder is your case. All I'm supposed to be doing is finding Abigail Longworth."

"Oh, you rotten field hand, you," Razoni said.

23

They drove up to the Marichal house on the West Side of Central Park, but there was no answer to their leaning on the doorbell and pounding on the door.

"Screw it," Razoni said. "Let's go get a drink."

"I think we ought to go talk to the captain first," Jackson said.

The black man was driving. He drove like a maniac and Trace was hard-pressed even to stay near their blue Chevrolet. Obviously a maniac lawbreaker, Trace thought, one who couldn't even be bothered to obey the traffic laws.

He followed them downtown, proud of himself for staying so close to them, proud of himself for being so inconspicuous.

Jackson said, "That black shit-wagon's still following us."

"I know," Razoni said. "I saw it."

"I wonder who it is," Jackson said.

"I'll find out now."

Razoni bent over on the front seat so he couldn't be seen from the car that was tailing them and talked into the radio to headquarters, giving it the license number and make of the old car that had been on their tail since they left the Salamanda headquarters.

He wrote down the identification as the woman radio

operator read back the name: Patrick Tracy, and an address in Middle Village, Queens.

"Patrick Tracy," Razoni said. "Mean anything to you?"

"No," Tough said.

"Well, screw him, then, who cares? Probably just another faggot attracted by your nice heinie. This whole city sucks." Razoni crumped up the piece of paper with the name on it and tossed it into the doorless glove compartment whose door had somehow broken off once when Razoni had locked his cigarettes inside and couldn't find the key.

They parked alongside police headquarters.

"Oooops," Trace said. He saw their car pull into a spot between squad cars and emergency wagons and realized he had been trailing two city policemen all around New York. "Not too swift," he mumbled to himself. But how could he have known? They certainly looked like criminals.

That was the trouble with New York. The mayor looked like your uncle, the Statue of Liberty looked like Sylvester Stallone. Naturally the cops looked like criminals. What else? He was just glad they hadn't seen him.

When Trace got back to the Salamanda headquarters, Sister Glorious was working the room. Obviously, the news coverage of the Swami's death had attracted a lot of curious people and the large meeting room was half-filled. Faint, vaguely Indian music played, and Gloria Alcetta slowly worked her way through the room, like a politician at a political banquet, stopping to chat with everybody, smile, pat shoulders, proselytize.

She finally reached Trace, who was sitting in the far corner of the room. He saw her and clicked on his tape recorder.

"Am I a suspect?" she said. She had a warm voice to go with a pleasant smile and an absolutely first-rate face and a body that was still marvelous, even though mostly hidden by a long white gown.

"Suspect?" Trace said. "I don't understand."

"I saw you hanging around before," she said. "I thought you were a policeman."

"Not me," Trace protested mildly. "Not me. You're . . . you're Sister Glorious, right?"

"That's right. And you're not a policeman?"

"No."

"I've really made a mistake. I'm sorry," she said. "One of our young people saw you around and thought you were a policeman."

"No. I think it's terrible what happened to the Swami. Have the police been harassing you?"

"No. I guess it's just their job. So what brings you here today?"

"I was wondering. Will Swami Salamanda's work go on?" Trace asked.

"It certainly will. Are you interested in our work?"

"Praise be," Trace said. "I certainly am."

"You don't look like the praise-be type," Gloria said. "Where are you from?"

"Nevada. I guess I was attracted to this by the Swami's message. The freedom he preaches."

"It is his way . . . was his way," the woman said.

"I'd like to follow, but . . . Well, it's embarrassing."

"You have a family," Gloria Alcetta said.

"That's right. How did you know that?"

"Many of us have families. Many of us have left them to join the Love Is All movement. Some have brought their families with them. All are welcome, you know."

Trace laughed. "My wife doesn't believe," he said. "She thinks I'm a dimbulb going into my second childhood."

Gloria shook her head sadly. "There are many like that," she said.

"It hurts," Trace said. "It was probably easier for you to join the movement."

"No easier than for you. I too left a family, a husband, to follow the path."

"What did your husband say about that?" Trace asked.

"He didn't like it."

"But he didn't try to stop you?"

"He tried. Oh, how he tried. He came here and threatened me. He even threatened the Swami. I asked him to join me in my new life, but he refused, so I had to live it alone. When he saw I would not be swayed, he left me alone. Take heart."

"I don't think my wife would ever let me alone," Trace said. He thought of Cora, his ex-wife. "I doubt it. She might try to kill me."

"Think of it honestly. . . . What is your name?"

"Devlin."

"Think of it honestly, Mr. Devlin."

"No, Devlin's my first name."

"I'm sorry. If you think of it honestly, Devlin, you'd realize that violence is very unlikely to happen. A lot of people talk about violence, but that doesn't mean they will do it when the time comes. It is just a way of ventilating their feelings and they need it because they don't have the power of love to use."

"I sure hope you're right," Trace said. "Your husband didn't come back, you say."

"Not after I made things clear to him," Gloria said.

"No phone calls in the middle of the night or any of that? I'm afraid of things like that," Trace said.

"Minor annoyances. Tell me, Devlin, what do you do?"

"I run an insurance company."

"Successfully?"

"One of the biggest in Nevada."

"Would you be prepared to give it up to follow our path?"

"I'm ready," Trace said. "If I don't get shot."

More people drifted into the room. Gloria stood up and said, "You won't be. I hope we see you on Sunday. When we move to Pennsylvania, to the City of Love, there will be many jobs to be done. Someone who knows insurance would be very helpful there."

"I'm going to do it," Trace said.

"Good for you." She patted his upper arm and turned

on the full-voltage smile for a split second, then drifted toward the new people who had just come into the room.

Trace hung around a few minutes more, and then left to go back to the office.

Zero. Meeting Gloria had been zero. Except for looking at her. That had definitely been in the plus column.

"I don't need this," Razoni said as the two policemen left headquarters.

"It's called a reaming," Jackson said. "We've had one before."

"Yeah, well, maybe you. But, goddammit, I'm working a million jobs, working Sundays, who needs this shit, and then he tells us 'Be careful.' Be careful ain't the way you do things. Be careful is what you tell morons. You don't tell us be careful."

"I think you need a drink," Jackson said, slipping behind the wheel of the car.

"No. Let's go to OTB. A little off-track betting sounds good now. We'll go watch the horses. Dammit, Tough, you're drinking too much and you'd better watch it."

"What do I want to go to OTB for? I don't bet."

"And that's another thing that's wrong with you. You're the only black man in New York City who isn't in hock to OTB. Act right. Go for a couple of bucks, you cheap bastard."

"I'd rather have a drink," Jackson said.

Razoni was rooting around in the open glove compartment of the car for a cigarette. He looked at a crumpled piece of paper, then dug into the side pocket of his jacket.

"I'll be a son of a bitch," he said. "Somebody's after us."

"After us? What the hell for?" Jackson said. "Of all the policemen in the world, the way we're going, we pose the least threat of anybody who ever lived."

"Shut up. Remember that license plate we got, Patrick Tracy, right?"

"Right," Jackson said.

"Well, remember the other day when we were fixing

that restaurant shakedown except you screwed it up because you couldn't work the tape recorder."

"I remember the broad outlines of the incident," Jackson said. "Yes."

"Well, I pulled a card off that guy, some card for a private eye. And here it is, Patrick Tracy. I knew it. This was the suit I was wearing then. And that ding-dong who was trying to trail us today, that was Patrick Tracy. And this other guy, what was his name?"

"Some wop name," Jackson said.

"That makes it harder," Razoni said, " 'cause all Italians aren't named Jackson or Washington, unlike some people I know. Wait a minute. I'm thinking."

"Alcetta," Jackson said.

"Right. I told you. Alcetta. Angelo Alcetta. You remember him?" Razoni said.

"Right. The sleazy greaseball, as opposed to the one who looked like a tractor trailer."

"You got it," Razoni said. "Well, that guy Alcetta had this Patrick Tracy's card on him and now this so-called private eye Patrick Tracy is following us around. What does that sound like to you?"

"Love at first sight?" Jackson said.

"No, wiseass. It sounds like somebody's trying to set us up for something."

"What, pray tell?" Jackson said.

"I don't know hhhhhhwat," Razoni said, imitating Jackson's precise pronunciation. "As soon as I figure out hhhhwat, I will hhhhhlet you know."

"Stop it. You sound like Jack Palance."

"I think we ought to go see this Patrick Tracy," Razoni said.

"I think we ought to go drinking," Jackson said.

"After we see Patrick Tracy. On to West Twenty-sixth Street," Razoni said.

Trace, expecting Chico, answered the telephone: "Tracy, Tracy and Friend Investigations, Our Eyes Never Close." He turned down the sound on the television.

"Trace. Is that you?" The voice sounded anxious, a little frantic

"Why, I do believe it is Walter Marks, noted executive with Garrison Fidelity Insurance Company calling to chat. How are you, Walter?"

"Did you send that lunatic up here?" The voice was changing to a whiny snarl.

"Please be more specific. Which lunatic?"

"That Mangini woman," Marks said.

"Chico? Yes, I sent her. Well, at least I knew she was coming. What's the matter? What did she do?"

"She threatened me."

"That's ridiculous. She's as small as you are. Almost," Trace said. "Actually, she's in better condition, but that's because she dances. Maybe you should dance."

"Dammit, I don't want to dance and you stop waltzing me around."

"Good, good, very good. Waltzing you around. Very good. Wurry good. That's how Frankenstein would say it if he could talk. Wurry, wurry good."

"Will you shut up?" Marks shouted. "She threatened me, I tell you. Guns and all. I don't want that woman around here."

"Love me, love my associate." Trace said. "You mean she threatened you with a gun? Like to shoot you?"

"That's what she was getting at. She was telling me that she'd shot other people before. With her gat."

"With her gat? Come on, Groucho, you're making this up, right?"

"No, I'm not. I know a threat when I get one and that woman was threatening me with her gat if I didn't give you all a lot of work."

"What'd you do?"

"What could I do?" Trace could almost hear Walter Marks shrug in absolution of his conduct. "The Dundee case was taken but I gave her something else. Trace, handle it, but I do not want that woman back here. She frightens me. She frightened me before, but now that she's carrying a .357 Magnum, she frightens me worse. I think that woman has a psychological problem."

"I think you're right, Groucho," Trace said. "When she comes in, I'm going to finish this once and for all."

"What are you going to do?" Marks asked.

"I'm going to let her have it, right between the eyes," Trace said.

"What?"

"I'm going to plug her, right between the eyes. I'm fed up with this."

"Trace, you're as crazy as she is."

"Well, only one of us is walking back out through that door, pardner. And I reckon it's going to be me. Thanks for calling, old buddy."

"Don't do anything stupid," Marks said.

Trace hung up on him and went back to working on what Sarge laughingly called his books.

Razoni and Jackson stopped at the bottom of the long flight of stairs leading to the second-floor offices. Razoni took his gun from the holster behind his belt and checked it.

"You're not going to need that," Jackson said.

"Hey, baby, you never know. First this guy's name winds up in the wallet of some Mafia ginzo that we leaned on."

"*You* leaned on," Jackson said.

"And now this guy is following us around town. It's not too far out to think that he works for Angelo there and Angelo said, 'Go teach these guys a lesson for pushing my face in the soup, especially the black one with the snotty kid.' Hah? Makes sense, doesn't it? Hah?"

"Don't go shooting anybody," Jackson said wearily.

The two men started up the stairs.

Before he left his ex-wife and children, before he packed it all in and moved to Las Vegas to be a gambler, Trace had been an accountant. Eventually, in Las Vegas, he had met Chico and Robert Swenson, head of the insurance company, and that had gotten him where he was today, wherever that might be. He had not looked at a ledger book in years, but it hadn't occurred to him that they might have changed so drastically. Income on the left, outgo on the right, that seemed pretty basic. Sarge seemed to have a different system: income nowhere, outgo nowhere, and just random lists of numbers and amounts written down.

He wrestled his way through it, trying to make some sense of the numbers, but the more he wrestled, the more sure he was that this agency was taking in very little, and if growth was projected on a bar chart, it would be the twenty-second century before the company made enough money to pay him and Chico a salary.

Maybe if he got a lot of work for the firm out of Walter Marks. That might help. And they'd have to start getting the firm some publicity. That might help. Advertise. Solve a big case.

He had it, a breakthrough. He could load up a gun for Chico and have her walk down Eighth Avenue shooting everybody over five feet tall. That might get them ink.

Something.

Anything.

24

Trace expected Chico, so he didn't look up when the office door opened. He was still trying to make some sense out of his father's ledger books so he just said, "I was told to shoot you."

"See? See? I told you," a male voice shouted.

Trace looked up. It was the two men he had seen talking to Gloria Alcetta at the Swami's headquarters, the two who had gone later to police headquarters.

The Italian-looking one in the shiny suit was jumping up and down, obviously gloating about something. He pulled a gun from under his jacket and leveled it at Trace.

The bigger one, the black one, said, "Easy, Ed."

"Easy, my ass," the one named Ed said. "You heard the sucker. He was told to shoot us."

"Yeah," the black man said, looking at Trace. "Yeah. What was that all about?"

"I didn't know you were there," Trace said. He made sure he kept his hands on the desk in full view of these two whackos. "I thought it was my partner. It was a joke between me and her. Just a joke."

"Boy, I've heard some horseshit stories in my life," the one called Ed said, "but that takes the prize."

"A poor thing, perhaps, but 'tis true, 'tis true," Trace said.

"What are you, an Englishman?" the one named Ed said.

"He's being literary," the black one said. "You're Tracy?"

"That's right. Who are you? If you don't mind my asking." He was staring at Razoni's gun pointed at him.

"I'm Detective Jackson. This is Detective Razoni. New York City police."

"Now that we know each other so well, do you think you can get him to stop aiming that gun at me?" Trace said.

"Not on your freaking life, buster," Razoni said. "Not until I find out what you meant by that I-was-told-to-shoot-you crack."

Trace noticed that the two policeman had separated. The white one, Razoni, was still standing just inside the door, but off to the side so he couldn't be seen through the glass of the office window. The black cop, Jackson, had moved to a point, ten feet away, near the couch. He didn't have a gun in his hand, but Trace had no doubt one could appear very suddenly. Standing apart this way, there was no way they could be surprised now, no way that Trace—if he had a mind to—could take them both out in one fusillade. They might be dopey, but they knew something about being cops.

"I told you, it was a joke," Trace said. "I thought you guys were my partner coming in."

"Do we look like your partner ?" Razoni said.

"You'd be amazed at how much you don't look like my partner," Trace said.

"You always threaten to shoot him?" Razoni said.

"It's a her, a her, and I hardly ever threaten to shoot her," Trace said. "Let me explain."

"That's what we've been waiting for, ace," Razoni said.

"I'll make it simple," Trace said.

"What do you mean by that?" Razoni snapped.

"What do you mean what do I mean?"

"You don't have to keep nothing simple. We can understand anything you've got to say. You think cops are dumb or something? You look like a guy who thinks cops are dumb."

Trace looked at the black cop for sympathy. Jackson said, "Tell us the story, mister. Please."

"I was talking to one of our clients," Trace said. "My partner was just there. This client doesn't like my partner and he told me on the phone that I ought to shoot her. That was all. It was a joke."

"You have a pretty funny way of joking, Tracy," Razoni said.

"Listen. Will you put that gun away? You make me nervous."

"You make me nervous," Razoni said. "This client that wants you to shoot people, that couldn't be Angelo Alcetta, could it?"

"Angelo Alcetta?" Trace said. He shook his head. "Not him."

"But you know him, right?" Razoni was barely able to disguise his triumph.

"Yeah. Our firm is doing some work for him."

"I bet you are," Razoni said sarcastically.

"What does that mean?" Trace asked. He noticed that the gun had never left Razoni's hand, nor had it deviated one millimeter from its position. If there was such a thing as relaxing one's guard, this Razoni had never heard of it. When he drew that revolver, it was aimed at the middle of Trace's forehead. It was still aimed at the middle of Trace's forehead. If Razoni had any kind of a seizure, Trace was deadmeat. "Can't you put that gun away?" he said. "Until I'm sure you don't have Parkinson's disease?"

"Not until I'm sure we're not going to need it," Razoni said. "You're working for Alcetta. He's a nickel-and-dime mob guy. Why does that make you have to follow us?"

Trace noted that the black man, Jackson, had sat down on the couch. Maybe that was a good sign. Maybe when he sat down, that meant that Razoni wasn't going to shoot anybody. He wished he'd put that gun away, though.

"Because I didn't know who you were and I was wondering why you were talking to Mrs. Alcetta," Trace said.

"G'wan," Razoni sneered. "We never talked to no Mrs. Alcetta."

"Sure you did. Down at the Swami's joint. That woman."

"Sister Glorious?"

"That's her," Trace said.

"She said her name was Gloria Charterman," Jackson said.

"I guess that's her maiden name. Then she married Alcetta."

"How do you know all this?" Razoni asked.

"Alcetta hired my father to check up on his wife for a divorce case," Trace said.

"Your father?" Jackson said.

"Patrick Tracy. It's his company. He's a retired city cop."

"Then who the Christ are you?" Razoni said. The barrel of the revolver lowered a millimeter.

"I'm Devlin Tracy, the son."

"You're a p.i. too?"

"No," Trace said. "I live in Las Vegas. I'm just visiting."

"And this partner of yours?"

"She's out somewhere. Damned if I know what she's doing," Trace said.

"So that was Mrs. Alcetta?" Razoni said. The gun lowered more.

"That's right."

"And you saw us talking to her so you decided to follow us?" Razoni said. Trace nodded and Razoni snapped, "Why? You think you got a right to follow anybody who talks to anybody else?"

Trace shook his head. "My father was trying to get some dirt on Mrs. Alcetta. I saw her talking to you guys. I just wanted to know who you were."

"Aaaaah," Razoni said. The gun dropped.

Jackson chuckled. "Put the gun away, Ed. What he means is that he saw us talking to her and he thought we were criminals."

"Well, maybe you look like a criminal," Razoni said to his partner. "A lot of black criminals in this city," he said to Trace. "You have to watch yourself." He put the gun back behind his belt.

"Don't pay any attention to him," Jackson told Trace good-humoredly. "You pay attention to him, he'll have you nuts in no time at all."

"You're working on the Swami murder case?" Trace asked.

"Looking into it," Jackson said.

"Yeah. That and everything else. We're looking for fagolas in our spare time," Razoni said.

"Why?" Jackson asked Trace. "You know anything about the Swami murder?"

"No," Trace said. "I was just wondering what a nice girl who marries an Italian goon from Brooklyn winds up doing in an Indian free-love cult."

"Ask her," Razoni said. "We're not 'Dear Abby.' " He looked across the room at Jackson. "We ought to do something with this guy."

"I don't know," Jackson said.

"Like what?" Trace asked.

"Like put you away for a while to keep you out of trouble," Razoni said.

"You ought to have a reason at least to put me away," Trace said mildly.

Then came Chico's voice. She stood in the doorway, wearing a long tan trenchcoat despite the July heat. Her right hand waggled menacingly in her pocket.

"Before you try to put him away, you're gonna have to deal with me, asshole," she said.

Razoni wheeled around at the voice. Jackson looked mildly interested. Razoni's hand went under his jacket.

Chico waved her finger inside her trenchcoat.

"All right, you. Over there." She nodded for Razoni to get to the sofa. He didn't move. "Go ahead, Trace," she said. "Call the cops. Tell them to hurry because my gat's got an itchy trigger finger."

Trace rolled his eyes.

"You got a gat?" Razoni said.

"That's right, brown eyes," she said. "Now get over there and sit down next to the other one. Trace, why aren't you calling the cops?"

"These *are* the cops. Believe it or not."

"Oh, for crying out loud."

Razoni had a gun on her.

Trace said, "Chico, you shouldn't threaten to shoot

someone with your gat when that someone is already holding his own gat.''

"That's right," Razoni snarled. "Hands out of your pockets, lady. Careful. Bring that gun out between two fingers.''

Trace shook his head. He looked at Jackson, who was shaking his head. As if by prearrangement, they both got up and walked to the window to look out at West Twenty-sixth Street.

"This happen all the time with you?" Trace asked.

"All the time," Jackson said morosely. "How about you?''

"Like clockwork. If that woman ever really gets a gun, we're all in trouble.''

They paused for a moment. Razoni and Chico were yelling at each other.

"Keep your hands out of my pockets, you moron, or I'll have you up on sex charges.''

"Hey, lady. You don't have no gat, don't talk about having a gat.''

"I want a lawyer before I talk to you.''

"You can have the whole Simple Liberties Union if you want," Razoni shouted, "but you're going to empty out your pockets.''

"Where's your father?" Jackson asked Trace. "He runs the agency, right?'' He was still looking down on West Twenty-sixth Street.

"Right. He's on vacation with my mother. All he had was this divorce case, keep an eye on Gloria Alcetta for Angelo, and so he asked me to handle it for him while he was gone. He said no heavy lifting.''

"You a detective in Vegas?" Jackson asked.

"No. I kind of check out claims for an insurance company. I just get paid to be nosy.''

"And the girl?"

"She's a blackjack dealer by trade," Trace said. "I think she wants to be a detective.''

"You're a moron," Chico was shouting behind them.

"I saw enough of you people in Vietnam," Razoni said.

"You always had hand grenades strapped to your body. I'm searching you."

"You ought to go back to Vietnam and search for your brain," Chico shouted. "M.I.A., M.I.A."

"They seem to be hitting it off pretty well," Trace said to Jackson.

"Yeah, I think so," Jackson said. "He hasn't punched her yet."

"He punches women as a rule?" Trace said.

"Ed would punch the fender off a truck if it made him mad. But don't worry. This is all for show. He likes to yell a lot."

"Hey, I'm sorry about tailing you two. I was just trying to check out everything about Gloria Alcetta."

"Just what I would have done," Jackson said. "Is there a good restaurant around here?"

"Downstairs," Trace said. "Bogie's. Good food, big drinks, and they leave you alone. You men aren't really assigned to the Salamanda murder?"

"No," Jackson said. "We work out of the commissioner's office. Trouble-shooters, sort of. We were down at Salamanda's on something else."

Behind them, Chico's voice raised to a scream. "I'll tell you for the last time, cement-head. I don't have a gat."

"Then, goddammit, you're the only person in New York who doesn't. Empty them pockets."

"No."

Razoni hollered, "Jackson, get over here. Hold her down."

Jackson moved even farther away from Razoni and said to Trace, "Any ideas who might have killed Salamanda?"

"Sorry, no. I just got into town yesterday."

"Well, if you find out anything or come up with any ideas, you let us know." He reached into his pocket. "Here. Take my card. Maybe it'll come in handy."

"Thanks," Trace said, pocketing the card. "You think we ought to break this up?" He nodded over his shoulder toward where Razoni and Chico were shouting at each other, face to face.

"You'll never get a gat in this town," Razoni was

yelling. "Not as long as I'm working here. You're a subversive."

"You'll probably be kicked off the force before I apply for my license. You're a moron."

"Before one of them gets hurt," Jackson said. "I guess so."

The two men walked back from the window. Jackson said, "Detective Razoni."

Trace said, "Miss Mangini."

The two stopped yelling.

Jackson said, "We really ought to be off."

Razoni looked at Trace and said, "What did you call her?"

"Miss Mangini," Trace said. "Her name."

"I thought she was some kind of Oriental," Razoni said.

"She is. But she's half a Sicilian too."

"Don't talk around me like I'm not here," Chico said.

"Ignore her," Trace said.

"And she's your partner?" Razoni asked Trace, who nodded. Razoni nodded too. "Mister, you've got some weird kind of partner," he said.

"Yeah?" Chico yelled. "Well, let me tell you—"

Jackson said, "Hush now, lady. Before you say anything you regret."

Razoni said to Chico, "You don't look Italian."

She said, "At times like this, you dumb greaser, I'm glad I don't."

Razoni snorted under his breath like a puzzled bull. "Tracy," he said.

"Yes?"

"You vouch that she's unarmed?"

"Yes," Trace said.

"The blood of innocent people will be on your head," Razoni warned.

"She's unarmed," Trace said.

"Let's get out of here," Jackson said.

Razoni said, "I'm still not convinced about you, Tracy. Stay off our tail."

Jackson said to Razoni, "I already told him all that."

Razoni said, "Well, it's about time, Tough. Let's get out of here."

Chico told him, "Go stand at the curb. They pick up garbage tonight."

"Yeah?" Razoni said from the doorway. "You're on my list, lady." He looked at Trace. "I really pity you," he said. "Come on, Tough," he said, and left.

They could hear his footsteps thunking down the stairs.

Chico smiled at Jackson. "Thanks," she said. "Why do they call you Tough?"

"Just a nickname."

"Are you really tough?"

"Naaah," he said with a soft smile. "It's from an old poem my mother used to say."

" 'Tough Alley'?"

Jackson smiled again. "You're Sicilian and Japanese. Don't tell me you're black too?"

"I just know the poetry," Chico said, shaking her head.

Jackson nodded. "Well, so long, miss. So long, Tracy. Remember. Call me if anything comes up."

"I will," Trace said.

The door closed behind Jackson. Trace sat down at the desk and smiled at Chico.

"So did you have a nice day?" he asked.

25

My name is Tough;
I live in Tough Alley.
The farther down you go,
The tougher they get.
I live in the last house.

Chico finished reciting and said, "An old street poem. Somehow I don't think that Detective Jackson is anybody to mess with."

"Me neither," Trace said. "That's why I'm glad you didn't really pull your gat and blow his partner away."

"That's a fine how-do-you-do," Chico said. "I come back to the office here and I see two big lugs terrorizing the man I tolerate; so at risk of life and limb, I jump into the fray, throwing my own personal safety to the winds to try to save him, and what do I get? Ridicule."

"Look at the bright side," Trace said. "On the job only one day and already you've threatened to shoot a New York cop. Some people probably don't have that experience for weeks . . . months even."

She giggled. "It probably would have gone down all right if I hadn't run into that Razoni character. He must be the only guy in New York who isn't afraid of a woman with a gat."

"Stop saying gat," Trace said. "And take off that trenchcoat. Where'd you get that trenchcoat anyway? What are you wearing it for? It's the middle of the summer, for crying out loud."

"I was going to buy a tape recorder like you use," Chico said. "You know, to tape all my suspects when I talk to them. But when I went into the store, I saw this darling coat and I knew I had to have it. It's got deep pockets for carrying equipment."

"God help me," Trace said. "We've been in this business one day and already my partner's going cuckoo and I run into the nuttiest cop in all of New York. I can't wait to see what tomorrow's going to be like."

Chico was hanging up her coat. "Don't knock it," she said. "I brought back our first case."

"I heard all about it," Trace said.

"Oh?"

"Yes. Groucho called and said you threatened him with your gat. Have you done anything today besides terrorize the denizens of New York and wave your gat at everybody?"

"Hey, whatever works," Chico said airily. "We got the case, didn't we?"

"Good. You handle it," Trace said.

"I intend to. You're the expert at this, though, phony insurance claims and all. Do you have any advice for me?"

"I mean, you're serious now?" Trace said.

"Deadly serious. I want advice from the old master."

"All right. Don't turn in your expense sheet until I go over it first. Groucho likes to cut your expenses in half, so what you have to do is triple them before you turn them in. This is the only way to show a profit."

"Actually I was hoping for something a little more technical in the way of advice," Chico said. "Like how do I trail people, worm my way into their confidence, stuff like that?"

Trace leaned back, looked at the ceiling, and tried to remember how he did things. "If you're going to trail anybody, it's best not to do it naked," Trace said. "People have a way of noticing you if you're naked. And don't dress like Magnum P.I. I know a private eye who dressed like Magnum P.I. once and got arrested for looking suspicious. Let's see. What else? You worm your way into people's confidence the way you wormed your way into mine. Be sneaky and devious. Let them talk. Don't be afraid of dead air.''

"What do you mean, dead air?''

"Well, sometimes," Trace said, "you ask a question and the guy gives you an answer, see, and then he stops. Now, most people ask another question right away, but that's wrong. What you do is just sit there and wait. People get nervous if they're no talking or listening, so if they give you an answer but you just wait, they start adding to their answer. That's where you get them 'cause most people only figure out their lie one sentence in advance. You get them talking four or five sentences and then they're out of their script, and that's when you got them. And smile a lot. Everybody talks to a woman who smiles a lot.''

"That's it?'' Chico said.

"You asked me for what I know. That's what I know.''

"Three years working on insurance claims and that's all you know?'' Chico said.

Trace hadn't noticed before how short her skirt was. Maybe, God willing, mini-skirts were coming back. She had beautiful legs.

"It's all you need to know," Trace said. "Let Sherlock Holmes figure out things by analyzing pipe ashes and nonsense like that. None of that means anything to us. All we ever have to work with is what people tell us, and if you talk to enough people long enough and often enough, you're going to start hearing conflicting stories. And that's when you got them, Babe. Time out. Something's on the TV.''

Trace turned up the sound on the small black-and-white set perched on the corner of his desk, and Chico came around to stand behind him and watch.

The well-known face of Theodore Longworth was on the screen. He was delivering an editorial about Swami Salamanda's death.

". . . certainly the killer or killers of Swami Salamanda should be caught. But what of the other five persons murdered in New York City over the weekend? Should not their murders be solved too? It is simply not right for the police department to throw massive resources into the murder investigation of Swami Salamanda—ignoring these other five killings—simply because Salamanda had the habit of making the headlines. John Donne said that 'Each man's death diminishes us all,' and that is true. Unfortunately, our police department seems to think that some deaths are more equal than others. This is wrong. There were six killings this weekend and New York City would be served better by having three of them solved than by having Salamanda's murder solved and the rest of them go unsolved. That's our opinion here at UBC. Ted Longworth reporting.''

Trace turned the sound back down softly but left the picture on.

"More bullshit," he said. "Who cares?"

Chico went and sat on one of the folding chairs alongside the desk. She crossed her legs. Yes, they were wonderful legs.

"Anyway," she said, "want to hear about my case?"

"If I can look up your skirt," he said.

"Look away," she said. Her purse was on the floor and from it she took a pile of papers and put them on her lap.

"Another thing," Trace said. "Don't carry around too many papers. It confuses the mind and it doesn't leave room in your bag for your gat. I don't know how you're going to get a Browning automatic rifle in there the way it is."

"Very funny," Chico said. "Just shut up and listen. This is in Teaneck. That's in New Jersey. This woman, let's see, Debbie Doblemeyer. Her husband took out a life-insurance policy on her three weeks ago."

"How much?" Trace asked.

"Fifty thousand. And one week ago, her car went off the road and she got killed. Marks wants us—our firm, that's got a good ring to it, doesn't it?—to look into it."

"Look away," Trace said. "What does the husband do for a living?"

"He's a druggist. Runs a store in a mall somewhere."

"Look away, but it was an accident."

"How do you know that? You don't know anything about it."

"He's a druggist, he makes a lot of money. If he were going to kill his wife for dough, it'd be a lot of dough. Fifty thousand he can probably borrow against the value of aspirins in his store."

"Is this the way you solve all your problems?" Chico asked. "By making snap judgments?"

"Not snap judgments," Trace said. "Rough cuts. Sarge taught me that. I say it's an accident."

"Well, I say it's murder, and I say the hell with it," Chico said.

"Have it your own way," Trace said with a shrug. "How you going to do it?"

"I'm going to do what you do. I'm going to go talk to people, friends, cops, things like that."

"The funeral home where she was buried. They'll probably have a list of people who visited at the wake. Double-check that against the phone book and you'll find some people in the neighborhood who'll talk. Skip the next-door neighbors. They never talk. But the people across the street will."

"Why's that?" Chico asked.

"Everybody hates the people who live across the street," Trace said. "Cops are tough, though. Usually you can't get to see their reports, but if and when you do, they don't tell you anything. But if you find the cops who handled the case, they'll usually be helpful. The ones who were at the accident, I mean. But you'll need identification because they're always afraid of talking to the wrong people and getting their ass in a sling."

"I've got identification. I had business cards printed today when I was in seeing Marks."

Chico fished back into her purse and brought out a small box, the size of two cigarette packs stacked side by side. She took a card from the box and handed it to Trace.

MANGINI AND TRACY
Private Investigations
249 West 26th Street, N.Y.C.

Michiko Mangini, Call: 555-0288
Agent
Ask us. We'll find out.

There was a silhouette of a smoking gun in the corner of the card.

"Pretty neat, huh?" Chico said.

"Love the billing," Trace said.

"Strict alphabetical order," Chico said. "M comes before T."

"Which T is that, by the way? Is that T for Sarge or T for me?"

"That's T for both of you," Chico said. "I didn't see any need to clutter up the card with a lot of excess verbiage."

"Like the names of the other partners, the senior partners," Trace said sourly.

"Cheez-o-man. Is this the way you're going to be from now on, picky and worrying about your billing?"

"I love the smoking gun, though," Trace said. "It lets people know exactly what you're up to."

"It's a kind of advertising. When you and I get our licenses to carry heat—"

"Carry heat?"

"Right. When we get our licenses to be packing, everybody in this firm'll be armed. Prospective clients ought to know that. That we fear nothing."

"Speak for yourself. I fear everything," Trace said. "And speaking of terror, my ex-wife called me today. I told you this was going to happen—that my mother would spill the beans, and Bruno would be calling here—and first day on the job and already it's happened."

"What'd she want?"

"Me to come to dinner."

"Go ahead and go," Chico said. "You should see your kids."

"Oh, shut up," Trace said, and turned the sound on the television up to full volume.

An hour later, just as Trace was beginning to wonder where Angelo Alcetta was, the telephone rang.

"This is Charlie Ribs, I work for Sonny Alcetta."

"Yes."

"Sonny says he'll be at your office in the morning."

"Fine."

"You be there," Charlie Ribs said.

Trace hung up and said, "That's enough threats for one day. Let's go home."

26

Trace's Log: Monday evening, first entry in the illustrious new career of Devlin Tracy, boy detective.

How do I let myself get conned into things like this? Here I am, in this stupid detective agency one day, and I run afoul of the New York cops already in the person of the only cop in the world dumber than I am. Something Razoni. Ed Razoni. That's it.

And Chico is turning out to be a homicidal maniac. Maybe I'll stay here and work with Sarge for a while at the agency, but I'll tell you, world, when it looks like her gun permit is going to be approved, I'm going to have to give some serious consideration to moving out and setting up residence in some other town under an assumed name.

Chico's finally asleep, dreaming, no doubt, of her first real detective job tomorrow. Christ, how you can look forward to working for Groucho and the insurance company is beyond me. But nothing bothers her. She cooked us a wonderful dinner tonight and then ate it all.

And that's another thing that's wrong. It wasn't until we got into the house here tonight that I realized I hadn't had a drink all day. I made up for that right away and I'm going to make sure it doesn't happen tomorrow. I've got my reputation to take care of, you know.

So now we come to the business at hand. Angelo Alcetta. Tomorrow I'll try to con him into giving the firm more work. For the life of me, I can't figure out what Alcetta wants to know about his wife or why he wants to know it, but my basic rough-hewn integrity demands that tomorrow

I give it a shot. As long as he pays. Maybe I'll try to find out something dirty about her. Just to keep the company's good name.

And who knows? I wouldn't mind seeing Sister Glorious again anyway, because that is one of the world's beautiful women. Close to Chico even.

Nice like Chico too. She told me something today. What? Oh, yeah. That Angelo had threatened her and the Swami too. I hope he doesn't threaten me when we meet tomorrow. I've been threatened enough already.

Chico says that I don't take things seriously and I don't think about things enough. Hah. It is to laugh, that's what it is. For instance, what just came to me was this wonderful idea for ending poverty in India. You see what we do, we ordain all the Indians. Make them ministers. And then send them, in shifts, to the United States. There is no Indian so dopey or so degenerate that some American somewhere will not throw money at him. This is a serious plan to solve a serious problem. Someday the world will recognize my genius.

I almost had to use bodily force to stop Chico from redecorating Sarge's house tonight and throwing out all the knick-knacks. She has never forgiven my mother for coming to our apartment, taking down genuine oil paintings, and hanging up in their place plaster clown masks. But the house remains secure. At least until tomorrow. At least until Chico gets a gun.

I'm going to be a lousy detective. I know it. I'm a lousy insurance investigator and in this job I feel about as useful as a puppy attacking its own paw. Dammit, I bet Sarge is having a grand old time out on the high seas.

What a day. And Hulk called and expects me to have dinner with her and What's-his-name and the girl on Saturday. Fatto chance-o.

Good night, world. I think I'm going up and get even for the attack on Pearl Harbor. With my luck, I'll lose this one too.

27

Before they rang the doorbell at the Marichal town house the next morning, Ed Razoni wanted to make his position perfectly clear.

"Dammit, Tough, this is the absolute wrong thing to do."

"A man's got to do what a man's got to do," Jackson said.

"This ain't 'do,' " Razoni said. "This is doo-doo. This is just trouble. Look, all we got to do is go through the motions, give all our stuff to those two stupid cops at the precinct, and the hell with it. We take none of the heat."

"It's our case," Jackson said stubbornly. "And our break."

"And our ass that's going to be in the garbage can," Razoni said. "Who's going to tell Longworth that his kid killed the lizard? Not me. And don't expect me to tell the captain either. Not me. Why? Last night you promised you'd sleep on it."

"I *did* sleep on it. I decided we go ahead and pick up the girl."

"That's what I hate about you, Jackson. You sleep on things and you still don't change your mind. Go ahead. Ring the goddamn bell. But this is on your head. I want you to remember that."

"If I forget, I'm sure you'll remind me," Jackson said.

He rang the doorbell a long time before the door was opened by the butler.

"Yes?" he said, having obviously obliterated any memory of having seen them before.

190

"Move aside, Lurch," Razoni snarled. "We've come to see the girl."

"Wait right here, please."

"We'll wait inside," Razoni said, and pushed his way through the door and into the foyer. Jackson followed him.

"Where is she?" Razoni asked.

"Miss Karen is, I believe, with her family. I shall see."

"Don't bother to announce us," Razoni said. "We can find our own way." To Jackson, he said, "Just follow the trail of peanut shells."

"And the smell of wine."

"And the cries of alley-oop," Razoni said.

"As you wish," the butler said.

They pulled open the double French doors. The scene was as they remembered it.

Ferenc Marichal floated back and forth above the room on a trapeze bar slung through the rings. Sitting on his shoulder as he swung was the spider monkey, wearing a red pillbox hat. Still standing in front of her canvas was Charmaine Marichal, her tight blond curls twisted under a railroad cap she wore. Mother Marichal was drinking at the table in the corner.

There was a difference.

A tall blond girl now sat on the paint-splattered sofa near her mother. Her legs were curled under her in the lotus position, her hands were folded in her lap; her eyes were closed.

"Karen," Jackson called.

"Hey, look who's here," called Marichal from overhead. "Our friends from yesterday. Hi there, fellows." He waved a hand at them insistently, trying to get them to wave back.

Razoni finally waved in a gesture that managed to combine hello, good-bye, and an anatomical impossibility even for a man in good shape.

"Karen," Jackson repeated.

The tall blonde opened her eyes. She seemed to take a moment to focus on the two detectives, and then she looked startled. After a moment, she looked resigned.

She rose slowly. "Yes?" she said. The voice was still smooth and liquid.

"We'd like to talk to you," Jackson said.

"I have nothing to say to you."

"Here or downtown?" Razoni said.

"Nothing to say, here *or* downtown," the girl said.

For all the attention they were attracting the two detectives might have been alone in the room with the girl. Mrs. Marichal kept painting. Mother Marichal kept drinking. Mr. Marichal and Monkey Marichal kept swinging merrily along.

"Let's go, dear," Jackson said.

Karen Marichal walked toward them, head down, resignedly.

Overhead, her father called out, "Hey? You all leaving so soon?"

Jackson nodded.

"Where you going?"

"We're arresting your daughter," Razoni growled.

"Oh, good. Things were getting so dull."

Sonny Alcetta stomped into the office looking annoyed. He was wearing a navy-blue blazer that he kept slapping at as if it were home for an ant colony. He wore gray slacks and another white tie, and Trace thought that Detective Razoni might be nuts, but his description of Alcetta as a nickel-and-dime mob guy seemed to be right on the nickel.

Alcetta sized up Chico and gave her a big smile before turning to Trace.

"Who are you?" he asked.

"Mr. Alcetta, I presume," Trace said.

He nodded. "You?"

"I'm Devlin Tracy. This is my associate, Miss Mangini." Trace reached under his jacket and turned on his tape recorder.

"Mangini, huh? That's funny. You don't look Italian."

"Really?" Chico said. "No one ever noticed before."

"Is there something wrong, Mr. Alcetta?" Trace asked. "Why are you slapping at your jacket?"

"Aaaah, I got wrinkled. Some guy bumps into me downstairs here and knocks me into a wall and I get all wrinkled and I bet I got all that dust from the hall all over me. Do I, lady?'' He spun around so Chico could inspect his jacket.

"You look beautiful, Mr. Alcetta," she said. "Absolutely beautiful."

"Hey. All right," he said. He looked at Trace and said, "Where's the other guy?"

"That's Patrick Tracy, the founding member of the firm. He was called to Washington on hush-hush business. We're from the West Coast office. He called us in for this job."

"You said your report's done?" Alcetta said.

"We've completed our three days of preliminary investigation," Trace said.

"Yeah?"

"We have made over twenty-five contacts with persons who know or are associated with your wife, beginning the very day that you contacted Mr. Patrick Tracy. Since that time, your wife has spent every day down at the religious temple—"

"Temple, huh? That's a big laugh."

"Right," Trace said agreeably. "Down at the House of Love or the food store next door. She spends every night at her own apartment. She has very few visitors, and when she does, they are always women. No men."

"Yeah, yeah, yeah. What I want to know is did she kill this Swami?" Alcetta asked.

"Do you think she did?"

"Hey. She walked out on me, didn't she? Who knows what she's likely to do?" Alcetta asked. He didn't wait for an answer but walked to the window and looked down into West Twenty-sixth Street.

"Miss Mangini and I conferred with the police yesterday about your wife's involvement in the case. Our firm has very close ties to the New York City police department. At this point in time, they do not regard your wife as a prime suspect in the killing of Swami Salamanda."

"Too bad," Alcetta said.

"You want her to fry?"

"Naaaah. Who cares?"

"Then what's too bad?" Trace asked.

"Too bad they didn't both get poisoned. That would have done some good."

"At this point in time, you seem to bear a lot of animosity toward your wife," Trace said.

"Animosity? Naaah. I just would like to hit her in the head. That Swami, too, if somebody didn't beat me to it." He flapped his arms out at the sides, palms up. "I've been doing some checking too about this church thing she got herself involved in. It'd be bad enough if she just shaved her head and went around begging in the street, selling bowls of rice or whatever the fuck they do. But this thing is like a big sex party, this Salamanda crap. Everybody's screwing all over the place. That's what he's into. What do they call it?"

"Free love?" Chico said.

"Right. Free love. A whole lot of humping. I don't want anybody associated with me to be involved in this. It'll ruin my reputation."

"I can certainly understand how that is a treasure to be guarded," Trace said. "It is our firm's opinion that your wife was Swami Salamanda's mistress."

"You mean she was screwing that sand nigger?" Alcetta said.

"At this point in time, that is our best judgment," Trace said. "It's all in our report."

"Oh, that bitch. I want you guys to get her. Get her good."

"You understand, Mr. Alcetta, that next weekend your wife is probably moving to Pennsylvania."

"What's in Pennsylvania?" Alcetta said.

"It's in our far-flung report," Trace said. "Next week, the Salamanda organization is opening a new headquarters in Pennsylvania called the City of Love. As an official in the organization, your wife will undoubtedly go there. At any rate, through a personal interview with her, I can tell you that those are her plans at this point in time."

"Next weekend, huh?"

"That's correct," Trace said.

"Well. You got five more days, maybe. You keep

checking on her. Get something on her for me. Something I can hang her with."

"For the divorce action?" Trace said.

Alcetta looked blank. Then he said, "Yeah. Yeah. For the divorce. Sure. You guys still want to be paid in advance?"

"It's five hundred dollars," Trace said. "Plus tax."

"Why don't you send me a bill?" Alcetta said.

Trace was about to protest, but Chico said, "Yes, Mr. Tracy, do that. Nobody carries around five hundred dollars in cash."

"Aaaah, the hell with it," Alcetta said. "I'll pay now." He pulled a bankroll from his pocket and peeled off bills. "Five hundred, you say?" He looked out of the corner of his eyes to make sure Chico was watching him.

"And twenty," Trace said. "Tax."

Alcetta tossed the money onto the desk and said, "You call me when you're done. Get that bitch."

Trace nodded. As Alcetta opened the door, Trace held up the file folder and said, "Don't you want the report?"

"Naaah," Alcetta said. "You hang on to it. I don't like to read much."

"At this point in time, we'll save it for you," Trace said.

The door closed and Trace nodded to Chico. "Good move on the money," he said.

"Hit 'em in the macho. It works every time," she said.

"Shhh. The television," Trace said. He turned up the sound and spun the set so Chico could see the screen, which was showing Gloria Alcetta's face. The announcer's voice was soft over the picture.

"Police still have no leads in the bizarre murder of Swami Salamanda, the love guru, in his headquarters two nights ago. The Swami's death leaves a void at the top of his organization, Love Is All, but unconfirmed reports say this woman—Sister Glorious—will probably be named Gurumayi (that's lady guru) of the organization next week when they move their headquarters to Pennsylvania. Nothing is known about the background of Sister Glorious except that she is an American."

Trace said to Chico, "See if he's still out in the street."

"Sure. Why?" Chico said, running to the window.

"Look for a Lincoln. He'll be in a Lincoln."

"Why a Lincoln?"

"They're always in Lincolns," Trace said.

"Too late," Chico said. "Oh, yeah. That's got to be his car."

"Why?"

"It's got a bumper strip that says Italians Make the Best Lovers."

"Best pizza too," Trace said. "Too bad we missed him."

"What'd you want him for?"

"I couldn't resist. He's so upset at the idea of his wife divorcing him. Wait until we tell him that she's God and God's going to divorce him. Well, we'll put it in our next report."

Later, Chico asked, "One question, Trace?"

"What's that?"

"When you were talking to Alcetta, why'd you keep saying 'at this point in time'?"

"Italians love that," Trace said. "It makes bullshit sound important."

Chico grunted acknowledgment and took her trenchcoat from the rack. "Well, I'm on my way. My first big job," she said. "What are you going to do today?"

"We got five hundred out of Angelo. I think maybe I'll nose around and try to get something that we can make another bullshit report out of."

He stopped Chico at the door.

"I know," she said. "I should be careful."

"That too. But most important, keep track of your expenses."

28

The two detectives were talking to Karen Marichal in a sparsely furnished interrogation room.

"Look, Karen," said Jackson. "Why don't you just help us and make it easier on yourself?"

His voice seemed to echo in the high-ceilinged room where he and the girl sat facing each other across a desk. Razoni paced back and forth behind the young woman.

"I have nothing to say."

"You're making it difficult," Jackson said. "We know you know Abigail, even though you told us the other night that you had never seen her before. So we're pretty sure you know where she is."

Karen Marichal clamped her lips tight.

"To hell with it, Tough. Let's just book her for murder."

Karen wheeled around in the chair to stare at Razoni. "Murder?"

"Yeah, murder. My partner didn't tell you everything we know. We know that you and Abigail picked up the flowers that the lizard choked on. We know that Abigail was the one who handed them to him in that ceremony. Murder."

"But . . . no . . ."

"What did you do with the flowers when you picked them up?" asked Jackson softly.

"Forget it," Razoni said, with a wink at Jackson. "Let's just book her."

"Ed, why don't you see if you can find us the statistical file on murders by poisoning?" He nodded.

"Okay, if you want. But I'll be right back and then we book her." Razoni was smiling as he left the room. He and Jackson had played good-guy, bad-guy so many times it had become second nature to them.

When the door closed behind Razoni, Jackson said calmly, "My partner is inclined to charge ahead. I think we could find the truth better if we all lowered our voices a little. Now what did you and Abigail do with the roses when you picked them up?"

"We brought them back to the ashram."

"And?"

"We put them in the refrigerator."

"Is that usual?"

"Yes."

"Now how did Abigail get involved in the ceremony?"

"She was a new member. It was an honor for her."

"So she got dressed, went to the refrigerator for the flowers and then went into the auditorium. Is that right?"

"I guess so."

"Weren't you there?"

"The ceremony was only for new members. I've been a member for almost a year," Karen said. "I was next door at the store when it all happened."

"How did it happen?" Jackson asked.

Karen Marichal thought for a moment, then said, "I don't want to talk anymore." She clamped her mouth tightly shut.

"Karen, do you understand what is happening? By your silence, you're making it look as if you and Abigail had something to do with the murder. You denied even knowing Abigail. Then when we went to your house, you disguised your voice so we wouldn't recognize you. Does that all sound like an innocent person with nothing to hide?"

The girl remained silent.

"I know Abigail is your lover," Jackson said. Karen's eyes widened in surprise. "But if she or someone else had something to do with the Swami's death, you shouldn't be the one to be punished. Now we can't help you unless we find Abigail. Where is she?"

There was no answer.

"Even when we talked to you the first time and you told us your name was Keri Ellison. You might have thought that was just a joke, but it wouldn't look good to a lot of people."

Silence.

"Some policemen go to church, you know. I'm one of them. I've been singing the Kyrie Eleison since I was a boy."

Finally she spoke. "I want a lawyer."

"Whatever you say, Karen. But I don't think I'm going to be able to stop charges from being filed against you. How do you think it's going to make your family feel when you're booked as an accessory to murder?"

"My family? They'll probably go out to buy new clothes for the trial."

Jackson sighed and rose. "I have some things to do outside. I'm going to leave you here. You'll be all right."

The girl did not answer.

In the hallway, Jackson called over a uniformed patrolman.

"I have to see Captain Mannion. There's a suspect in there. Make sure she doesn't leave and doesn't hurt herself."

The patrolman nodded. Razoni was pacing back and forth at the end of the hall.

"Well?"

"Nothing," Jackson said. "She won't give anything."

"Well, you'd better go upstairs and tell the captain," Razoni said.

When they walked into Mannion's office, Razoni said pleasantly, "Hiya, Schultz. How's everything in the weasel family?"

"He's been looking for you. Where you been?"

"Where we're supposed to be," Razoni said. "At police headquarters, doing police business. It's kind of interesting work, Schultz. You ought to try it sometime if you ever get tired of being a ribbon clerk." He leaned over the sergeant's desk. "I know, Schultz. 'Very funny.'"

Schultz pressed a button on the telephone. "Detective Jackson's here, sir," he said. Pause. "Yes, sir. He's here too."

He nodded them toward Captain Mannion's door.

The gooseneck lamp on Mannion's desk had been raised to the full intimidation angle. It shone sharply into their eyes as the two detectives sat down in the straight-backed wooden chairs. Behind the desk, they could barely see Mannion's outline, curled in a wreath of cigarette smoke.

"Okay, let's have it. First you, Jackson, on Abigail Longworth. The mayor's going batshit. The commissioner's going batshit. Longworth is screaming that he'll take the department apart on television. What about that girl?"

"Well, it's complicated, Captain," Jackson began.

"Complicated? Do you know where she is or not? How complicated is that?"

"Well, actually, Captain, yes and no," interjected Razoni, trying to be helpful.

"Quiet, Razoni. I'm talking to Jackson."

"No, Captain," said Jackson. "We haven't found her yet. But we've picked up somebody who we think knows where she is."

"Who's that?"

Razoni squirmed in his seat.

"Her name is Karen Marichal," said Jackson. "She's a friend of the Longworth girl."

Razoni drummed his fingers on the edge of his chair.

"I see, Jackson. And why do you think she knows where Abigail Longworth is?" Mannion asked.

Razoni could stand it no longer. "Because she and the Longworth brat are lezzies and they poisoned the lizard." He nodded to emphasize his words, as if congratulating himself on a job well done.

Mannion sank back in his chair. The two detectives could hear air sipping into his mouth. Then there was only silence in the room. And finally the silence was broken by a sound neither had ever heard before. Mannion was chuckling. Razoni found the sound terrifying.

Mannion chuckled a little more, then said, "Razoni, I've got to hand it to you. You really do have a strange sense of humor. You must be a barrel of laughs during the day."

"I'm not joking, Captain. They killed the guru. The one that ate the roses."

"What?" Mannion rose to his feet behind the desk, a gorgon rising out of some primitive darkness. His face was visible as he leaned forward over the gooseneck lamp. His neck was bulging, throbbing with tightened tendons, his jaw half-open, ready to scream.

Razoni decided he had done his bit. "Tough, you better tell him all about it," he said.

"Jackson?" Mannion spoke just the one word, phrased like a question, but managed to make it sound like a plea for Jackson to rescue him from this maniacal Italian.

"Well, Captain, we're not sure yet, but that's what it's beginning to look like."

"But why? What reason did they have to do in that bearded bastard?"

"If we knew that, Captain, we'd know it all," said Jackson.

Mannion sat back heavily in his chair and snatched his cigarette from the edge of the desk. It had already gone out. He puffed loudly anyway, then stopped and lit the cigarette, puffed again, and exhaled the smoke with the sound of defective air brakes.

"Okay. Let's let that go for a while. Now, where is the Longworth brat?"

"We don't know yet."

"But she hasn't been kidnapped?"

"No."

"But you don't know where she is?"

"No," Razoni interrupted, "but we've got an idea."

This was news to Jackson, who stared at his partner as intently as Mannion did.

"If we let out the word that we're holding this Marichal chickie in the lizard's killing, it might bring Abigail out of the woodwork."

"Why should it?" asked Mannion.

" 'Cause she's a fag," Razoni said. "These two are lezzies. You know how they are, Captain. Smooching up to each other and everything. Doing dirty things. Writing poems. When Abigail hears that her fag girlfriend is in the slammer, her little fag heart is going to say, 'Oh, oh, I've got to protect my little fag lezzie sweetheart,' and she'll show up.''

"You seem to have it all figured out, Razoni."

"Yes, sir, Captain. Comes from thinking ahead. Of course, a lot of the credit goes to Tough. It was his idea too," Razoni said graciously. "I mean, once *I* discovered that they were fagolas."

Mannion sucked on his cigarette again and shook his head sadly. "Oh, my God," he said. "I'm going to have to talk to the commissioner." He put the cigarette back on the edge of the desk. "All right. Here's what we do for now. Let the department p.r. man put out a statement that the Marichal kid is being questioned in connection with Salamanda's murder. But that's all. No reference, no reference at all, to Abigail. You got it?"

"Right."

"Right."

"When I say no reference, I mean not one word. Until we've got a charge on her, I don't think we'd better say anything. And Razoni, if I were you, I wouldn't say anything to Longworth, or anybody else for that matter, about his daughter being a fag, as you so delicately put it."

"He won't be upset," Razoni said firmly.

"Why not?"

"He's a fag too."

"Jackson, get him out of here," Mannion roared. He was still yelling when the door closed behind the two detectives.

"Now, what's he yelling about?" asked Razoni. "Did I say something?"

Jackson didn't answer and Sergeant Schultz looked happy to see Razoni discomfited. Razoni reduced his happiness by accidentally stepping on Schultz's foot.

In the hall, Razoni assigned Jackson to tell the public-relations officer exactly what to say "and make sure the dumb shit doesn't go running off at the mouth. The captain will hold you personally responsible."

"Yes, sir," Jackson said.

Razoni went downstairs to where Karen Marichal was held in the interrogation room. He had something important to ask her.

When he had chased the patrolman from the door, he went inside. The young woman was sitting rigidly at the desk. She looked up, alarmed, when she recognized Razoni.

"Don't you hurt me," she said.

"No, I won't hurt you. I just want to ask you something."

"What?"

"How does it feel to be a lesbian?"

"Oh, go screw yourself."

"That's what I mean," Razoni said.

29

"You said this was important, Mister . . ."

"Graham," Trace said. "My friends just call me Will."

"And it concerns . . ."

"I'm sorry I don't have any business cards with me. I left them back in my hotel room," Trace said.

"Would you please tell me what your business is?" said J. J. Gildersleeve.

They were sitting in the small office in the rear of the Salamanda headquarters.

"I couldn't help it," Trace said. "I was watching the television and I saw the report and I had to get right down here."

"What report?" Gildersleeve asked. He was a small man with yellow discolored teeth with large spaces between them. Handy for spitting pumpkin seeds, Trace thought. The man bit his nails too.

"About Sister Glorious, of course," Trace said. "How she is going to take over the work of the Swami."

"I'm not in a position to discuss that right now," Gildersleeve said.

Trace chuckled. "Heh, heh. I understand. Hierarchical problems, et cetera, et cetera, I truly do understand. But that's why I came."

"I was hoping that eventually you would tell me," Gildersleeve said, barely able to keep the annoyance from his voice.

"Sister Glorious," Trace said. "Well, I wanted you to know that she is a married woman."

"I know that," Gildersleeve said.

"But she is separated from her husband. I thought, well, I thought you had better know that. Think of the consequences to your organization."

Gildersleeve leaned forward across the desk. He was interested now. "What consequences?" he said.

"I can trust your discretion in this matter?" Trace asked.

"You can. You have my word. What consequences?"

"I happen to be close to the family that Sister Glorious is married into. The Alcetta family of Brooklyn. They are not the type of family that would normally be associated with the type of freedoms the Swami espoused."

"I know that. I've met Sister's husband," Gildersleeve said.

"You have?"

Trace waited and let the silence hang in the room. Gildersleeve waited too, but cracked first. "Yes. He was here one day to talk to Sister Glorious."

"Then you know what he is like?"

"I do."

"He told me once in private conversation that he would do anything—he stressed the 'anything'—to separate his wife from your movement. I think he is a dangerous man."

"He certainly is a noisy one," Gildersleeve said. "He came in here and threatened to kill Sister. He threatened to kill the Swami. I told him unless he left I was going to call the police and he threatened to kill me."

"That's what I mean," Trace said smugly.

"A lot of people talk," Gildersleeve said. He sat back in his chair. "You haven't anything to tell me that might compromise Sister Glorious's ability to head our movement, have you, Mr. Graham?"

"Call me Will," Trace said. He shook his head. "Just that family connection."

"Well, I thank you for your concern, sir, but I really have to be back to work. I have a national conference here this weekend. If the police have not moved toward a solution of the Swami's murder, I plan to expose their inefficiency to the world. I've many things to do before I get caught up. A potful of work," he said.

Trace rose. "Sister will be the leader, then?" he said.

"That decision won't be made by her alone," Gildersleeve said. "I really must ask you to leave."

Trace walked down the block toward Sarge's old car, thinking. Gildersleeve did not like Gloria Alcetta. That was pretty obvious. Probably he thought of her as some kind of interloper in a movement he'd been with for years. But did he really expect that he could be named guru? Guru Gildersleeve? Come on.

He passed a florist shop and next to it noticed a television store that advertised XXX TV tapes, taping equipment, and VCRs for sale or rent. He remembered something Sarge had told him on Sunday and walked into the store where a giant of a man was trying to fit kielbasa-sized fingers into the back of a television set designed to be serviced by the pencil fingers of Oriental dwarfs.

"I need some information, my good man," Trace said.

"The public library's on Forty-second Street. You can tell it by the lions out front."

Trace ignored the comment. The man had hunkered down closer over the set.

"I'm looking for somebody to shoot some television tape. My daughter's engagement party."

"Yellow pages. A lot of places do that."

"Well, it's not my favorite daughter," Trace said, "so I'm trying to hold the cost down. I really wanted somebody maybe not too professional."

"Rent the equipment and do it yourself. That's the cheapest way. You want to rent equipment? I rent equipment."

"I'm afraid I have no skill," Trace said. "I was down the block at the Temple of Love and they said there was a young man who used to tape there. I thought you might know who he is."

"Yeah. I know him. He always buys his tapes here. But you couldn't afford him."

"How's that, old chap?"

"He just got a job with United Broadcasting."

"He must be very good," Trace said.

"He's not that good. But he took some film of that cuckoo guru the day he went belly up and I guess the company liked them because they hired him."

"Oh? I never saw those films," Trace said.

"Me neither. But I guess they were pretty good if they hired him."

"What's his name? Maybe he's freelancing?" Trace said.

"Sam. Sam Silverand. He lives in that apartment building on the corner, that big red dump. Let's see, he's number 412."

"You know, I don't want some lunatic taking these films," Trace said. "He's not one of these Love people, is he?"

"Naaah, he's kind of nerdy and he used to hang out there because he likes that free-love crap. He told me once that people grope each other right at the meetings."

"It takes all kinds," Trace said. "Thanks for your help."

There was no doorman, no lock on the front door, and no lights in the hallway, which smelled like a dog's kennel on a holiday weekend. The stairs were bare splintering wood; the landings semicovered with linoleum whose print had long ago worn away, exposing a dirt-brown base. Sam Silverand had three visible locks on the door to his apartment and God knew how many inside.

But no one was home. Trace tried the bell but didn't hear it ring inside the apartment. Then he tried knocking on the door. He knocked a long time before giving up.

When he turned around, an old woman was watching him from an apartment at the other end of the hall. Two security chains were still in place as she peered out the crack. Trace could see a bit of the flowered cotton housedress she wore.

"He's not home," she said.

"I was figuring that out. Where is he?"

"I'm not authorized to give out that information," she said.

Trace nodded and walked toward the stairs.

"You want to leave a message. I'll tell him."

"I'm not authorized to leave a message."

"Ain't you a dummy?"

"Maybe I am. Hell. Tell him that Roone Arledge was here." He started down the steps.

The woman called after him. "Hey."

"What?" Trace said.

"You're a television guy, right? A big shot?"

"Right. I made Howard Cosell what he is today."

"He's a dork."

"And I put him there," Trace said.

"Roone Arledge?"

"Right."

"What kind of a name is Roone?" she asked.

"A first name," Trace said.

"I don't mean *that*," she said. "How'd you get to be so big if you're so stupid?"

"I had a lot of good people helping me."

"Is Roone German?"

"No. It's Guelph. I'm the last of the Guelphs."

"It's a dumb name. What do you want Sam for?"

"I wanted to talk to him about some tape he shot when the Indian down the street got poisoned."

"You're too late, Mr. Mogul. United Broadcasting beat you to it. They already bought it."

"I didn't see it. Was it good?"

"It was never on. Sam and me were looking for it, he even came over here, but it wasn't on. The big guy there bought it hisself but it wasn't on."

"I guess Sam was disappointed," Trace said.

"Well, he got a job out of it from the big guy, so I guess it all worked out."

"What big guy?"

"The big guy what runs United Broadcasting," she said. "Longneck or something."

"When's Sam usually get home?"

"I don't know. He just started."

"Maybe I'll catch up with him tomorrow," Trace said.

"I'll tell him you were here."

"Thanks," Trace said, and started down the stairs.

"Hey, Arledge," the woman yelled as Trace neared the next landing.

"What?" Trace yelled back.

"Fire Cosell. He's a dork."

Using a tavern telephone, it took Trace twenty minutes to track down Razoni and Jackson.

"This is Ed Razoni."

"This is Devlin Tracy."

"Who the hell are you?" Never much for charm, Razoni sounded even grouchier than usual, Trace thought.

"Is your partner there?"

"Yeah, but he doesn't talk to nobody unless I tell him to talk to somebody," Razoni said. "Who are you?"

"I'm with the State Lottery Office," Trace said. "I'm checking a winning ticket."

Trace heard the phone drop and Razoni's voice saying, "Get this one, Tough. It may be important."

"Detective Jackson."

"This is Devlin Tracy. We met yesterday in my office while our partners were threatening to shoot each other."

"Right. What can I do for you?"

"I thought you might be interested," Trace said. "I tracked down that TV tape of the Swami dying."

"What TV tape?" Jackson said, and suddenly Trace remembered that Sister Glorious had told Sarge about the tape and he had never passed the message on to the two city detectives.

"Well, there was a tape shot," Trace said. "By some guy named Sam Silverand, who used to hang out at the House of Love. United Broadcasting bought the tape, but I don't think they showed it. Then they hired him as a cameraman. I think he's working tonight."

"That's good," Jackson said. "How'd you happen to run into this?"

"I was nosing around at the Swami's place. My divorce case. I stumbled on it."

"You're not playing hotshot and getting involved in that murder investigation, are you?" Jackson asked.

"No. Divorce is more my speed. Why?"

"Sometimes people who kill other people start to kill people who are looking for them."

"I'm not afraid," Trace said. "Remember? I've got my partner to protect me."

"The girl with the invisible gat," Jackson said.

"What harm could come to me?"

In the background, Trace heard Razoni roaring, "Tell that guy to go fuck himself. Tell him to stay out of our business. Tell him, Tough. You tell him."

"You heard that?" Jackson asked.

"Half of New York did," Trace said.

"Thanks for the tip."

"Anytime. If I run into anything else, I'll keep you posted."

"Well?" Razoni said as Jackson hung up the telephone.

"Interesting. There was a TV tape shot when the Swami died."

"Screw that," Razoni said, waving a hand in dismissal. "Screw the lizard. We try to do our jobs and we get our asses reamed out and we get assigned to look for some faggot's faggot kid, screw it all. And I don't want you talking to that Tracy anyway."

"Why?"

"Because of that homicidal Jap he's got working for him. She's gonna get one of us killed."

"But listen to this anyway," Jackson said. "The TV film was bought by United Broadcasting, but they never showed it."

"I don't think that's interesting," Razoni said.

"I do. I think I'm going to look at it," Jackson said.

"Don't volunteer," Razoni said. "Christ, didn't you learn anything in reform school?"

"No," Jackson said. "That's why I kept getting left back."

There was another phone call for Jackson. He answered it, then came back looking worried.

"What now?" Razoni said.

"We've got to roll. That was the captain. He wants us to meet him right away."

"Where?"

"At Theodore Longworth's house."

30

They parked in the circular driveway behind an old Subaru that they recognized as Captain Mannion's. He was on the front steps waiting for them.

"Great idea, Razoni," he said.

"Thanks, Captain. But remember it wasn't all my idea. Tough helped a little bit too. He takes notes and things."

"So the girlfriend would show up if we announced we were holding the Marichal kid?" Mannion said.

"Right," said Razoni. He detected a change of wind and asked cautiously, "She's home, isn't she?"

"No, dopey, she isn't home. You two better come inside."

Inside the house, Theodore Longworth paced back and forth, being comforted by a man the two detectives recognized well. The police commissioner. At the sight of the two detectives, Longworth's face gathered red like a spanked toddler.

"You two. You two. You two said you were going to bring back my little girl."

Razoni noticed that Longworth had a glass in his hand and liquid slopped over the sides as he waved his arms for emphasis.

Jackson remained silent, content to let the television executive yell himself out. Razoni, however, was not about to be abused by a fag, probably husband of a fag, certainly father of a fag, even if he did own the biggest television network in the world.

He started to say something but was silenced by Captain Mannion's squeezing his shoulder.

The police commissioner said, "Perhaps, Ted, we ought to brief these two men on what has happened."

Longworth looked angrily at the commissioner, then paused, nodded, and slumped into a chair. More of the liquid slopped from his glass.

The commissioner walked to a small table. "This arrived just a little while ago. It was brought by a cabdriver who said he had been given it by a man to deliver here."

On the table was a small tape recorder. The commissioner pressed a button. The machine whirred, then scratchily, hesitantly, a voice sounded out. A young woman's voice.

"Daddy, thith ith Abigail. Daddy, two men are holding me in an old building. They're going to hurt me, Daddy, unleth you do jutht what they thay. Two of your polithemen picked up Karen Marichal today. One of the polithemen wath named Detective Jackthon. They thay you have to let her go if you ever want to thee me alive again. Daddy, pleathe do what they thay. I'm thcared."

The recorder clicked the end of the message and the commissioner looked up. "We've called the FBI, of course, and they should be here any minute." He stopped short when he saw that Razoni was using his hand to cover a large smile on his face. Razoni saw the commissioner looking at him and tried unsuccessfully to stop smiling.

"Can I ask a question?" he said.

"Go ahead," said the commissioner.

"Mr. Longworth, does your kid always talk funny like that?"

"Like what?"

"Thpitting her wordth. Anything with an S in it."

Longworth glared at him. "She has a slight lisp, if that's what you mean, Detective."

Razoni looked at Jackson, who nodded. "When did this tape arrive, Mr. Longworth?"

"Just a little while ago."

"Before six o'clock or after six o'clock? Do you remember?"

"Why? Is it important?"

"The story about Karen Marichal was on the six-o'clock news," Jackson said. "It's worth knowing if this tape was made before or after that."

"Before that," Longworth said. "I was just getting ready to watch the news when the cabbie brought the tape."

"Did the cabbie say where he got it?"

"From a tall man, a very tall man, up on the West Side someplace."

"Tall man with blond hair?" Jackson asked.

Longworth nodded.

"Captain, can we talk to you for a minute?" asked Razoni. Mannion looked at the commissioner. When he nodded, Mannion went into the hall with the two detectives.

"What is it, Razoni?"

"When the FBI comes, stall them for a while. Tough and me are going to go get the kid."

"You know where she is?"

"We can find her," Razoni said.

Mannion studied their faces carefully as if deciding whether or not he trusted them. Finally, he agreed. "Okay, but don't slip. This time it'll be your ass. Mine too, probably. Longworth's going nuts."

"We'll get her, Captain," Razoni said. "And if you think he's nuts now, you might start preparing him for the fact that we're going to charge the little faggot with murder. See how he likes that."

"Razoni," Mannion cautioned, "you're on thin ice, so you'd better step easy." He looked at Razoni's stubborn dark eyes and softened. "I'll talk about it with the commissioner. Hurry up now."

The two detectives ran toward their car and skidded away down the long semicircular drive in front of the mansion.

"Ed, you're the picture of couth."

"Why the hell do I always get in trouble?" Razoni asked.

"You didn't have to say his kid talks funny."

"But she *does* talk funny. No wonder she's a fag. No

man'd want to talk to her. He'd spend all his time wiping his face.''

"Funny, we noticed Karen's voice was different, but I thought the lisp was to disguise it.''

"Sure," Razoni said. "But those two dirty things were probably there in the dark, and when we came, Karen got afraid that we'd recognize her so she turned out the lights and had Abigail make believe that she was Karen.''

"Thank God they're not too smart. Handing over that tape recorder to the cabbie.''

"Right. Tall, blond. Lurch, the butler. And it was dumb to send it before the news was on. The only people who knew about it were the ones in Karen's house. And even your name on the tape. I knew you'd get in trouble if you keep giving everybody your business card.''

"I just hope we're right," Jackson said. "I don't want to go back on traffic duty.''

"Don't worry about it," Razoni said. "We're right.''

The Marichal's brownstone was dark when they pulled up. No lights shone through to the street.

"Maybe no one's home," Jackson said.

"They're home. They're down in the cellar drinking bats' blood," Razoni said.

Razoni leaned on the bell at the top of the steps but got no answer. He pounded on the door with his fist. "Come on, Lurch, open up. I know you're in there," he yelled.

There was only silence from the other side of the door.

Razoni shrugged. "Do you please want to look the other way?''

"Why?''

"I'm about to break the law.''

"If it's good enough for you, it's good enough for me," Jackson said.

The two detectives moved lightly down the front steps and through the small flagstoned alleyway that ran alongside the brownstone. Halfway to the rear of the house was an old wooden door with windows in it.

Razoni pressed his face to the windows and peered inside.

"Black as you," he said. "Nobody there, dammit.''

"Maybe they're eating pigeons on the roof, instead," Jackson said.

"We'll see." Razoni drew his revolver and, using the butt of it, crisply and sharply smashed the pane of glass right next to the doorknob. There was a string of small tinkles as glass bits hit the stone floor of the cellar. Then again there was silence.

Razoni reached carefully through the broken window and unlocked the door. He and Jackson moved into the building, then waited to acclimate their eyes to the darkness.

"A ground-level basement," Jackson said. "I thought all these buildings had real cellars."

"This one used to," Razoni said.

"Yeah?"

"But when it got filled with bodies, they decided to pave it over."

Razoni led the way up the stairs toward the first floor of the house.

"Man, it's dark in here," Jackson said.

"Follow me. I can see in the dark."

"I knew I should have spent my youth breaking into warehouses at night."

"The exercise would have been good for you, Fatty. Instead, you sat home eating chitlins and ham hocks and look at the shape you're in."

The first floor was dark and empty. They pulled open the French doors to the sitting room but no one was inside. The trapeze hung motionless from the ceiling. It seemed strange not to see Mrs. Marichal's blond curls in front of the canvas on the far side of the room.

They searched the first floor carefully but found no one. In the kitchen, Razoni knocked over an empty wine bottle.

Jackson led the way upstairs. Razoni trooped slowly after him through the dark. He heard something and froze on the steps.

"Tough," he whispered.

"I hear it."

The sound was a rustling, a small scraping noise. It seemed to come from the top of the stairs. In the silence, it echoed loud and ominous. A drape blowing against an open window? The start-up hiss of air from some kind of central air-conditioning?

It continued.

Slowly, carefully, Jackson again started up the stairs, pausing on each step to listen. He drew his pistol. Razoni's was already in his hand.

They reached the top of the stairs before it attacked.

Razoni felt something slam against his face. It was pressed against his face. Something was smothering him.

"I got it," he shouted. He reached up with his hands and grabbed a handful of hair. He wrenched.

There was a squawking and a chattering and a hissing. Razoni held on fiercely to the handful of hair. He felt sharp teeth bite into the back of his hand.

"Owwwww," he yelled.

Jackson, pistol cocked, moved alongside him.

"Oh, for Christ's sake," he said, "will you stop fooling around with the monkey? We didn't come here to play with the monkey."

Razoni held the monkey by the neck in one hand. The animal was hissing and chattering. Razoni heaved him away down the corridor. The chattering stopped and again, all was silent.

"Are you ready to stop fooling around?" Jackson asked.

"That's right. Get smart. It wasn't you that fucker was trying to rape."

"He must have thought he recognized you," Jackson said.

They turned to the right, toward the door of Karen Marichal's room. From inside, they heard no sound. Jackson reached out his hand for the doorknob.

He turned it slowly. The door lock clicked, the door began to swing open, and then the sharp report of a shot cracked out. Above Jackson's head, the wood of the door frame splintered as a bullet slammed into it.

Razoni dived into Jackson, dragging him to the floor and pushing him to the side of the doorway. The two of them went down in a lump, Razoni's body covering his partner's.

The monkey, who had been hiding out of reach, saw the

two men on the floor, decided that they had changed their minds about playing, and with one large bound landed on top of them.

Razoni had been scrambling toward his feet, gun cocked, ready to charge into the room, when the monkey hit him, and he went down again.

"Ed, don't shoot," hissed Jackson as Razoni clawed over his head, trying to get the monkey off him. "It's probably the girl."

Razoni punched the monkey in the stomach. The animal, ooofed, chattered, jumped, and ran. They heard it skittering down the hallway.

Razoni, from a crouch, leaned forward and with his left hand pushed the door wide open.

"We're coming in," he shouted.

"Come another thtep and I'll thoot."

Razoni stood up

"Oh, for Christ's sake," he said. "It's the twit. Hey, don't thoot. We're poleeth."

Jackson got up from the floor. "Abigail, I'm Detective Jackson. Remember? We were here yesterday?"

"What do you want?" the girl called.

"We've come to take you home," said Jackson.

"Ith Karen all right?"

"Karen's being released right now," said Jackson.

"Very good," Razoni whispered. "Always lie."

"Karen's being released and there's no reason for you to hide here anymore."

There was a silence from inside the room, then the young woman's voice said, "Oh, I gueth it'th all right."

"We're coming in," Jackson said.

"Okay."

They turned on the light and found Abigail Longworth huddled in a corner of the sofa, where she had been the first time they had encountered her. She wore jeans and a sweatshirt that read LOVE IS ALL and in her hand was a .38 police special.

Razoni stepped up and snatched the gun away from her.

"You could have hurt somebody," he said.

"I thought you were burglarth," Abigail said.

"Shoot first and ask questions later?" Razoni said.

"Why not, Ed? It's what you do," Jackson said.

"Oh, shut up. Who asked you? Come on, Abigail. Daddykins is waiting for you."

"Where is everybody else, by the way? How come the house is empty?" Jackson asked.

"The Marichalth all went to picket poleeth headquarterth."

"For what?" Razoni asked.

"To make you releathe Karen. I told them they thould hire a lawyer but they wouldn't lithen."

In the car on the way back, Jackson asked the young woman, "Why did you run after you gave Swami Salamanda the roses?"

"I wath afraid. I didn't know what happened and then I thought my daddy wath going to be embarrathed if my name wath involved. Tho I panicked. Karen thaid I thould thtay in her houth for a while. Then we didn't know what to do becauth it thounded like I killed the Thwami."

"A likely story," Razoni said.

"It'th a true thtory," said Abigail heatedly.

"I think it's a little queer," said Razoni, underlining "queer." "I think there are a lot of queer things in this case, starting with you."

"You're hateful," Abigail said.

"Right. And as far as I'm concerned, you're murder-suspect number one. You and Karen got the flowers for the lizard and you gave the flowers to the lizard and then the lizard died and that makes you and her the two people involved in his death."

"By why would we kill our Thwami?"

"I don't know. But you just tried to kill us when we opened the door to your room. We'll find out."

"Where'th Karen?"

"In jail, where you belong too," Razoni said.

"Let me out of thith car," Abigail screamed. "You tricked me. You told me Karen wath releathed. Let me out of here."

She swung her small fists toward Razoni, but Jackson smothered her arms with his right hand, pinning her fists in her lap.

"You know what they say, kid," said Razoni. "Never trust anybody over thirty."

"That'th not what I thay," Abigail said.

"No? What do you say?"

"I thay fuck all pigth."

"You keep that up and I'm going to tell your daddykins on you," Razoni said.

31

Chico found Trace sitting at the bar in Bogie's and slumped onto a stool next to him.

"Look at you," he said. "I thought you'd come bellying up to the bar, order a double Scotch on the rocks, and threaten to blow away the bartender if he didn't step on it. You look like something the cat dragged in."

"You never told me this was such shitful work," Chico said.

"Tough day, huh?"

"Whoever said economics was the dismal science wasn't ever an investigator," Chico said. "An awful day."

"Well, let me get a drink to put myself in the right frame of mind, and then tell me all about it," Trace said.

"What gets me is I did everything right," Chico said as Trace signaled the bartender to refill his glass. "I went to the funeral home, I went to the neighbors, I talked to the cops, I even talked to bartenders. Christ, what sleazeballs. They're always hitting on you. And I still come up empty."

"How so?" Trace said.

"Trace, that woman's death was an accident." She grabbed his arms and turned him on his stool so she could stare into his face. "A freaking accident," she said.

"That's why you're so depressed?" he asked.

"Well, wouldn't you be? I wanted to show off for Garrison Fidelity. I wanted to save them a hundred thou on a double-indemnity payoff. I wanted this to be a murder and I wanted to solve it. Dammit, I hate druggists. Druggists are never murderers," Chico said.

"Hey, Babe, that's the way it goes sometimes," Trace said. "Most of the time those accidents that you read about, they're really accidents. If they weren't, insurance companies would never pay off and they'd own the whole world instead of the half of it they have now."

"It's still depressing," Chico said.

"Now you know why I drink," Trace said.

"Oh, hogwash. You drank like a fish before you ever investigated a case. Don't try that on me," she said.

"Well, I thought it was worth a shot," Trace said. "So what happened today? Lady drove off a road, just like the report said?"

"Sort of. There was a little more to it than that," Chico said. "This Debbie Doblemeyer, that's the dead woman, she and her husband were childless. Then finally, age forty, she got pregnant. It was a tough pregnancy and I guess that's why the husband insured her in the first place. Well, she lost the baby, and that was her last chance at having one. Make a long story short, she started to drink, all the time, in the house, out of the house. She closed this cocktail lounge the night she died, drove home and got killed."

"You think she wanted it to happen?" Trace asked.

Chico shrugged. "Maybe. The bartender remembered that she made a big point out of saying good-bye to everybody at the bar, all the regulars."

"There," Trace said. "You have it. You can make a case for suicide. Garrison Fidelity won't pay on a suicide."

Chico looked at him with total surprise on her face. "I wouldn't do that," she said.

"Why not?"

"I don't believe you," she said. "Poor woman had a miscarriage and was unhappy and maybe she did try to drink to get herself killed. I don't know, but I'm not going to be the one to tag her with the suicide label."

"I thought you wanted to make a big splash for Groucho," Trace said.

"Not by jumping feet first into liquid excrement," Chico said.

"You don't have the heart to work for an insurance company," Trace said.

"I've got a big heart," she said.

"Exactly," Trace said.

When Razoni and Jackson reentered Theodore Longworth's study, four more men were there, all in business suits with vests and regimental striped ties.

"Look at those clothes," Razoni mumbled to Jackson. "Are they awful or what?"

"That's so nobody will recognize them," Jackson said.

The two detectives led Abigail between them. She had stopped struggling.

Longworth saw his daughter, dropped his drink, and ran toward her. She broke loose from the detectives and ran to him. They embraced in the center of the room.

"Oh, baby," said Longworth.

"Oh, Daddy," said Abigail.

"Disgusting," said Razoni.

The four FBI agents were very brisk. They demanded to know if there had been a kidnapping.

"No," Razoni said.

"We'll still have to make a report on this," said one agent, apparently the leader because his suit almost fit.

"Why?" said the police commissioner, stepping forward, Captain Mannion at his side.

"Because it is a violation to make a false report to federal authorities."

"I think you might reconsider," said the commissioner smoothly. "If you recall, we asked you here in an advisory capacity. No one made any formal report of a kidnapping. We just wanted you to be aware of the incident, in the unlikely event it turned out to be a criminal act."

"Well . . ." began the agent.

"It'll be much easier this way," said the commissioner. "Just a family matter, and we do appreciate your taking the trouble to come here, even though no action was warranted. I plan to call your director tomorrow just to thank him personally for your thoughtfulness."

The FBI man knew a threat when he heard one, but glad to be taken off the hook so smoothly, he nodded agreement.

"All right," he said. "We'll let it go at that. Men," he called to his assistants. As one they rose from their chairs. The agent in charge nodded to Longworth, who broke the embrace with his daughter and stepped forward to shake his hand warmly.

"I want to thank you," he said.

"There's no indication here of any violation of federal law," said the agent. "We'll be leaving."

"Thanks again."

The four agents were at the door to the study when Abigail pointed a finger at Razoni and Jackson across the room. "Brutality," she shouted. "Violation of my righth."

"Oh, shit," said Razoni aloud.

This apparently was the incorrect thing to say under Longworth's roof because he wheeled on Razoni. "What did you say?" he demanded, glancing back over his shoulder as if wondering if his daughter had heard the terrible epithet.

"I said, 'Oh, shit,' " said Razoni. "I said it before too when Abigail said, 'Fuck all pigth.' "

Longworth shrank back as if struck. The FBI agent in charge paused in the doorway. "Police brutality is a federal violation," he announced solemnly.

"They abuthed me," Abigail Longworth shouted. "They mithtreated me. They lied to me."

Razoni nodded his head in disgust. "Tell them how you tried to kill us, Abigail. Tell them about the shot you took at us."

The commissioner stepped forward quickly and put his arm around the FBI agent in charge. "We'll take care of this, Fred. Sounds like a personality conflict to me."

"It might be serious, Commissioner."

The commissioner chuckled and said softly, "Just temper, I think. We'll handle it."

The agent looked at him, then at Razoni as if filing his face in memory for the next time a brutality complaint was lodged and he lacked a suspect. Razoni stuck his tongue out. Although the agent was startled, he allowed himself to be steered from the room by the commissioner. Mannion pulled the two detectives off into a corner of the room.

"Okay. Good work. You found her, now calm down."

"Tough wants to ask you something," Razoni said. "He wants to know did you tell him."

"Tell him what?"

"One, that his daughter's a freaking fag. Two, that she probably killed the lizard. Three, that she's been hiding out of her own free will, and four, the kidnapping tape was a fake, and that's a crime. And five . . . No, you couldn't tell him five because you didn't know about it, but when we went to get her, she tried to kill us. She fired a shot at us. From a big old gun. A big gun. Bang. Right over our heads. If I hadn't moved fast, she might have plugged Tough. Fortunately, I was there to protect him. And I would have shot her right between her freaking lesbian eyes if that goddamn monkey hadn't jumped in my hair."

"Monkey, Razoni?"

"Yeah. That monkey that rides the trapeze. It got on my arm and I couldn't shoot her the way I should have."

"Jackson, have you two been drinking?"

"No, Captain. Ed's telling you the absolute truth. Almost."

"Captain, did you tell him?" demanded Razoni.

"No. But I told the commissioner." Mannion seemed apologetic.

"And *he* told Longworth, right?"

"Well, not exactly," Mannion said.

The commissioner reentered the room. He raised a cautionary finger toward the two detectives, then stepped forward to speak to Longworth, who was still consoling his daughter in the middle of the room. He talked to him in tones so low the detectives could not hear. They saw Longworth nod, then put his arm around Abigail and walk with her toward the door.

"Daddy," she said, "I want to file chargeth againtht thothe two."

"Not now, honeybunch. Plenty of time for that." He kept steering her toward the door.

"That makes us even," Razoni growled. "Murder, filing false kidnap reports, firing a gun within city limits, being a dirty fag within city limits, spattering a policeman's face."

The door closed behind Longworth and his daughter and the commissioner said, "Marvin, Jackson, Razoni. Come on over and sit down."

"Who's Marvin?" Razoni whispered to Jackson.

"The captain."

"His name's Marvin?"

Jackson nodded.

"Nobody's named Marvin."

The commissioner waved all three to spots on the couch and walked to the liquor cabinet. "Anybody want a drink? I know I can use one."

"No," said Mannion.

"No, thank you," said Jackson

"What kind of bourbon's he got?" asked Razoni.

The commissioner looked surprised. "I don't know. Let's see. Jack Daniels."

"Okay," said Razoni. "Just as long as it's not some cheap shit. I'll have a double bourbon on the rocks with a splash of soda. Not too much soda."

"Do you have any favorite kind of glass?" the commissioner asked puckishly.

"Yeah. A clean one," Razoni said. He wondered why Jackson was looking at him strangely and Mannion appeared to be going into cardiac arrest.

Dutifully the commissioner made the drink, then poured himself a small neat Scotch. He handed the drink to Razoni, then sat in a wing-back chair, facing all three.

"I think we'll agree that we have a problem," he said soothingly. Razoni stopped drinking and was about to say something when the commissioner quickly went on. "It's obvious that Miss Longworth is somewhat upset. I gather you two men are somewhat upset also."

Razoni nodded. He looked off toward the bar, wondering if Longworth had any peanuts.

"Now, let's see if I understand this. You two men were assigned by Marvin here"—Razoni snickered—"to investigate the murder of Swami Salamanda and then you became involved also in Miss Longworth's disappearance. I take it now that you have found that Miss Longworth and a friend, Miss Marichal, picked up at the florist the roses that were later used to poison Salamanda. You also have found that Miss Marichal lied to you about not knowing Miss Longworth's whereabouts and you picked up Miss Marichal largely to force Miss Longworth to reveal her whereabouts. Is that correct?"

Mannion and Jackson nodded. Razoni said, "No."

"No?" said the commissioner.

"No," said Razoni. "It leaves out the fact that the poisoned roses the guru ate were handed to him by old Spitmouth there. It leaves out the fact that she turned in a false kidnapping report to try to get her fag friend out of jail, and it leaves out the fact that she tried to kill my partner and only my fast action saved his life."

"Are you saying Miss Longworth murdered Swami Salamanda?"

Razoni shrugged and sipped his drink. "She's the best suspect we've got. She gives him flowers, he keels over, and she runs away. We've booked people for less."

"Maybe in the old days, Detective. Not now. You don't have enough to book her for murder."

"We've got enough to detain her for questioning."

"Man, you can't just go detaining Ted Longworth's daughter for questioning."

"How about attempted murder for trying to shoot my partner?" Razoni said.

"What is it about you, Razoni, that you're trying to put that girl in jail?" the commissioner asked. His face was starting to flush.

"Because I don't know whether or not she killed the lizard, but if she did, she's going to skip as soon as everybody turns their backs and maybe this time, Tough and I won't be able to find her so easily. She'll wind up hiding out in that goddamn City of Love with all the other dykes."

The commissioner turned from Razoni and spoke formally. "Captain Mannion, the investigation into Salamanda's death is to continue. Miss Longworth is not, repeat not, to be bothered. Unless a formal charge can be filed immediately against Miss Marichal, she is to be released. No mention of any possible involvement by Miss Longworth will be made at all and she will not be questioned, nor will this matter be brought to Mr. Longworth's attention until your unit has a great deal more evidence and many fewer wild suspicions. Do I make myself clear?"

Mannion nodded.

"I also recommend that you assign new men to the death of Swami Salamanda—to get a fresh viewpoint, as it were. Use the entire resources of the department if necessary. Again, do I make myself clear?"

"Yes, sir," said Mannion.

"Razoni, Jackson, I want to commend you both for your quick, efficient work in bringing Miss Longworth safely home. I know that Mr. Longworth is probably a little hot now, but when tempers cool, I'm sure he will share my view and I'm also sure that he will let you know personally how he feels. Are there any questions?"

"Yes, sir," said Razoni.

Mannion's face grew red. Jackson stifled a groan.

"Yes, Razoni," the commissioner said with a sigh.

"Does Longworth have any peanuts?"

32

They were told by Captain Mannion to wait for him out in their car, but Razoni decided that if he had owned a hat, he might just have left it in Longworth's hallway so he had better look for it and so he just happened to overhear Mannion and the commissioner speaking.

COMMISSIONER: Marvin, you've got blood in your eye.

MANNION: I'll do what you say.

COMMISSIONER: Fine.

MANNION: But you're wrong and you're downgrading two fine detectives.

COMMISSIONER: I don't know. That one looks unstable to me. It seems as if Razoni has a grudge against Miss Longworth.

MANNION: Can I speak?

COMMISSIONER: Go ahead.

MANNION: Grudge, my ass. If he says there's a reason to suspect her in a case, you'd better believe there's a reason to suspect her.

COMMISSIONER: And you don't think it's just hatred at first sight?

MANNION: Those two don't hate. They're cops. They'd book you if they thought you killed Salamanda.

COMMISSIONER: You seem to be taking this kind of personally, Marvin.

MANNION: Commissioner, I've been a cop for thirty-five years. In all that time, I've met five, maybe six people I'd trust to walk down a dark alley with. Two of them are out there in that car. Or, knowing that insane Italian bastard, out in the hall trying to hear what we're saying.

Razoni decided his hat was nowhere to be found and he was sitting next to Jackson five minutes later when Captain Mannion came out of the house.

"I don't want any arguments. I want you two to go downtown and let the Marichal brat go. Tell her not to leave town without letting us know."

"And then what?" Razoni said.

"Then tomorrow I'll find something new for you to do before you both get me thrown off the force."

"I guess you don't want us to solve the Salamanda case for you," Razoni said.

"Look. It's been nothing but headache. That asshole Gildersleeve says if we don't solve it by the weekend, we'll have rioting in the streets outside headquarters. Okay, let there be. Let the precinct bulls handle the murder. It's been nothing but a headache for you two."

"You're telling us to get off that case?" Jackson said.

"No. I am specifically not telling you to get off that case. However, you will have another assignment for which you will be responsible. Of course, I can't tell you men what to do in your off-duty hours. I'll see you in the morning."

He walked off to his car, parked directly in front of theirs.

"All right," Razoni asked Jackson. "What the hell does that mean?"

"That means the captain thinks we may be right. That means he's been ordered to take us off the case and he doesn't want to."

"Why not?" asked Razoni.

"Because he trusts us more than any other detectives he's got."

Razoni nodded slightly as Jackson started the car's engine. "I can understand him trusting me. But why you?"

"Because I'm charming and bright and lovable," Jackson said.

*   *   *

"I'm drunk," Chico said.

"I'm getting tired of you being plastered all the time," Trace said.

"All I had was a little sip of a little glass of wine," Chico said apologetically.

"You've done this every year since I've met you," Trace said. "You take a little sip of wine and then you faint on me."

"Japanese cran't dink," Chico said. "Whooops." She giggled. "Can't drink, I mean."

"I know what you mean," Trace said.

Chico tried to count the number of cocktail stirrers on the bar in front of Trace, evidence of the number of drinks he had. She kept getting confused at five.

"How many drinks you have?" she said. "You never get drunk."

"I've had *on dorduncu* drinks," Trace said. "Fourteen. And I don't get drunk because I'm big and experienced and Irish. And you get drunk because you're little and you're Japanese and alcohol is poison to you."

"That's why I never be a businessman," Chico said.

"Why?"

"Two-martini lunch would kill me."

"*Ikinci* martinis," Trace said. "Very tough."

"Stop turking talkish," Chico said. "Whooops." She giggled again.

Trace had another drink and had the bartender bring Chico a cup of black coffee, which she dutifully sipped, and five minutes later the drunk attack was over.

"Feel better now?" he asked.

She nodded. "Stupid, isn't it? A half a sip of wine and blotto. And what's worse is I have a hangover the next day."

"That's why I drink so much," Trace said.

"Why?"

"I'm drinking for two."

Later, Trace said, "I feel stupid doing this alleged checking up on Gloria Alcetta."

"Why?"

"Because there's nothing to find out. She's a religious zoonie and her husband's a nut and I'm wasting his money. I don't mind wasting his money, I just don't like wasting my time."

Still later, Trace said, "I'm going to make a phone call."

He did, and when he came back to the bar, he said, "Sister Glorious must be home. She's not at the mosque and she's not at the granary."

"Granary?" Chico said.

"The food store next to the headquarters. Listen. Let's stop by her apartment on the way home."

"What for?"

" 'Cause I want to look in her eyes and tell her that we're snooping after her for her husband and see what she's got to say to that," Trace said.

"There's a couple of problems with that," Chico said.

"Name two."

"One, doesn't that destroy your ability to find out anything bad about her? I mean, if she knows what you're up to? And two, isn't that betraying your client's confidence?"

"Answers. *Birinci*. One. Probably, but I'm not finding out anything anyway, and if I'm going to fail, this will at least save time and let me spend more time out drinking with you. *Ikinci*. Two. About betraying our client's confidence. Who cares?"

"Good thinking," Chico said. "Let's go."

When they saw what was outside police headquarters, Razoni and Jackson almost wished for the return of the pickets from Salamanda's movement.

Standing in a straggly line before the building were a man wearing leotards, ballet slippers, and a shiny knee-length leather coat; a woman in an artist's smock with Harpo Marx blond curls peeking out from under a railroad cap; a man over six and a half feet tall with long blond hair and a formal suit; an elderly woman in a satin dress and white fur stole who paused every so often in marching past the front door to take a sip from a Thermos bottle she had around her neck on a lanyard.

"Oh, oh," Razoni said. "The Addams family's here. I'll still take the old lady."

The picketers were carrying signs. Ferenc Marichal's read: END POLICE BRUTALITY. Charmaine Marichal carried one with the legend: NEVER AGAIN. The butler's sign read: FREEDOM NOW.

And Mother Marichal carried a sign that Razoni and Jackson had to cross the street to read. It was hand-lettered and said: " 'The law has no claim to human respect. It has no civilizing mission; its only purpose is to protect exploitation.'—Kropotkin."

"What do you think, Tough?" asked Razoni as they approached the Marichal menagerie.

"I kind of think that that Kropotkin may have something."

Mother Marichal saw them first. The Thermos bottle was at her lips and she sputtered in surprise, spattering the front of her white gown with drops of red wine.

"There they are," she cried. "There are the despoilers."

"Calm down, Mama," said Razoni.

She raised her sign to strike Razoni on the head. He danced back nimbly and the sign missed by three feet.

"Listen, you can all go home," Razoni said. "We're releasing Karen now."

"We don't want to go home," Mr. Marichal said.

"What?"

"We're going to stay. We want to draw the spotlight of world opinion to the abuses of our outmoded law-enforcement system."

Razoni turned in disgust. "Just hang on a few minutes and you can have another recruit. We're sending Karen out."

On the steps, Jackson consoled his partner. "They won't stay long," he said.

"No?"

"No. Mama is almost out of wine," Jackson said.

Inside a holding cell, Razoni told the young woman, "We're letting you go, sweetie."

"Oh?"

"Yeah. I still think you did it, but everybody else wants to let you go."

"What about Abigail?"

"She's home, honey. We found her where you had her hid," said Razoni.

"Is she all right?"

"She's fine," Jackson said. "Your family's outside."

"I think they're picketing." said Jackson.

"Or having a picnic," Razoni said. "It's hard to tell. Try to get them out of here, will you? And you're not allowed to leave town."

"Why not?"

"Because the investigation is still going on. And unless somebody finds somebody else killed the lizard, you and your sweetie there are still suspects one and two."

"You're hateful."

"I'm lovable," Razoni said. "Too bad, you'll never find out."

After Karen Marichal left, the two detectives sat quietly in the room for a few minutes before the silence exceeded Razoni's attention span and he said, "Tough, I'm going to let you do something I never thought I would."

"What?"

"Buy me a drink."

At the Red Horse Tavern, Razoni said, "I don't think that fag really had Jack Daniels in his house. I bet that was some cheap crap poured into a Jack Daniels bottle."

"You think the head of the biggest television network in the world pours cheap mash into expensive bottles?" Jackson said.

"Sure. Then he bills his company for Jack Daniels."

"You know, Ed. You're probably right. I bet he could knock down fifty or sixty dollars a year that way."

"Damn right I'm right."

On the next drink, Jackson said, "You know what's wrong with those girls as suspects?"

"What?"

"They don't have any motive," Jackson said.

Razoni said, "That's not so. They just don't have any motive that we know about."

Jackson said, "That's true."

During the next drink, Jackson said, "Who does have a motive?"

"I'll play your silly game," Razoni said. "Who does have a motive?"

"Nobody that I know of." Jackson said.

"Me neither," Razoni said.

Fourth drink, Razoni said, "One thing puzzles me."

Jackson said, "Add it to the list of the many things that puzzle me. What?"

Razoni said, "The flowers. In the refrigerator."

"What are you talking about?"

"If the lizard ate the roses, why was there another dozen roses in the refrigerator? I saw them when I was looking for a beer."

"Yeah. I saw them," Jackson said. "Maybe somebody just likes roses."

"Sure," Razoni said. "Why not? Even Marvin likes roses. Marvin. Our captain's name is Marvin." His laughter was interrupted by the telephone ringing.

There was no doorman in sight inside the elegant marble-walled lobby of Gloria Alcetta's apartment building. A directory over the doorman's desk showed that G. CHARTERMAN lived in Apartment 317.

"Charterman?" Chico said as they walked to the elevator.

"Her maiden name," Trace said. "Let's surprise her. Maybe we'll find her in bed with the Italian national soccer team."

Gloria's apartment was at the end of the hall, its front

door hidden from view in a small alcove. The door was ajar.

Trace rang the buzzer set into the frame alongside the doorway, then rang it again and again. No answer.

"Not home," Chico said.

"A true detective is persevering above all things," Trace said. "And also a snoop."

He pushed open the door and called out, "Mrs. Alcetta?"

No answer, and he and Chico stepped inside, leaving the hallway door open.

"Mrs. Alcetta?" Trace called again. The living room they were standing in was furnished in that elegant way that only underfurnished apartments managed. There were two small sofas in the center of the floor, facing each other across a marble-topped coffee table. There was a small dining table in a far corner and a stereo set against the other wall. Dried flowers sat in tall vases on the floor. There was a fireplace in the long wall and above it was a painting of Salamanda, seated majestically, wearing white robes. Trace recognized him from all the newspaper photos he had seen in the past two days.

"Mrs. Alcetta?" Trace called out again.

Chico looked around the apartment. "We should send your mother up here," she said. "Can you imagine how a few plaster knickknacks would look in here?" She looked at the stereo rack of tapes and said, "Sitar music. I didn't think anybody really listened to that anymore."

Trace walked to the back of the apartment. The small kitchenette was empty. He pushed open the door to another room, started to call out, "Mrs. . . ." then stopped and Chico saw him run inside.

When she followed him, Trace was in the center of the floor, kneeling alongside the body of a woman.

"Is that Gloria?"

Trace nodded. "Somebody bashed in her head."

"Is she. . . ?"

"Yes. And a while too. She's cold."

He stood up and looked around the bedroom. The living

room had been sparsely furnished and elegant; the bedroom made up for it. It was crammed with furniture—dressers, a desk, cardboard boxes—and the room gave signs of having been ransacked. Papers from the desk were strewn on the floor. Contents of some cardboard storage boxes had been emptied out.

"Looks like somebody tossed the place," Trace said.

"What do we do now?" Chico said. She tried, but was unable to keep her eyes off the face of the beautiful dead redhead.

"Much as I hate it, I think we've got to call the cops," Trace said.

"There's something under the bed," Chico said. Trace bent down and started to reach for it and Chico said, "No. It might be a weapon."

Trace lifted the edge of the bedspread and peered under. "I think you're right," he said. "It looks like a blunt instrument to me. Some kind of statuette or something. And it's got blood on one end."

"Nice," Chico said. "There goes my appetite."

"If you think that's going to ruin your appetite, wait until you see what comes next." Trace said.

"What's that?"

"I've got to call Razoni and Jackson."

"You know what I hate? Besides you two?" Razoni snarled.

"I'm sure you'll tell us," Chico said.

"The way you two beanbags keep pestering us. Don't you think we have anything else to do but run around after you two?"

"Sorry," Chico said. "Our mistake. We thought the police would be interested in a murder."

"The police, the police. Right," Razoni said. "You get the police by calling Nine-Eleven if the goddamn number isn't broken. You don't get the police by pestering Tough and me every chance you get. Do we look like the police?"

"He does," Chico said, pointing to the burly black detective who was standing next to Trace on the other side of the bedroom door. "You sort of look like somebody from the ten-most-wanted list."

"Oh, yeah?"

Trace said to Jackson, "They're at it again."

"Good," Jackson said softly. "Keeps them occupied. Did you touch anything, Tracy?"

"No. That looks like the weapon under the bed, but I kept my hands off it. Didn't even touch the doorknobs."

"Good. That may make things easier."

"Chico found out something important, though," Trace said.

"What's that?"

Behind them, Chico and Razoni had worked their way up to full-throated shouting.

"Let her tell you. It'll make her feel good and maybe it'll cut the noise level in here."

"Good idea," Jackson said. He called out, "Miss Mangini."

Chico stopped in midyell and looked at him.

"What was it you learned?" Jackson asked her.

"I was trying to tell this idiot, but he wouldn't listen."

"I don't listen," Razoni said. "He's the listening partner. You want to say something, you say it to him, not to me, 'cause I don't ever want to have to listen to you again."

"Suits me, Guido," Chico said, turning her back on him. "I went downstairs to talk to the doorman," she told Jackson. "He said he didn't see anybody coming in or asking for Gloria Charterman. But he said there was a car parked in front, in that no-parking spot near the garbage cans, earlier today. He recognized the car."

"Oh?" Jackson said. Behind her, Razoni was shifting weight from foot to foot in an obvious wish that she would get on with it.

"Yeah. He said it was a brown Lincoln and it had a bumper strip on the front that said ITALIANS MAKE THE BEST LOVERS."

"That's true anyway," Razoni said.

"Harrr," Chico said. "Anyway, the doorman's seen the car before, and so have we. Angelo Alcetta. He's got a car like that with those bumper strips." She looked over her shoulder at Razoni. "Another Italian monument to bad taste and poor judgment."

"Car's not there now, is it?" Jackson said. "I didn't see any car."

Chico answered, "No, the doorman said he saw it just before noon. It was there about an hour and he was thinking of calling the police about moving it."

"He could have called us," Razoni said. "All the pests call us. Why not him?"

"I gave him your number so he can do that next time," Chico said. "Anyway, he said he had to go to the bathroom, and when he came back, the car was gone."

"You've seen the car?" Jackson asked Trace.

Trace nodded. "Alcetta was in the office to tell us to keep looking into his wife's affairs. When he drove away, we saw the car with that stupid bumper strip on it."

"Okay," Jackson said. "I guess maybe we ought to get the precinct cops here and see that somebody picks up Alcetta. You two are going to have to hang around to give statements."

"Not to to me," Razoni said. "I'm not taking any statements. I don't work twenty-four hours a day. I want to go home."

"We'll get rid of it when the others get here," Jackson said. He reached for the telephone, picking it up carefully with a handkerchief.

"When you call them, tell them to book these two for withholding evidence," Razoni said.

"Get lost," Chico said. "We didn't withhold anything."

"For impeding an investigation," Razoni said.

"All we did was call you," Trace said.

"That probably qualifies," Chico said.

Jackson hung up the telephone and Trace said, "Another thing. We heard from Gloria herself and from that

Gildersleeve at the Temple of Love that Alcetta had threatened both the Swami and Gloria.''

''Don't tell us.'' Razoni said. ''Tell the precinct cops.''

Jackson ignored him. ''It may just be that Angelo's temper has gotten him into real trouble,'' he said.

''That's the way it is with Italians,'' Chico said.

33

Trace's Log: Three o'clock in the bleeding morning and Chico has finally gone to bed. I know she's mad because she spent an hour rearranging my mother's plastic ashtrays and genuine-wood plaques that say WELCOME TO WILDWOOD, NEW JERSEY.

What's she got to be mad about? So she expected I'd buy her dinner after her own very first case, and so I didn't get a chance to because we found that stupid body, but it's not like she didn't eat. Every cop in New York kept trying to hit on her and bring her a Big Mac. Aaah, she'll get over it and I'll buy her dinner tomorrow or sometime. Maybe I'll get her something nice in a T-shirt. Maybe with the legend ITALIANS MAKE THE BEST LOVERS.

You know, world, when I came to New York on this misbegotten adventure, I thought I might hang up my tape recorder. Put the little frog microphone away in the bottom of a drawer somewhere and never use it again.

Hah! Fat chance. Now I've got a jacket pocket filled with tapes and I don't think it's ever going to get any better.

Somehow Chico conned them and she doesn't have to, but the cops have warned me that I'm going to be called before a grand jury most likely. And then the grand jury is going to indict Angelo Alcetta and then I'm going to spend eternity standing up on the bottom of the Hudson River with my feet embedded in cement. Way to go, Trace. Way to go. The only good thing is that the cops tonight were

240

professional and we didn't have to deal with that lunatic Razoni.

Where is Sarge when we need him? Why is he gallivanting around Puerto Rico or the high seas or wherever he is by now?

So why did Angelo Alcetta kill his wife? Was he that mad that she was leaving him? He killed her. The cops found a button from his jacket on the floor in the bedroom. That and parking that stupid recognizable car of his right in front of the building make a pretty good case.

He must have a temper, but I still don't figure him for killing Salamanda, even though Brother Gildersleeve told me today that he had threatened the Swami and Gloria too. Poisoned roses don't seem like the thing Angelo would do. Maybe Brother Gildersleeve killed them all. Why not? He's from Pittsburgh, and people from Pittsburgh will do anything. Chico's mother comes from near Pittsburgh, and she loots for the Pittsburgh Pilots or that's what she tells me. How do I know Gildersleeve's from Pittsburgh? Aha, and here you thought I wasn't a great detective. I know he's from Pittsburgh because he said "pot" and "caught" and pronounced them both the same way, and they do that only in Pittsburgh. Trust me, this is just another one of the things in which I am expert. I have a good ear. Like I know people from Philadelphia say they're from Full-uff-ya, and if I were from Philadelphia, I'd try to hide the fact too.

It occurs to me I'm going to get my ass hauled before a grand jury and I may wind up losing my private-eye license before I ever get a chance to apply for one. They may put a black mark next to my name and never let me get a gun. I don't want to live in a world where Chico's armed and I'm not.

Maybe I'll be a writer. Antiwar tracts. *Johnny Got His Gat* has a ring to it, doesn't it?

I think when they try to blacklist me they should take into consideration the fact that I found out about who took that TV tape of the Swami getting killed and I did what a good citizen would do, I told the cops, or at least the Razoni and Jackson contingent of them. That's a good service. And I made one old lady happy by making her think I was Roone Arledge and I was going to fire Howard Cosell. Do all our acts of kindness go unnoticed in this world?

Gloria Alcetta told me her husband threatened her. I told that to the cops too, and it occurs to me that I have not really bent over backward to protect the best interests of our client, Angelo.

Well, that's it, folks. *Birinci, icinci,* and *ucuncu.* One, two, three, I'm going to bed. If Chico will have me. I wonder why Angelo Alcetta didn't close the door behind him when he left Gloria's apartment.

34

"You are Mr. Tracy?"

The man who asked the question was courtly and, despite the summer heat, was wearing a homburg and carrying a dark gabardine raincoat over his arm. His almost-dancerly shoes were mirror-shined; his silk handkerchief matched his silk tie; his skin was olive-tinted tan.

Trace nodded and the man said, "I am Armando Alcetta. May I come in?"

"Please do," Trace said. He rose behind the desk and Chico got up from the sofa where she had been sitting. Alcetta smiled when he saw her. Trace turned on his recorder.

"This is my associate, Miss Mangini," Trace said.

"Yes. I saw your name in the paper, Miss Mangini. I did not expect you would look quite so . . ."

"Un-Italian?" Chico said.

"Beautiful," Alcetta corrected.

"Thank you," Chico said as she took the man's raincoat and hat and hung them on the coat rack in the corner of the room.

"I am Angelo Alcetta's father," the old man said as he shook Trace's hand, then sat down on the threadbare sofa. Young Alcetta had declined to sit on the couch because he didn't like its looks and alibied that it might wrinkle his trousers. The elder Alcetta obviously didn't worry about wrinkled trousers, and looking at him, Trace knew why. His trousers wouldn't wrinkle because they didn't dare.

"What can I do for you, Mr. Alcetta?" Trace asked.

243

"You can prove my son innocent, Mr. Tracy," the man said wearily.

Trace looked at him for a moment, then glanced away. Through the frosted glass of the office door, he could see the figure of a man waiting outside. Armando Alcetta had not come alone.

"Your son hasn't been charged with anything yet," Trace said. It was odd, he thought. Angelo Alcetta tried his hardest to look like a Mafia don and wound up looking ridiculous. His father tried to look like an Italian bank president and wound up looking like the King of Sicily in mufti.

"But he will be," Alcetta said. "I would want you to help him if you could."

"I don't know how I can do that," Trace said. "You probably know, Miss Mangini and I found the body last night. I've been warned I'll have to testify before a grand jury. I will have to tell the truth." Trace thought the old man was a real presence because, instinctively, Trace had slipped into Alcetta's formal speech patterns. It vaguely annoyed him.

"I would not ask you to lie," the old man said. His fingertips were bridged in front of him on his lap and he had the sleek bulged belly of the elderly well-fed. He looked off at the far wall where the *Playboy* centerfolds had once hung, as if he could see back in time and still saw them and was weighing their qualifications.

"Why me?" Trace asked. "There are a lot of detectives in this town."

"You are Devlin Tracy," Alcetta intoned emotionlessly. "You live in Las Vegas, where you own a condominium. You are employed as a freelance investigator by Garrison Fidelity Insurance Company. This agency is owned by your father, Retired Police Sergeant Patrick Tracy. The two of you have the same reputation: that you are honest and trustworthy. On a case, you were both described to me as dogs with bones in their mouth, not letting go until you had chewed your way through. That is not meant to be unflattering, Mr. Tracy. It is a compliment. You will, neither of you, be bought off or run off. My Angelo needs that kind of help."

He looked up and Trace said, "And you are Armando Alcetta and I suspect that you run a small food-importing business—olive oil, no doubt—and I think I resent you having your henchmen go prying about into my father's and my business."

Alcetta held up a hand in a defensive gesture. "Forgive me," he said. "I understand your feeling. Please try, though, to understand mine. My only son is about to be charged with one murder, possibly two. I want help for him and I want to be sure that that help is good help."

"Suppose we find that Angelo committed both murders? He was heard to threaten both people. His car was seen outside his wife's apartment. His jacket button was found in the murder room."

"I want you to look and find the truth," Alcetta said. "You will not find Angelo to be a killer. He is innocent."

"If he has an alibi for the murder, why do you need us?"

"There are people who will swear, truthfully, that they saw Angelo. He was busy on company business. If possible, I do not want those witnesses dragged into this matter and will call on them only as a last resort. There is another reason. I can clear Angelo, but that will not bring about the apprehension of the real killer. You can do that."

"I still don't know why us," Trace said.

"First of all, because you already know Angelo through your work regarding his wife. Second, because you are already involved in the case from having discovered poor Gloria's body. Third, for the reasons I mentioned earlier. I have cause to believe you will not be frightened from seeking the truth, no matter what handy conclusions the police wish to jump to."

Trace would have sworn the man used a kind of tooth gloss because his teeth were snow-white and sparkled like pearls. Then he realized that what they were was just a very good, very white set of false teeth. This was an old man worried about his only son.

"Let me ask you this," Trace said. "Why was Angelo

so upset about his marriage breaking up? Lots of marriages do.''

"We select our spouses," the old man said, "but God selects our children.''

"What exactly does that mean?''

"It means that my son is basically a good boy at heart. But he has a loose lip and I suspect that he feared he had spoken to Gloria of things he should not have told her. Family matters. I am sure he feared offending me if she should repeat any of the things that he said in some divorce matter.''

"I don't think threatening her life in front of witnesses was the way to get her to cooperate," Trace said.

"My son is not always discreet or wise. Sometimes, the boy is a fool. I wish it were not so, but that is it. And there you have it. Will you take this case for me?''

"My father is the senior partner in the firm," Trace said. "I think I should talk to him first.''

"What do you think his answer will be?" Alcetta asked.

Trace thought of the company's ridiculous ledgers inside the center desk drawer. "I think he'll say take the case.''

As Alcetta rose, Trace said, "But with one proviso. If we find Angelo innocent, we'll tell you. If we find evidence that makes him guilty, we will tell the police.''

"That is fair enough, Mr. Tracy," Alcetta said. He handed Trace a business card. "I can be reached at that telephone number twenty-four hours a day. I will not interfere with your conduct of the case. However, as a concerned parent, I wish you would keep me abreast of anything you may find.''

"Assuming my father says yes," Trace said.

"Of course." Alcetta withdrew an envelope from inside his jacket. "Against that likelihood, I have a retainer for you in here." He put the white silk-threaded envelope on the desk in front of Tracy. "There is five thousand dollars in there. I trust that will suffice for a start. Please let me know when you need more.''

He extended his hand and Trace shook it. It was a firm hand, dry, not sweaty, surprisingly large.

Alcetta took his hat and coat from the rack, nodded to

Trace, then stopped at the door and said formally, "Miss Mangini."

"Mr. Alcetta," she said.

He let himself out. Chico started to speak but Trace silently shushed her with a finger across his lips.

He waited a full thirty seconds, then went to the door and looked out into the hallway. Satisfied there was no one there, he went to the front window. Chico joined him, looking down into the street, where a large black Lincoln limousine was slowly pulling away from the curb.

Chico jumped up into the air and squealed, "I love it," she said. "Michiko Mangini, Mafia detective. You think he can help me get a gat?"

"I think he could probably help you get a Sherman tank," Trace said.

"He seems like a nice man," she said.

"You always respond to threats that way?"

"What threats?" she asked.

"Do you really think he did all that research just to satisfy himself that we were pure heart and clean hands?" Come on. The next sentence out of his mouth would have been 'Ve know vere your family liffs.' All that courtly bullshit. It's all threats."

"Oh, come on, Trace. You're paranoid."

"When you deal with the Mafia, it doesn't hurt to be paranoid."

"I think he's just worried about Angelo," Chico said.

"I don't doubt it. I just don't know if Sarge will want anything to do with these people. It might not be good for his reputation."

"Talk him into it. Mangini, Mafia detective. Talk him into it. Besides, we need the money."

She was standing at the desk. She had fished the yellow rose Sarge had given her from the waste-paper basket where Trace had tossed it. She pressed the sharp angle-cut stem against Trace's throat. "Otherwise you're really in trouble," she said.

The telephone rang and Trace said, "You get it. It might be the ex."

Chico said, "Mangini and Tracy investigations," then

said, "Hello, darling. Yes, I changed the billing. Whoever answers the phone gets top billing. It's Sarge," she said to Trace, handing him the telephone.

"Hello, son, from the sunny isle of Puerto Rico. How's it going?" Sarge said.

"Terrific," Trace said. "I'm having my ass hauled before a grand jury and I've got you a great new client."

"Who?"

"The Mafia," Trace said.

"Don't take any checks," Sarge said.

"Levity. I'm going before a grand jury and what I get is levity."

"I think maybe you ought to explain what's going on," Sarge said.

"Remember the dead Swami we had when you were here?"

"Right."

"Well, now we've got a dead Gloria Alcetta." Briefly, Trace filled his father in on the facts of the case.

"So they're going to book Angelo?"

"It seems that way. Unless we get him off the hook for the old man."

"Your client is going to be arrested, the woman you were watching is murdered. You've done real well in your first case, son," Sarge said dryly.

"I don't need you abusing me," Trace said.

"And you're really going before a grand jury?"

"The cops told me I probably would," Trace said.

"Hallelujah," Sarge said.

"Hallelujah? I'm going up the river and I get hallelujah?"

"You're not going up the river. And yes, hallelujah, because now I have an excuse to get on the next plane and come home."

"Cruise is that bad, huh?"

"Son, you never saw the like of it. Five hundred fat women who look exactly like your mother and their miserable husbands playing horse-racing on the deck with six-inch-square dice and brooms with horses' heads on them."

"How you doing?" Trace asked.

"I'm behind six dollars. And then they eat. Seven times

a day they eat. And don't skip a dessert or you're being cheated. I sweat cholesterol. I've got to get out of here before I die. Everybody on this ship has had a coronary bypass already. I've got to get home before I'm next.''

"Sarge, I need you. Come home,'' Trace said.

"I knew you'd understand,'' Sarge said. "Let me ask you something.''

"Go ahead.''

"Do you think Angelo did it?''

"I don't have a better suspect,'' Trace said.

"What does Chico think?''

"She thinks no,'' Trace said.

"I'm on her side,'' Sarge said. "Five thousand dollars, you say?''

"In hundreds.''

"I'm on my way, son. Don't spend it till I get there.''

35

"Look at it this way, Ed. It beats doing traffic duty."

"Serving warrants is the same as doing traffic duty," Razoni said. "It's for somebody with no experience."

"Or somebody on the shit list," Jackson said.

"It's all right if they want to punish you, but why they've got to drag me down with you I'll never know," Razoni said. He glared at Jackson belligerently as if the huge black man were the source of all Razoni's problems, past, present, and future.

"It's just Captain Mannion's way of protecting us," Jackson said. "Keep us out of sight until things blow over."

"But, dammit, that's what's wrong. We were supposed to find that little fagola and we found her. If they leave us alone, we'd solve that freaking lizard murder too. I saw those two bastards, what's their name, Gault and Gorman, those two precinct bulls up at headquarters, and they did everything but spit at me."

"What'd you do?" Jackson said.

"I spit at them. What the hell else could I do? I'll tell you, Tough, they *knew* we were going on warrants. Everybody knows. We're humiliated," Razoni said.

"Our day will come again," Jackson said philosophically. "Then we'll get even."

"You bet your butt we will. They'll have some job nobody else can do and they'll have to give it to us and we'll do it, and then somebody will get mad at you for something and I'll take the blame," Razoni said. "Stop all the talk. Just keep your eyes open for"—he looked at a card on his lap—"Pedro González. Can you beat that? Trying to find Pedro González in this town is like trying to find Booker T. Washington."

"You're behind the times," Jackson said. "This year it wouldn't be hard to find a Booker T. Washington. I'd hate to be looking for a Muhammad X, though. There he is."

Casually, Jackson slid the car into a parking spot, a half-block down the street from a neighborhood tavern.

"Where?" said Razoni.

"He was in the doorway of the saloon. He's little."

"Of course, he's little. Did you expect Pedro González to be playing tackle for the Jets?" Razoni was getting out of the car. He started walking casually back toward the corner.

The small man in powder-blue shirt and slacks who stood in the doorway of the tavern saw the big hard-faced man coming toward him and instinctively ducked back inside the tavern.

Over his head, Razoni waved toward Jackson, then went into the bar. The room was crowded and reverberated with the sounds of Spanish chatter, which always had sounded to Razoni like people yelling "Meeta, meeta, meeta."

He found room at the bar. While he waited for the bartender, he watched two old men playing dominoes at a table across from the bar. Each one slammed his domino down as if it were the delivery of an insult.

They talked as they played. "Meeta, meeta, meeta."

The bartender arrived in front of Razoni. "*Señor?*" he said.

"Right," said Razoni. "*Sí.* Pedro González. See Pedro González? I look for Pedro González. Meeta, meeta, meeta meeta."

The bartender looked Razoni over carefully. "I think I saw Pedro go into the back." He motioned toward a large back room where people sat sipping drinks and playing dominoes and dice.

"Muchas thank you," Razoni said. He walked toward the broad flower-bordered archway entrance to the back room. He stood there looking around at the tables. Ten seconds. Twenty seconds. Of course, Pedro González was not there. Thirty seconds. Forty seconds. Enough. Enough time for Pedro González to have scooted out of the men's room where he was hidden and to have run out the front door behind Razoni.

He turned and walked back toward the bar's entrance.

"You find him, señor?" asked the bartender, eyes twinkling. The others at the bar chuckled.

"No, Fidel, I didn't find him because I didn't look in the men's room. But I'll find him out front. Meeta, meeta, meeta."

He waved at the confused bartender and strolled out the front door where the small Puerto Rican in the powder-blue shirt and slacks was struggling in the massive arms of Jackson.

"Pedro González," Razoni said. "It is my great pleasure to inform you that you are under arrest."

"Foke you, peeg."

"Listen to him, Tough. He can't even say pig. If you people are going to come to this country and use up all the black folks' welfare money, why don't you learn to talk right?" He sounded more interested than annoyed and paused as if truly waiting for an answer.

There was none so, each holding a wrist, they walked Pedro González back to the car. Razoni pushed the small man into the front seat between the two detectives.

"Why you peek me up?"

"We peek you up because there is warrant for joo arrest," said Razoni. "Joo no pay the two thousand dollar in traffic teekets. Now shut joo mouth, you make me seek."

Three blocks away was a precinct house, and Jackson waited while Razoni went in and turned Pedro González over to the desk sergeant, along with the warrant and a few thousand well-chosen words about how, if the precinct detectives were more efficient, major criminal masterminds like Pedro González would not be free to walk the streets, eating up the time of important detectives who had other things to do.

When Razoni got back outside, Jackson was not in the

car. He returned after a few minutes and Razoni said, "Well?"

"I called the captain. The precinct bulls, Gault and Gorman, want to talk to Karen Marichal and Abigail Longworth about the Swami's murder."

"Good. I hope they fry," Razoni said.

"Who? The girls or the detectives?"

"All of them," Razoni said. "They're all fags."

36

"God, I hate this traffic," Trace said.

"Will you stop complaining?" Chico said. "You've done nothing but complain since we got back to New York."

"I have very carefully not complained since we got back to New York," Trace said. "But I wouldn't mind if you'd take out your gat and jump out and shoot about ten thousand of these bastards. We're going to be late."

"Don't worry," Chico said. "Sarge will wait for us, and besides, those planes from San Juan are always late. You know what I would have done if I were Angelo Alcetta?"

"Kill your wife with a bat instead of a club?"

"Don't get smart. I think if I wanted to kill my wife, I wouldn't have parked my very identifiable car right in front of her apartment for one and all to see."

"No," Trace said. "That's what you wouldn't do if you were Angelo Alcetta with *your* brains. But Angelo Alcetta with *his* brains might very well have done just that."

"It doesn't ring true," she said. "Nobody's that stupid."

"Angelo Alcetta is."

When Sarge saw them waiting for him in the terminal building, he dropped to the floor and kissed the ground like the Pope returning to Rome after a world tour.

He had no luggage. "I left it on the ship with your mother," he said. "What the hell, they were all her clothes anyway." He hugged Chico and said to Trace, "Had an interesting few days, haven't you?"

"You know me. Do anything for a buck. I figured being a Mafia private eye would probably be good for business." Besides, the ex called to invite me to dinner. Maybe if it gets in the papers that I work for the mob, she'll leave me alone."

Sarge opened the windows of the car as they drove back to New York. "Oh, what a pleasure to breathe dirt again. I've inhaled so much salt air in the last two days, my legs are swollen."

Trace and Chico filled him in on the events since he'd gone. He started to chuckle as Trace told him of the run-in with Razoni and Jackson, who thought that Trace was following them.

"That doesn't seem so funny to me," Trace said. "The one's a homicidal maniac, if I ever saw one."

"Just funny your running into them," Sarge said.

"You know them?"

"I've heard of them. They're special cops."

"Sure are," Trace said. "Homicidal maniac cops."

Sarge shook his head. "They work out of the commissioner's office. I know the guy who works there, Marv Mannion. We were rookies together. And this Razoni and Jackson, I'm told, get everything nobody else in the department can handle."

"It's hard to square Razoni that I met with somebody who can do something," Chico said. "All that lunatic does is yell and complain."

"Just telling you their reputation," Sarge said.

Trace got lost with the two of them shouting directions, so instead of going back to Sarge's house in Queens, they wound up in Manhattan. Sarge offered to buy them dinner at Bogie's and before Trace could say a word, Chico had accepted for the two of them.

"Sam Silverand?"

The young man who answered the door was rail-thin, acned, and had scarecrow hair. He nodded, and his Ad-am's Apple jumped up and down nervously, like a neurotic elevator trying desperately to find a floor it liked. His eyes were bloodshot.

"I'm Detective Jackson and this is Detective Razoni. We'd like to talk to you."

"Sure. About what?"

"Swami Salamanda," Jackson said.

"Oh. Okay. What do you want to know?"

"Can we come in?" Jackson said.

"Sure. Sorry. Come on in."

He led them into a large one-room apartment that looked as if it had been rented to Dr. Jekyll and Mr. Hyde. The right half of the apartment was a stove, a refrigerator, a small kitchen table, a couch that opened into an unmade bed, and a television set, all of it looking as if none of it had been cleaned since he had moved in. The left side of the apartment was a different story: a whole wall of complicated-looking camera equipment, console boards, and TV monitors. It looked as neat as an IBM laboratory.

Jackson took out his notebook as Silverand gestured then to the kitchen table, which he cleaned by lifting up the plastic tablecloth with everything in it and depositing it all in the sink.

"Can I get you something? All I've got is coffee," the young man said.

"Not in this place," Razoni said.

Silverand shrugged. As the two detectives sat down, he went to the stove and lit the gas under a pot of water. "I'm going to have some anyway. What can I do for you?"

"We understand you took some TV film of the Swami the day he died," Jackson said.

"Tape," Silverand said, and when Jackson looked up, he said, "TV tape. Half-inch. Not film."

"Right," Jackson said. "Do you have it?"

"No. I sold it to United Broadcasting. I took it up there and they liked it so they bought it from me."

"But they never showed it?" Jackson said.

"That's right."

"Why?" Jackson asked.

"I don't know."

"That must have been pretty disappointing."

Silverand shook his head and gave a slow wide-mouthed grin.

"No. It got me a job."

"How'd that happen?" Jackson said.

"I got a call from Theodore Longworth himself. He's the boss at United Broadcasting."

"A faggot," Razoni said.

Jackson glared at him and nodded to Silverand. "Go on, please."

"Well, he called and said that he'd reviewed the tape—he reviews all news tapes—and while the technical quality was a little low, he thought it showed real promise and he offered me a job as a cameraman. It's what I always wanted."

"Were you a follower of the Swami's?" Jackson asked.

Silverand shook his head.

"But you shot a lot of film . . . excuse me, tape, there, didn't you?"

"I was there a lot," Silverand admitted. "A lot of girls there. You know, House of Love and all."

"You went over there to score?" Razoni said.

"Cheaper than singles bars."

"Did you know Sister Glorious?"

"Yes," Silverand said. "The nicest lady, and beautiful. I told her I wanted to do a documentary on the Swami so she let me film there. None of the raunchy stuff where everybody was playing grab-ass but everything else."

"You know anybody who might want to kill her?" Jackson said.

"No. The paper said her husband killed her," Silverand said. "What a jerk he must be."

"Always checking," Jackson said with a shrug. "Just to make sure our case is solid."

Silverand made a cup of instant coffee. He spilled half of it on the kitchen-sink top.

"Did you notice anything unusual the day Salamanda got killed?" Jackson asked.

"No. A usual thing. They did it every Sunday, welcome new members and all."

258 — Warren Murphy

"The girl who brought in the roses, you got her on tape?" Jackson asked, writing in his notebook.

"Sure. I shot the whole ceremony, but when the Swami turned up his heels, I split and came back here to check out the tape. It was real good stuff, I thought."

"And now United Broadcasting has it?"

Silverand sipped his coffee, then shook his head. "It got destroyed. Longworth told me. That's one of the reasons he felt so bad, I think, and offered me the job. Do you know how long I've wanted to work for a TV station?"

Razoni was standing at the TV console board, looking through a pile of tapes.

"Detective, excuse me. Please be careful over there. All that equipment's real delicate."

"Hey, pal. I never break anything," Razoni said. He was looking through a stack of eight-by-ten photos.

"So there's no way for us to see this film and the girl who brought in the flowers," Jackson said.

"I've got a picture of her."

"I thought you said the tape was destroyed."

"It was. But before I took it up to the station I made a couple of prints from it in case nobody wanted the tape. I thought I might be able to sell a couple of the stills to one of the newspapers or something."

"Did you try that?"

"No. Mr. Longworth told me that all the stuff on the tape was theirs exclusively when he offered me the job."

"You still have the still photos?" Jackson asked.

Silverand walked across the room to where Razoni was looking through a stack of glossy photographs.

"All you take is pictures of women," he said.

"Some people take pictures of trees. I like women."

"Me too," Razoni said as Silverand took the stack of photos from his hands. He looked through them quickly, then brought out two.

"Here," he said, walking back and handing them to Jackson. "That's her coming through the curtain and that's her sprinkling the flowers on the stage."

"Dear sweet Abigail," Jackson said to Razoni.

"We knew that," Razoni said.

"You're not going to get these published or anything, are you?" Silverand asked. "It'll cost me my job."

"No," Jackson said. "It's just for the investigation. They'll be returned when we're done."

"I guess that's all right, then," Silverand said.

Outside, Jackson said, "Very strange."

Razoni said, "Not strange. Ridiculous. That ugly guy thinking he could score."

"I'm not talking about that," Jackson said. "I'm talking about Longworth getting that tape and seeing his daughter killing the Swami, and then he destroys the tape and he calls the cops to secretly find his daughter."

"I think the bastard ought to be booked for destroying evidence," Razoni said. "Those faggots will do anything to keep another faggot out of jail."

"It's his daughter," Jackson said.

"Who cares?" Razoni said. "All I know is he busted our chops and he knows damn well where his daughter is. She's out killing lizards."

"I think we ought to do something with these pictures," Jackson said.

"Like what?" Razoni said.

"Like send them to Gault and Gorman, those two cops that are handling the case."

"Good," Razoni said. "But do it anonymously. I can't stand those bastards."

"Of course, anonymously," Jackson said with a grin. "Is there any other way?"

37

Trace's Log: Sorry, folks. I've got a lot of things I'd love to tell you, but I work for the Mafia now and they're not too hot on their people making tape recordings.

Try to understand.

38

J. J. Gildersleeve was on page one of the *Times* attacking the inept New York City police.

"It was bad enough," he told a reporter, "that the police have been totally unable to solve the murder of our great leader, Swami Salamanda. But now, Sister Glorious has been murdered too and the police still have taken no action."

He warned that thousands of Salamanda's followers will be in the city this weekend "and they will demand action from the New York City police."

Sarge, Chico, and Trace had coffee in the office and Trace received a phone call telling him to appear forthwith at the Manhattan district attorney's office.

Chico volunteered to drive him, and when she let him off, Trace recognized J. J. Gildersleeve walking into the building. "They must have called him too," Trace said.

Chico looked at Gildersleeve's back and nodded. "Hurry up, get out," she said. "I've got things to do."

"Stay out of trouble, will you please?" Trace said.

"Of course. Don't I always?"

In a rough, street-Irish kind of way, Retired Police Sergeant Patrick Tracy and Captain Marvin Mannion resembled each other. Both were red-faced and white-haired, although Sarge was much the bigger of the two men. But each had the same laugh crinkles at the corners of the eyes, the eyes of men who had seen a lot and had realized that if you were going to last, you had better learn to laugh.

It would have taken no imagination at all to picture each of them in a heavyweight blue uniform, swinging a nightstick out on a walking beat, being the terror of local neighborhood toughs.

That was, in truth, how both of them had started, in the same graduating class from the New York police academy. But while Tracy had stayed in the patrol division, finally becoming a sergeant and supervising men who walked a beat, Mannion had lucked into a good arrest and turned it into an appointment as a detective. Starting there, he had parlayed some solid skills as a detective, a rough-hewn kind of integrity, the tenacity of a bulldog, and an underappreciated political sense to move up the ladder until he had been promoted to captain and sent to the commissioner's office.

Some felt he actually ran the department because the police commissioner was a civilian and he trusted totally Mannion's judgment about what was happening in the department. The commissioner was the technical boss, but in the police world, which was broken down into "us" versus "them"—with them being anyone who wasn't a police officer—he was barred from close contact with the thirty thousand men he commanded. Mannion was his eyes, his ears, his adviser and confidant, and the one man in the department that the commissioner knew he could rely on for the plain, unvarnished truth.

Although they had been on the force during the same thirty years, Sarge and Mannion were not close, never drinking friends, but each had known of the other. At several times in their careers, cases had brought them together and they had worked well, hit it off well, did their work, talked about getting together afterward but never had. It was probably that they were too much alike.

Sarge had thought he might feel out of place in Mannion's office, but while Mannion had moved up in the hierarchy, he had not gone far from his roots. His suit was as cheap and rumpled as Sarge's, and his desk as marred with cigarette burns. Piles of papers were stacked seemingly without sense or order on a long bank of file cabinets behind his desk.

Mannion came from behind the desk to greet him. "Pat, how are you?"

"Good enough, Marv. But I'm disappointed."

"Why's that?" Mannion said as he steered Sarge to a chair before his desk.

"Big shot like you. I thought you'd be wearing silk jackets and T-shirts like all the real cops do nowadays. Come on, make me feel good; tell me you've got a red Corvette parked outside."

"There go your illusions, Pat. I've got a '79 Subaru wagon."

"No wonder this city isn't as crime-free as Miami," Sarge said as Mannion sat behind the desk.

"So what are you doing these days? You don't look like the fishing-at-the-Jersey-shore type to me."

"No. I'm running a little p.i. agency."

'How long you been doing that? Why didn't you let me know?"

"About a year," Sarge said. "I'm doing all right, so I figured I'd save you for when I was ready to move into a welfare hotel. But the agency's why I'm here."

"Anything I can do," Mannion said.

"It's the Alcetta case," Sarge said.

For a moment, Mannion looked blank, then snapped his fingers. "There was a Tracy involved in that. Found the woman's body the other night."

"My son," Sarge said. "He's probably coming into the agency with me."

"He a cop?"

"Insurance investigator," Sarge said. "He's all right, though. He's going straight."

"Let's see," Mannion said. "He was, well, I guess *you* were representing Alcetta in a divorce investigation. Is that what it was?"

Sarge nodded. "But now Old Man Alcetta has asked us to see what we can do for young Angelo," he said.

"We're off the record, right?" Mannion said. When

Sarge nodded, he said, "Sonny Alcetta is a two-bit punk and it looks like we got him cold."

"It might not be that easy," Sarge said.

"How's that?" Mannion asked. He leaned back and lit a cigarette. "You want some coffee?" he asked.

Sarge shook his head. "Now, this is confidential from my side, too, right?"

Mannion squinted at him through a wreath of cigarette smoke and nodded.

"When Old Man Alcetta talked to my son, he made it pretty clear that Alcetta's got an alibi for the day the woman was killed, but he'd rather not have to use it."

"We'll have to cross that bridge when we come to it," Mannion said.

"You don't believe that, Marv," Sarge said. "You know what's going to happen. If you bring Alcetta in on just circumstantial evidence, if it ever gets to a trial, the family's going to bring in two hundred witnesses, half of them priests, who are going to swear the kid was doing a novena in Chicago the day of the murder. Then they'll get somebody who'll take a fall and say he used the kid's car to frame him. You're going to come up empty."

"Another killer walks," Mannion said. "That's probably what drove you off the job. It's what makes me upchuck most mornings before I drink my coffee."

"It doesn't have to be this time," Sarge said. "Maybe."

"I'm listening."

"This was the deal my son made with the old man. If we find out the kid's innocent, we tell him. If we find out the kid's guilty, we tell the police."

"You really expect that he'd let you do that?" Mannion said.

"You know me, Marv. I think you know what I'll do," Sarge said.

Mannion stubbed out his cigarette and leaned over the desk, resting his chin on his hands.

"Yeah, I guess I do. So what can I do?"

"Those two guys who work for you. Razoni and Jackson. They're working this case for you?"

Mannion simply stared at him without confirmation in his face.

"Tell them to give us a hand, that we're on the same side," Sarge said.

"What do we get out of it?"

"We have access to the Alcetta family. Your guys can help us and we've got an idea of where to look from the police end. We'll find out if Alcetta's phonying any kind of alibi up. One hand washes the other." Sarge leaned forward over the desk, so that his face and Mannion's were only a foot apart.

"Before you say no, Marv, think about it. You got that guy in the paper this morning, rapping the force because they haven't made an arrest yet. My son's already been called up to the DA's office and you know some asshole assistant district attorney is going to try to get a quick indictment so he can get his ugly stupid mug on the six-o'clock news and later Alcetta gets off. The DA won't care, he got his headlines, but the department gets a black eye and some damned killer gets free. Let's find the real killer. If it's Alcetta, we'll help you nail him. If it's not and we find out who is, we give him to you. We need help, though. Think about it before you say no."

"What made you think I was going to say no?" Mannion said. "You got it, Pat. What else?"

Sarge squinted his eyes. "Wait a minute. Just like that?"

"It sounds like a good deal to me," Mannion said. "What's to argue about?"

"Why do I get this feeling that I've just played into your hands?" Sarge asked.

"Because you've got a suspicious nature," Mannion said. "You going to be in your office today?"

"Yeah."

"I'll have Razoni and Jackson contact you there. Where is it?"

"On West Twenty-sixth Street. They know where it is. They were there the other day."

"Okay," Mannion said. "Just one thing."

"What is it?" Sarge said.

"Nobody knows about this. Nobody. You, me, Razoni, and Jackson. Nobody else. Nobody talks to the press. Nobody talks to the Alcetta family. My ass is in a bind, Pat, if this gets out."

"Not a word," Sarge said.

The captain rose from the desk and the two policemen shook hands. Marv walked around the desk and escorted Sarge to the door.

"Thanks, Marv," said Sarge.

"Maybe something good'll happen," Mannion said.

"I just wish I knew why I think you put one over on me."

"Sleep on it," Mannion said. "Maybe it'll come to you."

Mannion closed the door behind his old companion, went back to his desk, and told the radio room to have Razoni and Jackson call in immediately.

He allowed himself another cigarette—even though he was trying to cut down—and an unaccustomed smile. He had not liked his two top detectives being sent to Siberia because of some big-shot television executive with high-level friends. Now, perhaps, they could keep working on the case without officially working on the case. Nobody had to be the wiser.

Of course, it all depended on Patrick Tracy keeping his word and his mouth shut, but Mannion had always played hunches. He had a hunch that he could trust Tracy's word.

He hoped so.

If not, he was in real big trouble.

39

From the newsstand in the lobby of the Hotel Palmer in midtown, Chico dialed the hotel's number.

"Hello," she said. "Would you please connect me with Mr. Gildersleeve's room?"

She heard the phone ring a long time and then the operator came back on. "I'm sorry. Mr. Gildersleeve doesn't answer."

"What room is that?" Chico asked. "Is that four-eighteen?"

"I'm sorry, ma'am. I can't give out that information. May I take a message?"

"No. That's all right. I'll call later," Chico said.

She hung up the telephone, bought and ate a candy bar as she looked at the headlines of the newspapers in the small stationery shop. Gildersleeve's picture was on page one of the *Post.*

Being a detective wasn't as easy as she thought. Things that you took for granted just couldn't be taken for granted. Like how did you find out what room someone was staying in when hotels would never tell you that. If Trace were around, he'd probably bribe a bellhop, but she didn't think she could pull that off easily. Maybe if she had a gun, she could threaten someone and make them tell her. No, that wouldn't work either.

She looked around the stationery store, then wandered to the greeting-card rack and bought a birthday card that came in a long thin pink envelope. It was one of the new wave of cards that equated insults with humor and said,

"You're only as old as you look." On the inside, it continued, "And you look like shit. Old shit."

The card cost two dollars. Chico paid for it and with a pen from her purse wrote on the envelope, "Mr. J. J. Gildersleeve, Hotel Palmer."

She sealed the card and brought it to the front desk. She told the clerk, "I'd like to leave this for Mr. Gildersleeve, please."

"Yes, ma'am," he said, and took the card.

Chico walked across the lobby, sat in a chair, and watched the clerk. He put the envelope on the counter while he answered a telephone call. After a long conversation, punctuated with much laughter, he hung up, took the envelope, and slipped it into one of the little rectangular mail slots in the large rack behind him.

She waited until the clerk was busy with a customer at the far end of the counter before walking over. The bright-pink envelope was clearly visible in the room slot marked Number 624.

The door to Room 624 was open and the maid was inside. Chico was a little disappointed because she had hoped to try opening the door with a credit card. But maybe, she thought, it would be better to practice that one at home before taking it on the road.

She breezed into the room as the maid was making the large double bed, dropped her purse in the chair, and said, "Dear, would you mind terribly if I asked you to come back in five minutes? I've got some important business calls to make." The young maid nodded and smiled when Chico pressed a five-dollar bill into her hand.

"I really appreciate it," Chico said. She closed the door behind the maid and locked it, then looked around the room. She knew that police detectives called searching a room a "tossing," and it certainly would be easier to toss a hotel room than an apartment. She searched the night tables on each side of the bed, but found nothing except a Gideon bible and two New York City phone books, one with white pages, the other with yellow.

In the center drawer of the small desk across the room, she found only a guidebook to New York City, a folder with hotel stationery, and a small note pad. She held the note pad at an angle, looking at the top blank page to see if she could read any impressions that might be on the paper, but couldn't see anything.

"So much for the movies," she mumbled to herself softly. She skimmed the pages of the guidebook. None of them had been dog-eared, but as she skimmed the pages, she saw an advertisement circled. It was for the E-Z Rider auto-rental agency. She jotted down the address on a piece of paper in her purse, then replaced the book inside the drawer.

The waste-paper basket produced nothing but Kleenexes.

A leather traveling bag was on the floor of the closet. Chico opened it and looked inside. The bag appeared empty, but she felt around with her fingers and touched something. She brought it out. It was a rose petal. A yellow petal. She put it in her purse.

She closed the door behind her and put out the sign for the maid to make up the room immediately, then rode down in the elevator.

She walked to the front entrance of the hotel without looking back. So she did not see J. J. Gildersleeve standing at the front desk, talking to the clerk, and she did not see the clerk point at her and she did not see J. J. Gildersleeve follow her toward the front door.

Sarge met with Razoni and Jackson at a corner table in Bogie's. Trace and Chico had been right, Sarge thought. Razoni *was* a grumbler and complainer.

"I don't know what the hell we're doing here," Razoni said. "Since when do we go into partnership with amateurs?"

"Amateur?" Sarge said. "Sonny, I was on the job when you were still stealing hubcaps."

Razoni started to answer, but Jackson said, "We're here because the captain told us to be here and maybe it's not a bad idea."

The three men finally got down to business and compared notes. There was precious little hard information to share.

The bartender called Sarge away to take a telephone call.

Chico said, "I thought I'd find you there. What are you up to?"

"Just having lunch with your old friends. Razoni and Jackson."

"Terrific. I need to know something," she said.

"What's that?" Sarge asked. Chico told him and Sarge left the phone dangling and walked back to the table.

"Chico's on the phone," he said.

"Who?" asked Razoni.

"The woman who works with us," Sarge said.

"I don't want to talk to her," Razoni said. She's nothing but bad news."

"She doesn't want to talk to you. She wants to know about the roses that killed the Swami. How were the stems cut?"

"What a stupid question," Razoni said. "Everybody's a goddamn rose expert."

"Did you see the roses?" Sarge asked.

"I saw them at the police property room," Jackson said. "What does she mean about how the stems were cut?"

"Whether they were cut at an angle or just sliced straight across?" Sarge said.

Jackson closed his eyes, trying to visualize. Finally, he said, "Straight across."

Sarge went back to the phone and gave the information to Chico. She whooped over the telephone. "Great. Sarge, I'm onto something."

"What?"

"I'll have it this afternoon. I'll let you know."

"You be careful," he said.

"No. You be careful. Don't let that mug stick you with the check," Chico said.

When the two detectives left the restaurant and returned to their car, the radio was squawking.

"Car One-one-one, call your office."

"Oh, Christ, now what?" Razoni said. "What dumb thing does Mannion want now?"

"He probably wants to give us a commendation for how well we served warrants," Jackson said.

"Yeah. By tomorrow we'll be meter maids," Razoni said. He went back inside Bogie's to use the telephone.

"Down to the office," he said as he got into the car.

"What's up?"

"Gault and Gorman must have gotten the photographs we sneaked to them of Abigail feeding the lizard the poison. They want to talk to Abigail and Karen. Mannion wants us there."

"How nice," Jackson said.

They had to wait in the hallway outside the commissioner's office. The two precinct detectives were there. Gault had a thin complacent smile on his face.

"What's going on?" Jackson said.

"The commissioner and Mannion are inside telling Longworth what's what. The girls are in there too."

"And what is what?" Razoni said.

"We've just solved the Salamanda murder," Gault said.

"Good for you," Razoni said.

"Yeah, we solved it," Gault said. "So that tells you how much you know, Razoni. We made the biggest mistake detectives can make, huh? Well, we busted the case after you blew it."

Gault's partner, Gorman, nodded a lot, Razoni noticed. He was nodding now.

"The big men from the commissioner's office," Gault said. "Well, you two are one big pair of duds, as far as I'm concerned."

"Nice to know, Gault," Razoni said. "And here I was going to sponsor you for the detectives' hall of fame."

When the door opened and Mannion waved them all into the commissioner's office, they saw Theodore Longworth sitting in a soft leather chair alongside the commissioner's desk, a glass of whiskey in his hand. The two young women, wearing matching outfits of brown leather slacks and leather bolero jackets over kelly-green gauze blouses, sat side by side on a large sofa.

"They're into leather now," Razoni whispered to Jackson.

The commissioner was behind the desk. As he rose so did Longworth, who looked at the four detectives and said, "I want you to know that this entire thing is absurd. If it turns out that you people are harassing these young women, you're going to spend the rest of your lives in misery."

Razoni raised his hands. "Not us, Mr. Longworth. My partner and I don't have anything to do with this case. We just serve warrants on notorious criminals like Pedro González."

"We asked Razoni and Jackson to be here, Ted, just in case they have some background in the case that the other detectives don't have," the commissioner told Longworth.

"This is not the usual practice," he said, "but we thought we owed you the courtesy of hearing what these detectives have to say." He nodded toward Gault and Gorman. The two men began to pace back and forth across the center of the room.

"Miss Longworth," Gorman said, "where were you Sunday morning?"

"I wath at the Thwami Thalamanda athram," Abigail said.

Razoni covered his smirk with his hand.

"Who did you meet there?" Gorman said.

"It should be 'whom,' shouldn't it, Tough?" Razoni whispered to Jackson. Jackson nodded and Razoni said aloud, "He means 'Whom did you meet there?' "

Gorman glared at him. Abigail looked unhappy.

"All right," Gorman said. "Whom did you meet there? Did you meet Karen Marichal?"

"Yeth."

"And did you have occasion to go to a florist shop on that street?"

Abigail looked at Karen Marichal, who seemed bored by the proceedings, preferring instead to glare at Razoni across the room.

"Yeth," said Abigail.

"And what did you do at that florist shop?" asked

Gorman. He had started out at a slow leisurely striding pace, but was now moving back and forth almost on the gallop, wheeling and spinning at each end of the room. His partner, Detective Gault, was trying to keep up with him, but couldn't walk as fast as Gorman and kept having to wait for his partner to wheel around and come back.

"We bought a dothen rotheth," said Abigail.

"Is that right, Miss Marichal?" asked Gorman.

Karen nodded.

"Note that she agrees," Gorman told Gault.

"Right," said Gault.

"He talks," Razoni whispered to Jackson.

"And what did you do with the roses?"

"We brought them back and put them in the refrigerator," Abigail said.

"What for?"

"For the welcoming theremony for new memberth."

"And then during the ceremony, you brought the roses from the refrigerator, out to Swami Salamanda, is that right?"

"Yeth."

"Where were you during this, Miss Marichal?" Gorman asked.

"The ceremony was only for new members," she said in her cold imperious voice. "I worked at the food shop next door."

Gorman stood in front of Abigail. "So you gave the Swami the roses and he ate one of them and died."

"But I didn't poithon any rotheth," she said.

"Just answer my question. He ate a rose and died," Gorman said.

Abigail looked in panic at her father, who sat in his chair, drinking his drink, looking sick.

"Yeth."

"And then you fled?"

"Yeth."

"Why?"

"Becauthe I wath afraid."

"Afraid, Miss Longworth? If you had nothing to do

with the brutal murder of Swami Salamanda, why did you run? Why were you afraid?''

''I don't know.''

''And then you hid out in Miss Marichal's home?''

''Yeth,'' Abigail said.

''This is ridiculous,'' Razoni said softly to Jackson. ''We know all this.''

''Don't stop him,'' Jackson said. ''He thinks he's Sherlock Holmes. This is the big scene in the living room at the end of the story where he reveals who the murderer is.''

''Will you two be quiet?'' Mannion hissed.

Gorman was talking again. ''Now, Miss Longworth, Miss Marichal, I want you two to think very carefully before answering. Why did you murder Swami Salamanda?''

Trace found Sarge sitting at the bar in Bogie's.

''Have you seen Chico today?'' he asked.

''Only this morning,'' Sarge said. ''Then she called this afternoon and said she was onto something but wouldn't tell me what. It took you long enough to get back.''

''Goddamn bureaucrats,'' Trace said. ''Gildersleeve was in and out of the place in ten minutes. I spent the whole day cooling my heels until they decided to talk to me, and then they asked me two questions and told me to await a grand-jury summons. I wonder where Chico is.''

''Let's go upstairs and see if she left a message on the phone.''

They walked up the wooden uncarpeted steps to the second-floor detective office.

''I didn't notice that before,'' Sarge said. ''What happened to my centerfolds?''

''Chico took them down. She said they made the place look shabby.''

''Not by themselves, they didn't,'' Sarge said.

''Don't worry about it,'' Trace said. ''Now that we're big private eyes for the Mafia, who knows what comes next? The Pentagon? The CIA? You can hire your own bunnies to take coats.''

The red light was flashing on the telephone-answering machine and Sarge went over, turned the volume up, and pressed a button.

"Hello, Devlin. This is Michiko. I'm home and I've cooked up a wonderful dinner, so I wish you'd hurry home. But please, no company tonight. Tell your friend Pat to go eat in a restaurant. See you later. 'Bye."

"Something's wrong," Trace said. He dialed the telephone number at Sarge's house and Chico answered.

"Hello, Chico."

"Hello, Devlin. Are you coming home soon?"

"Is everything all right?"

"I've cooked your favorite. Eggplant. Got to run now. Are you coming right home?"

"I'll be right there."

"Good," she said. The phone clicked off in his ear.

"Something is wrong," he said. "We'd better get out to the house."

"She say something?" Sarge asked.

"She called me Devlin. She never calls me Devlin. And she said she made my favorite eggplant. She knows I won't eat eggplant. And before, she called you my friend Pat."

"Somebody's there with her," Sarge said.

"Let's go."

Trace moved to the door. Sarge pulled out one of the desk drawers. Taped to the outside of the back panel was a small .32-caliber revolver. "Take this," he said, tossing it across the room to Trace, who caught it and shoved it into his jacket pocket.

"Go over to the parking lot and get Billy's car," Sarge said. "I'm calling those two cops in case we need backup."

"Hurry up." Trace said as he turned and ran down the steps. "Just hurry up."

40

Gault and Gorman were working up to their big finale. The room had been shocked when they asked the two young women why they had killed Salamanda.

Theodore Longworth had started to rise to his feet, but the police commissioner had touched his shoulder. "Let them go on, Ted," he said.

Gorman said to Longworth, "I'm sorry, sir. But the evidence is there. And here." He nodded to Gault, who handed him a briefcase. Gorman opened it and took out two photographs and handed them to the commissioner.

"They show Abigail Longworth in the rose ceremony at the time the Swami was murdered," Gorman said. "Here is one of the roses." He pulled a withered rose from the briefcase. It was wrapped in Saran kitchen wrap. He held it up and showed it around the room.

"Let me see that," Jackson said, and took the rose from the detective's hand.

"Isn't this stupid?" Razoni said.

"Abigail," Longworth said, "did you have anything to do with this?"

"No, Daddy. I didn't kill anybody."

Jackson showed the rose to Razoni. "Look at the end," he whispered. The stem had been cut straight across. "That's what that girl in Tracy's office meant. The girls bought one batch of roses but the poisoned ones came from someplace else."

Gorman was talking aloud. "I'm sorry, Mr. Longworth, but we can't ignore the evidence. We could have done this all earlier and maybe less painfully if the case hadn't been botched at the start by incompetents."

"I'm not taking any more of this shit," Razoni said to Jackson. "Commissioner," he called out, "can I ask a question?"

"Go ahead."

"Abigail, sweets," Razoni said, "when you went to the refrigerator to get the roses for the ceremony, were there any other roses there?"

The girl thought a moment. "No," she said.

"Gorman? You look in the refrigerator?" Razoni asked.

"Yeah. There were roses there. We've got them in the property room."

"Where'd they come from?" Razoni asked.

Gorman stopped pacing. For the first time, a worried look appeared on his face.

"Somebody must have bought them," he said. He shrugged.

"Unpoisoned roses, right?" Razoni said.

"That's right. The lab said they weren't poisoned."

"Why would somebody buy them after the lizard was already dead?" Razoni asked.

He stared at Gorman, who stared back malevolently.

"I don't know," Gorman said.

"You don't know anything," Razoni said.

"These photos," Gorman said. "She was there."

"Of course she was there. We knew that. We sent you those pictures, you numbskull."

There was a knock on the door and Mannion rose to answer it. Sergeant Schultz from his office stood there, said a few words to Mannion, and then came inside. He stopped by Jackson.

"You got a phone call from a Tracy. He said he thinks the case is broken; get to his house in Queens right away."

"On our way," Razoni said. He and Jackson rose.

In the center of the room, Theodore Longworth was glaring at Detective Gorman. "You're in trouble with these false accusations."

Razoni stopped in midstride and wheeled about. "I'm about tired of you, Longworth," he snapped. The commissioner looked startled. "If you hadn't bought a goddamn television tape of your daughter at the Swami's and if you hadn't burned the goddamn tape and if you hadn't jerked the police department around trying to find her because you were afraid she was going to get arrested, this would have all been cleared up earlier. Take a hike, Longworth. You're a pain in the ass."

He turned and followed Jackson out the door.

"Who did it?" Mannion yelled after them.

"Damned if I know," Razoni said. "But I think we'll find out now."

Trace parked down the block from Sarge's house. The retired policeman checked his gun, a long-barreled .38 Special.

"Okay," he said. "Give me thirty seconds to cut through the neighbor's back yard. Then you make your move."

"Right," Trace said. "Hurry."

Sarge got out of the car and darted into an alley between two houses. Trace tried to count the seconds; they each seemed to take an eternity.

Finally, he got out of the car and walked down the street toward his parents' house. The unfamiliar weight of the pistol in his right jacket pocket slapped against his hip.

He whistled as he walked up the front steps and rang the bell.

There was no answer and he rang it again.

"Who is it?" Chico's voice called out.

"Devlin, honey. I forgot my key. Open up."

Slowly, she opened the door. There was a look of horror on her face. As Trace stepped inside, Chico darted her eyes toward the right, but before he could move, Trace felt a gun jabbed into his back.

The door slammed shut and Trace was pushed roughly against it.

"Don't move a muscle," a man's voice snapped at him, then began patting down his sides. He quickly found the gun in Trace's jacket, reached his hand in, and took it out. The gun was removed from Trace's back and he turned in time to see Gildersleeve putting Trace's pistol in his own jacket pocket.

"All right, you two. Over on the couch," Gildersleeve said. He held another gun in his hand and waved it at them. As Trace turned away, toward the couch, he winked reassuringly at Chico, then helped her to the couch.

"Are you all right?" he asked.

"I'm fine. I'm sorry."

"It's okay," Trace said. He put his arm around her shoulders and pulled her toward him. "Everything's okay," he said.

Gildersleeve was standing in front of them.

"I don't know why you two are so nosy, but it's going to cost you," he said. "You should have left well enough alone."

"I don't think your killing two people is 'well enough,' " Trace said. "You did kill them both, didn't you?"

"Ask your girlfriend," Gildersleeve said. "She knows all about it."

Trace looked at Chico, who nodded. "He killed Salamanda," she said. "I found the store down near his hotel where he bought the other roses that he poisoned. Then Gloria caught on and he had to kill her. He's the one who took that button from Alcetta downstairs from our office. And I found the place where he rented the car like Alcetta's. It still had the gum on it from the bumper strip he put on it."

Trace said, "That's what didn't ring right. If Angelo was going to kill his wife, why park his car in front where everybody would see it?"

"But it wasn't Angelo," Gildersleeve said. "I wanted everybody to see it."

"But why?" Trace asked.

"Why what?" Gildersleeve said.

"Everything. Why everything?"

Gildersleeve shrugged.

Chico said, "He was in charge of building that City of Love in Pennsylvania. He was going south with the money and Salamanda found out."

"And one thing led to another," Gildersleeve said. "And now it leads to you. I'm going to make it quick," he said. "It'll look like a lovers' quarrel."

Suddenly Sarge's voice rang through the room.

"Drop that gun or you're film at eleven," he roared.

Gildersleeve tensed. He looked as if he were about to turn.

"Don't turn around," Sarge barked. "Just drop that gun."

Gildersleeve dropped the gun onto the carpet. As Chico watched, he half-turned his body so that his right side was away from Sarge. He glanced toward the big ex-policeman standing in the doorway to the kitchen, and Chico saw his hand slip into his right jacket pocket, where he had stashed Trace's gun.

She started to yell. "Sarge! Watch out!" and as she did, Gildersleeve yanked the pistol out and wheeled toward Sarge. The gun was out in front of him, aimed across the room.

The .38 Special in Sarge's hand barked. Gildersleeve's arms flew up into the air. The gun dropped and he flew back onto the couch between Trace and Chico, who shrank away from the man. There was a hole in his chest big enough to push a golf ball into.

"Holy shit," Chico said as she got to her feet.

"Double that," Trace said, leaning over the man. "I think he's dead."

Sarge was at the telephone, calling the police, calling for an ambulance.

Chico shook her head. She was unable to take her eyes off Gildersleeve. She looked at Sarge with worry in her eyes.

"I thought he had you," she said. She went to him and put her arms about him as he stood at the telephone. "I thought he had you."

Absently, Sarge patted her head. "Not with that hairy old trick," he said. "I'm too old a cat, honey, to be screwed by a kitten."

Razoni and Jackson arrived three minutes later, even before the ambulance came.

Razoni looked at Gildersleeve's body on the couch, then at Chico, and said, "Jesus Christ. Why don't you people go back to Las Vegas? What pains in the ass you are."

41

The party was Jackson's idea. At first, Razoni resisted it because he said he was afraid to be anywhere with a homicidal maniac Japanese woman, but finally he relented when Jackson explained that not only had the murder been solved but they had been taken off punishment detail. Razoni agreed finally and pointed out that he had managed to solve the crime with his usual efficiency and had also managed not to be assaulted by any dirty, creepy, disgusting fags, male or female, who were sick and making a sick city sicker with their disgustingness.

Trace had agreed instantly because having something else to do on Saturday night meant that he had a reason not to accept his ex-wife's dinner invitation. Chico said she would go if the food was good. Sarge said, "Anything to get out of the house."

Razoni picked the restaurant, a "great place" he knew in Little Italy. Jackson, with his wife in the back seat, drove through the twisting little streets as if they were straight and followed Razoni's orders to park on the sidewalk in front of a small storefront restaurant that had the same quaint glamorous look as Anzio in 1945.

"Why did I park on the sidewalk, Ed?" he asked.

"Because the junkies sneak in here to crap in the streets but they wouldn't dare mess up a car that's got the nerve to be on the sidewalk."

Trace, Chico, and Sarge were already inside, at a large table in the far corner of the room. A jug of wine sat in front of them. Jackson made all the introductions while

Razoni busied himself figuring out how he could sit as far away from Chico as possible and still stay at the table.

A very thin, nervous old man was skittering about from table to table, muttering in Italian, and when he reached them, Razoni insisted upon ordering for everybody. The old man's hand shook furiously as he tried to hold a pencil and pad.

"We'll have melon and prosciutto, chopped baked clam, enough for everybody, bracciole, lasagne, your vegetable of the day, and another two jugs of wine."

The old man read the order back and Razoni nodded and said, "I want those clams chopped."

"Chopped," repeated the waiter as he tried to aim his shaking pencil at the pad. Razoni started to say something to Jackson's wife when the waiter began bellowing next to Razoni's ear. He was shouting their entire order to a gigantic woman who sat in the back of the restaurant peeling garlic. Jackson shrugged. Chico laughed aloud. Razoni jumped up.

"What the hell did you write all that down for if you were just going to shout it from the table?" he yelled at the old waiter.

"So you know what you're paying for," the old man said, shaking. While he was explaining, Trace and Chico could hear their order being bellowed by the fat woman to a cook who was behind a wall.

"Charming places you take us to, Ed," Jackson's wife said.

"It used to be great."

The waiter brought back more wine and more glasses, and Razoni poured for everyone, then lifted his glass in a toast.

"Here's to Abigail Longworth. And Karen Marichal. And Theodore Longworth. And the United Broadcasting network. And its entire staff. And all the other fags who are making this city unlivable for us normal people."

Chico muttered, "Name one."

"Name one what?" Razoni snapped.

"One normal people," she said.

"Well, I sure didn't mean you," he said.

Sarge raised his glass. "And here's to Captain Mannion and the two best detectives in New York."

"Gee, shucks, Sarge," Chico said.

"He meant us, lady," Razoni said.

They drank again, draining their glasses. Razoni refilled them all.

It was Jackson's turn. "Here's to the new famous detective agency. Long may it prosper to torture Razoni."

His voice was almost drowned out by the fat garlic lady screaming in Italian at the shivering waiter.

They drank and Jackson asked Razoni, "What's she saying? Does that language really have a meaning? I always thought it was just a lot of sounds."

"Go beat on a log with a drumstick," Razoni said.

The waiter appeared with a platter of baked whole clams. Razoni sniffed. "I wanted them chopped," he said.

"Never mind," said Jackson. "We'll be here all night."

"That's the trouble with you, Jackson. You settle too easily. Since you're paying for this, I should think you'd want things to be just so."

Jackson divided the clams anyway onto small appetizer plates. Suddenly he saw something shiny whiz past his right hand. The garlic woman was chasing their waiter down the center aisle of the restaurant, wildly waving her butcher knife in the air.

They disappeared through the front door out into the street.

Jackson excused himself. "This party's missing something," he said.

Razoni said, "This whole city's going to hell in a bucket."

Chico nodded, then plunged mouth-first into her plate of clams.

When Jackson returned, Razoni said, "Where'd you go?"

"I made a phone call," Jackson said.

"To who?"

"To whom?" Jackson said.

"All right, to whom?"

"I called the Marichal family."

"What for?" Razoni demanded.

"I invited them to dinner. I told them we found a great place where they'd feel right at home."

Razoni said, "Did you invite the monkey too?"

"I had to," Jackson said.

"Why?" Razoni demanded.

"He answered the phone."

Trace raised his glass in a toast. Everybody else lifted their glasses also.

Trace said, "God bless us every *birinci*."

Barr Job
201 767-1900

DIAL SIGNET FOR MURDER

A
1350
125
269
4174

B
1350.
151
2976
4477

*Prices slightly higher in Canada
†Not available in Canada